The game was b
Thea.

She was also beginn
mother had been so determined that they
should not meet. Why, he's nice, she thought,
and then, Perhaps he's charming to everyone,
and he's only being charming to me because
there's no one else about. Not a happy
thought, that.

Gis was wondering why it pleased him to
embark on such a childish flirtation with a
young woman of such marked lack of obvious
attractions. Pity, perhaps? Or was it that he
must do everything in his power to be as
different as possible from the sexual pirate
and robber whom she had surprised at
Mereside?

Dear Reader

We complete Paula Marshall's trilogy this month, moving outside our usual limits to the restless world of 1920. Kate's son has discovered his true origins and is a changed man. Elizabeth Lowther gives us a sparkling Regency where Lord Kirkham finds himself saddled with an unwanted wife!

In our American books, Caryn Cameron charts the brink of the Civil War, and Elisabeth MacDonald looks at how differently the Spanish and the English dealt with California in the 1870s.

Absorbing reads for your pleasure!

The Editor

Paula Marshall, married with three children, has had a varied life. She began her career in a large library and ended it as a senior academic in charge of history in a polytechnic. She has travelled widely, has been a swimming coach, and has appeared on *University Challenge* and *Mastermind*. She has always wanted to write, and likes her novels to be full of adventure and humour.

Recent titles by the same author:

TOUCH THE FIRE
THE CAPTAIN'S LADY

THE MOON SHINES BRIGHT

Paula Marshall

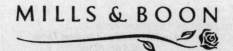

MILLS & BOON

MILLS & BOON LIMITED
ETON HOUSE, 18–24 PARADISE ROAD
RICHMOND, SURREY, TW9 1SR

*First published in Great Britain 1994
by Mills & Boon Limited*

© Paula Marshall 1994

*Australian copyright 1994   Philippine copyright 1994
This edition 1994*

ISBN 0 263 78252 2

*Set in 10½ on 12 pt Linotron Times
04-9405-81562*

*Typeset in Great Britain by Centracet, Cambridge
Printed and bound in Great Britain by
BPCC Paperbacks Ltd
Member of BPCC Ltd*

CHAPTER ONE

GIS HAVILLAND lay on a *chaise-longue* on the terrace at Padworth Manor, near Longthorne in Berkshire, his uncle Lord Longthorne's home. All six feet of him was draped with supreme elegance along it, his eyes were closed, and it was apparent that nothing on earth could disturb or fret him.

So his half-sister, Sophie Moreton, thought. She gave an exasperated sigh, said 'Gis!' in a voice half pleading, half commanding.

Gis's response was to open one bright blue eye — then shut it again.

'What is it, Soph? Do let me rest, there's a good girl. I've a head like a concertina. . .'

'Gis, I need you. . .really need you. There's no one else. . .no one.' This last came out in a long wail, quite unlike Sophie's usual bright and confident tones. Gis's response was to open both eyes and lever himself up a little.

'Good lord, Soph, what is it? You sound dire, quite dire.'

Sophie's eyes filled with tears. 'I am dire,' she said. 'And truly, there's no one else. And even you might not be able to help me.'

Gis leaned back again, picked up his discarded panama hat and placed it over his face. His voice, muffled by the hat, was as calm as it usually was, 'Can't help you, Soph, if you don't tell me what's wrong. Cough up, there's a love.'

His old pet name for her, left over from his childhood, nearly undid Sophie. Gis, at twenty-four, was seven years younger than she was but she sometimes thought that the age difference was the other way round. She looked at him, exasperated. 'At least take that hat off your face,' she said fretfully.

'Can't,' came back. 'Light hurts today. Do get on with it Soph. Want to go back to sleep.'

Only Gis, thought Sophie, could look quite so carelessly and remarkably handsome whatever posture you found him in. He would surely arrive at the gates of heaven, in perfect command of himself, instructing St Peter on the best way to organise the entry of those privileged souls destined for Paradise.

'Very well,' she said, voice resigned, 'it's this. . .' She stopped again, and was suddenly grateful that Gis couldn't see her face as she spoke. Was that why he had put the panama hat over his eyes? And if so, how had he known? She shivered. There were times when Gis frightened her.

'You remember,' she began, 'when I was organising nursing at Haverford Hall in 1917, when George was at the front, and just before he came home, shell-shocked, we had a procession of wounded officers through. . .'

'Never visited you there,' came from Gis. 'But yes, I know you did your bit for the war effort — nobly.'

'If only that were all,' breathed Sophie numbly. 'Well, I met Hector Dashwood that autumn, and he made a dead set at me. . .'

'He would.' Gis was laconic.

'Well, yes. I took no notice of him, at first. And

then, George came home, shell-shocked, they said, and was in such a state, and what with one thing and another he finally had to go to that sanatorium to be treated. We were both shattered, I think, and then. . . I went to London for a long leave, the doctor said I was in danger of breaking down myself, and I met Hector again. . .only this time, I didn't . . .send him away. We had an *affaire*. . . I don't know why. . .but everything seemed so dreadful. . . and he was so pleasant. . . Except. . . I wrote him some letters when I went back to Haverford. . .and then suddenly it was over. George recovered, and it was just a piece of wartime madness. Not at all like me really. I thought that was the end, I'd quite forgotten it, but Hector is blackmailing me, threatening to send the letters to George if I don't pay him a large sum of money. . .he's on his beam-ends, you know; Mereside is in a bad way. . . And I haven't any spare money. . . Papa put it all in trust. . .Hector doesn't believe me, thinks what with Papa's wealth and Kate's millions I must have access to plenty, but I haven't. And oh, God, Gis, what am I going to do? George won't stand for it. You know how upright he is, an MP. . .and Hector has threatened to send the letters to the Press. . .as well. . .'

She thought she had never been so relieved about anything as she was at the sight of Gis's panama hat covering his face which stopped him from seeing hers as well as her from seeing his.

'Say something. . . Gis,' she almost shouted, her distress at having to tell him such a tale overcoming her. 'He's given me a fortnight from yesterday to come up with the money.'

'Hush, Soph, I'm thinking,' was all she got back from him, and then, 'Are you sure he's not bluffing? He still has the letters?'

'Quite certain. He sent me a page from one of them. . .if George ever saw it. . .my marriage would be over.'

Lying quiet beneath the panama hat, Gis decided that he had never liked George Moreton much, and had been surprised when Sophie married him. He was as pompous and self-righteous as one might imagine a rising politician in the Tory party of the early nineteen-twenties to be, and he could understand Sophie's fears of his possible reaction to this disclosure.

Useless to point out to Sophie that she never ought to have married George in the first place, or that, having done so, she should have avoided Hector Dashwood like the plague.

'He couldn't blackmail you if he hadn't got the letters,' he offered suddenly.

'Well, that's a self-evident truth,' returned Sophie despairingly, thinking that she had hoped for more from Gis in the way of help than that sort of comment.

'So it is.' Gis's voice was as lazy as it usually was. 'Neat problem in philosophy, eh, Soph? Old Prof. Dunstan would be good on the subject—"x-thousand words on the nature of proof, Havilland". . . don't worry, Soph, I'll save you somehow.'

'Oh! Thank you, Gis, thank you!' Sophie sat down suddenly on one of the marble benches which decorated the terrace, alternating with ornate stone urns, filled with flowers—only the best of everything would do for Gis's uncle, Gerard Schuyler, Lord

Longthorne, recently ennobled by a monarch grateful for his wartime efforts to bring the USA, his original homeland, into the war on the side of the Allies. 'But how? Gis, How?'

'Don't ask,' replied Gis, wriggling himself into an even more comfortable position on the *chaise-longue*. 'Best not to know. Forget about it; consider it done.'

Which was, he thought wryly, when Sophie had disappeared into the house, breathing gratitude and affection, being rather more confident than he actually felt, but he had the beginnings of a plan in his mind, so that when, five minutes later, his mother, Kate, Lady Havilland, sister of Lord Longthorne, came on to the terrace to find him on the edge of sleep, and said reproachfully, 'Really, Gis, you promised to come with me to Mereside this afternoon, and look at you!' he said,

'Did I? Then hang on a moment while I make myself pretty; nothing would suit me better.'

He had learned during the war that reconnaissance before battle might not ensure success, but could certainly help to insure against failure.

'Gis worries me,' said his mother that evening, to her husband, Sir Richard Havilland, KCMG, her brother, Gerard Schuyler, now Lord Longthorne, and his wife Torry. Gis had disappeared before dinner, gone God knew where, and now they were seated in the drawing-room. Sophie and her husband had disappeared, too, moving on to stay with George's mama, a widow, at Hayforth, over the border into Oxfordshire, not far from the Longthornes' home.

'Oh, I thought that he had settled down beautifully—considering everything,' said Torry gently.

Richard gave a short laugh before he poured himself some more whisky. Talking about Gis always made him want to drink whisky.

'Oh, yes,' he offered, a trifle bitterly, 'apart from combining being well on the way to a double first with living the wildest life between here and the North Pole, I suppose we could call it settling down, after a fashion. At least his behaviour is all of a piece, and he won't listen to anything I say—or what anyone else says, for that matter.'

'Well, he always did go his own sweet way,' said Torry equably; little ruffled her.

'But he was such a charming little boy,' Kate almost wailed, 'so gentle and loving, and now, well, he's still charming, at least, everyone tells me so, but underneath it he's as hard as nails, and, as Richard says, will take advice from no one.'

Gerard, that all-seeing man of power, said nothing. At just over sixty he had, remarkably, retained the mental elasticity of his youth, but combined it with the mature judgement of the senior senator which he had become. A government reshuffle after the war had seen him elevated to the Lords. The war had changed everything, he thought, including his nephew, Gis, but it was also true that more than the war had changed Gis.

'You should have told him the truth about his birth, Kate, while he was still a child,' he finally said, once he had got his cigar going. 'I always thought that you were wrong not to do so.'

Kate's face began to crumple a little. She sprang to her feet, and walked away to the window, to stare

out at the black night. 'I lacked courage once,' she
muttered to the window, 'and it was nearly fatal,
but I learned nothing from it. He was so happy, and
I. . .we—didn't want anything to spoil that
happiness.'

'Then at least you should have told him before he
went to public school.' For Gerard was certain that
Gis had found out the truth about himself and his
origins some time in his seventeenth year—and did
not like it. No spirited young man, who had been
greatly loved, almost spoiled, because of the sweet-
ness of his nature and his intellectual precocity,
could have learned with equanimity that he had
been conceived and born nearly eight years before
his parents had chosen to marry, and that although
he had called Kate and Richard Mother and Father
from that marriage onwards he had always thought
that the titles were honorary, not a true statement
of what they actually were.

Richard Havilland, still handsome in his early
fifties, walked over to his wife, and put an arm
around her shoulders. 'Don't fret, Kate. What's
done is done, and I am as much to blame as you.
He hero-worshipped the pair of us, and I was
frightened of what the knowledge of the truth would
do to him if we told him while he was still a child.
Somehow, there was never a right time to tell him.
I agree with Gerard, we should have told him the
truth, but he was such a happy child, and so proud
of us both—and I didn't want to see that happiness
and that pride destroyed.'

'At least he's not jealous of Richie,' said Kate
desolately, Richie being Gis's legitimate brother,
the son born to Richard and herself after they had

married. 'He loves Richie, and the two girls as well,
that's plain, but he's so. . .' She sought for a word,
could not find it, could only think of 'wild', but Gis
was not wild, he was something worse, she thought,
and the old rapport between them had vanished, for
good, apparently. And then the War had come. . .
and she shuddered at the memory of that, and at
what Gis had done. . .

'And he's with Diana Troy tonight, I'm sure of
it,' she said suddenly. 'Diana's over at Tom
Moidore's place, and she only has to crook her little
finger, and he goes running, and she's fifteen years
older than he is, and married.'

Richard laughed a little ruefully at this. 'You
make it sound as though she winds him round her
little finger, Kate. You know Gis better than that.
He only does what he wants, when he wants to and
damn all else. He's twenty-four now, very much a
man, and he has to go his own way, and that's the
end of it.'

'Richard's right, Kate,' Gerard said, gently for
him. 'There's little you can do, and one day — who
knows — you may get the old Gis back.'

Kate wanted to wring her hands and shriek like a
character out of an old Greek tragedy, to howl for
the lost Ghysbrecht Schuyler, who had become
Ghysbrecht Havilland, and who had once said to
her when she had reproached him for his wild life,
'Don't worry, Mother, Gis Havilland, Gis Schuyler,'
and he had spoken of himself as though he were a
stranger, 'whatever his name is. . .for he hasn't
really got a name. . .will get his double first, you'll
see, and after that, who knows? I'm sure I don't.'

Which, all in all, was as unlike anything which the

happy boy he had been for sixteen years would have said as anything could possibly be. . . .

'Oh, Thea.' Her mother's voice was as severe as that redoubtable matron could make it. 'Is that the best you and Harvey can do? What a pity you take after your father's side of the family and not mine! Why on earth are you not more like your cousin Lilian? There is a model for you. I don't ask that you emulate Diana Troy.'

'I shall never look like Cousin Lilian, never, if I live to be a hundred,' said Thea quietly, 'and as for being like Cousin Diana — you surely cannot want that.'

'I almost wish that you were,' replied her mother sharply. 'Anything would be better than your present appearance. No looks, no style! Anyone would think that you don't want to get married. I'm sure Hector would propose if you gave him the slightest encouragement.'

If Thea Dunstan presented a problem to her parents, it was not because she was wild, nor because she was, as Gis Havilland was, remarkably beautiful and attractive to the opposite sex, who fell in droves before him, but rather because she was his complete opposite.

Gis talked. He talked brilliantly and entertainingly, his looks were those of an Apollo, his mind was first-class, like the degree which he was about to achieve, while Thea was quiet, apparently placid, retiring and plain. Oh, her eyes were good, and her hair was an interesting shade of chestnut, but once you had said that you had said everything. Her figure was shapely and graceful, but her clothes, all at odds with current fashion and chosen for her by her mother, did little to enhance it.

As a nineteen-year-old commodity on the marriage market the only virtue which she possessed was that her mother, Lady Edith Dunstan, wife of Theodore Dunstan, Professor of philosophy at William and Mary College, Oxford, was unexpectedly and enormously rich, being the last of her line, Lady Edith's three brothers, all much younger than she was, the product of her father's second marriage, having been killed in the Great War. The family title was destined to pass into oblivion, since all the cousins who might have inherited it had also been killed while serving in various branches of the armed forces.

'You could at least *try*,' scolded Lady Edith. 'You know that Hector Dashwood likes pretty, amusing women, and he would be a great catch — oh, not because of his money, he hasn't any — but the title is old, and you would be Countess Dashwood.'

The defiant imp who lived inside Thea's head and who rarely spoke aloud, said quietly, Hector Dashwood would not mind if I had an ass's head like Bottom in the play so long as I brought several million pounds along with it, in land and shares. He would even kiss it, and me, with every appearance of enthusiasm, if he thought that that would bring me to the altar.

Aloud, she said coolly and pleasantly — Lady Edith could never criticise her daughter's perfect manners, 'Oh, I don't think Hector would expect me to be a mannequin, Mother, quite the contrary. He wants a lady for his Countess, I'm sure. And remember, you choose my clothes for me, so if you do think that I ought to resemble a mannequin, or dress like Diana Troy. . .' and she let her voice trail off, leaving Lady Edith to take the hint—which, of course, she wouldn't.

Mannequins and beauties will do for Hector's mistresses, not his wife, observed the imp.

'Well, you may be right. At least, if he married you, Hector would not have to watch his wife gallivanting with all and sundry, like poor Troy does with Diana.'

'So I will do as I am. We are agreed on that, Mother?'

'Oh, very well,' sighed Lady Edith ungraciously, before sailing off like the battleship she was to fire her torpedoes at her husband for the rest of the afternoon, her child having managed to avoid all that she had so far aimed at her—a not uncommon occurrence. Remarkably, Lady Edith, despite her adroitness, had never managed to grasp that the daughter whom she so frequently deplored invariably came off best in all their encounters—she was too busy despising her for lacking those virtues which she thought that she ought to possess to recognise those which she did.

Thea watched her handsome mother, superbly caparisoned, corseted and coiffured, swim through her father's study door, and laughed soundlessly to herself before she returned to her room to put the final touches on her simple dress of fine grey wool, see that her stocking seams were straight, and that Harvey had, as instructed, trimmed her new cloche hat with a single white posy, as chaste in appearance as Thea herself.

Marry Hector Dashwood! She could think of no

worse fate, for all Hector's good looks, his old title
and his pedigree which went back to the Conquest.

I don't want to marry anyone, said the imp
defiantly; I should be much happier as an old maid,
laughing at the follies of others, but I really musn't
tell Mother so. I shall be coolly civil to Hector while
we stay with him at Mereside. I wonder who else
will be there? I suppose Lord Moidore will come
over from Poyns and bring Cousin Diana with him.
Well, at least *that* will provide me with some amusement. And Mereside does possess a good, if
neglected library, even if Hector never opens a
book! That will please me as well as Papa. Mother
will be cross with us.

The thought brought a smile to Thea's lips, trans-
forming the undistinguished face, so that her father,
watching her come down the stairs, dressed for the
short journey to Mereside, thought that, for a
moment, he could see once again the pretty girl
whom he had married, who had turned; through
time and disappointment at him and herself, into a
dragon with one idea in her head, to arrange a
splendid marriage for her daughter to make up for
losing her two little boys, neither of whom had
survived their difficult births, unlike their unwanted
and unvalued sister.

Gis Havilland took something like twenty-four
hours to work out what to do to try to save Sophie.
He had walked around Mereside, quietly inspecting
it, charming Hector, whom he had never liked, and
now liked less than ever since Sophie had told him
her story. Charming people was Gis's speciality. He
had once done it unconsciously, but ever since he

had found out who he was, or, rather, who he wasn't, using the charm had become a conscious weapon.

'Expectin' guests today,' Hector said. 'Old Mother Dunstan's bringing that gel of hers along. Plain as a pikestaff and dull with it, but stands to inherit everything, Lady Edith's brothers all dead, so the house and the Freville money all goin' to the dowd. Can't call her a flapper, don't flap!' And he laughed noisily at his own joke.

'Professor Dunstan's daughter, you mean?' queried Gis. Dunstan was the professor of philosophy who was to be Gis's tutor during his last year at Oxford, and he had heard — as who had not? — of Lady Edith. He had heard of the poor plain daughter, too, and felt sorry for her. At least the old Gis would have felt sorry, he had had a kind heart, but the one who had taken over seven years ago was rather amused at the idea of Hector, that connoisseur of beauty, having to marry a plain and dreary dowd. Like Thea Dunstan's imp, Gis had no illusions about the reason for such a marriage.

'Still seein' Diana Troy, are you?' queried Hector, looking sideways at the Golden Boy, as he knew Gis had been nicknamed at Eton, partly because of his blond good looks, partly because of his mother's share of the Schuyler wealth.

'Now and then,' said Gis airily. 'Now and then.' He was watching his mother talking to Hector's faded maiden aunt who acted as his hostess, and would do so until Hector married, which she hoped would be soon, and to money. He did not inform Hector that Diana had telephoned him that morning, and with a bit of luck he would spend the night

in Diana's bed at Poyns where both Tom Moidore
and Diana's complaisant husband, Bernard Troy,
would turn a blind eye. Bernard was given to
boasting about Diana's conquests rather than regret-
ting them.

With Gis and Diana it was difficult to tell who
had conquered whom. On the one hand Diana had
been thirty-one when she and the sixteen-year-old
Gis had first gone to bed together, which might
mean that the palm would have to be handed to
Diana. On the other hand, Gis was Gis, and had
been as precocious in sexual matters as he was in
everything else. He was like a drug to Diana, and
the four war years in which society and Europe had
apparently not known him were years of regret for
her. Meeting him again in early 1919 had been one
of the high points of her life. He had changed and
matured for the better in every way—or so Diana
thought.

'Mind you,' said Hector, ploughing on, 'I suppose
I shall end up marryin' the dowd. Can do with the
tin, don't you know? Small price to pay.' He paused,
glanced sideways at Gis. Like all the world he knew
of Gis's reputation for wildness and for women.
'Come to town with me when I've finished entertaining the bores here, why not? Visit Kate Merrick's,
eh? Make a nice change from the lovely Diana—
gettin' a bit long in the tooth, what?'

He laughed explosively. On reflection Gis liked
him less than ever. Any compunction about what he
might have to do to recover Sophie's letters was
rapidly disappearing. And how his sensitive, cul-
tured and gentle half-sister could have found herself

in bed with such an ass was beyond him. One had to blame it on the War, he supposed.

'A change is as good as a rest,' he said sardonically, tailoring his wit to what he thought Hector might appreciate, which Hector did, laughing uproariously and poking Gis in the ribs, so that Gis closed his eyes and wondered all over again what the attraction could be which earned him his reputation with women.

'On the other hand,' he added naughtily, dredging up as many well-worn phrases as he could think of to inwardly bait Hector with, 'all cats are the same at dusk, eh!' and he poked Hector in his ribs for a change, to ease his own sore sides.

It was like taking sweets from a child, he thought, and he had the brief hope that getting Sophie's letters back would be as easy. They had arrived at Mereside's superb, if neglected and shabby library, one corner of which, he discovered, was Hector's study. He wondered why Hector was taking him there, but soon discovered that Hector might be an oaf, but was not so stupid that he couldn't take advantage of Gis's other known reputation — of encyclopaedic knowledge and intellect.

'Might have to sell all this if the dowd don't turn up trumps,' he confided, waving at the once lovely room. 'They say you know all about such things, Havilland. You have a look and tell me if you think there are any treasures here. The pater always said so — but much he knew about such things.'

Gis, intrigued, and grateful to Hector for unwittingly making his task of reconnoitring easy, began to examine the room and the books arranged behind the tarnished lattices. He left the library with real regret. His remarkable memory had already logged everything in the room, including Hector's desk, and the possible whereabouts of a hidden safe. He spent the next hour charming Hector's aunt, and the first arrivals for his house-party, before taking his mother back to Padworth in his little open tourer, and getting himself ready to slip over to Poyns for the night, to keep his assignation with Diana Troy.

The Dunstans arrived at Mereside immediately after Gis and his mother had left so Gis was not given the opportunity to pass judgement on Hector's dowd. Lady Edith was annoyed to learn that she had missed Lady Havilland, but happy to learn that they had missed Gis. He was already notorious in Oxford, and when her husband had told her that young Havilland was to be one of his scholars in his final year she had said frostily, 'I hope you make sure that he's kept away from Dorothea, then.'

'Why?' asked her husband, who was not as unworldly as he looked and sounded. 'He's rich enough, surely.'

'Dubious,' announced Lady Edith firmly. 'Rich he may be, but — who is he? And what did he do in the war? Skulked in America, they say. Money doesn't whitewash everything, you know.'

'But a title does?' offered her husband, thinking of Hector Dashwood. He was not sure that he wanted his little Thea married to such a boorish philistine.

'You do talk nonsense sometimes, Theodore.' Lady Edith was dismissive. 'You know perfectly well what I mean. And Thea will not need money.

She does need a well-founded pedigree — and who is Gis Havilland?'

Her husband, who knew Sir Richard slightly, could have enlightened her, but chose not to. He was also beginning to ask himself what relevance well-founded pedigrees had to the new world of 1920, the War having changed so many things. He sighed, told himself not to worry; after all, he was pretty certain that his wife did not have the slightest idea of the true nature of the daughter whom she spent her days organising and bullying.

He thought that it might not be long before she received an unpleasant surprise. . .

CHAPTER TWO

THEA DUNSTAN, unaware that she had been the subject of discussion, not only between her parents, but between her would-be fiancée, Hector, Lord Dashwood, and his acquaintance, Gis Havilland, lay sleepless in her bed on the second night of her stay at Mereside. She found it beautiful, if neglected, and she could understand why Hector wished to marry her: her dowry, and her inheritance from Lady Edith would go a long way to restore the Dashwood fortunes.

She sighed, turned over in bed, sat up and switched on the bedside lamp; this wing of the house had been wired for electric light, and also possessed some antique plumbing—a large iron bath stood in the dressing-room next to her bedroom. A glance at her watch told her that it was half-past two.

It was useless. She knew from of old that when insomnia struck, as it often did, the only thing which would save her was an interesting, if frivolous novel—and she had forgotten to bring a book to bed with her. There was no help for it, she would have to go downstairs to the library which possessed a fine collection of late Stanley Weyman and early Rafael Sabatini. A romantic historical novel to lull her to sleep. . .what could be better than riding down the pathways of medieval Picardy or Renaissance Italy with a handsome young man?

No need for a candle. Other than the bedrooms,

Mereside's windows were uncurtained, and there was a full moon. Besides, she did not want to be caught wandering around in the middle of the night by someone attracted by the candle — who knew where they might think she was going. . .

Thea thrust her feet into sensible slippers, her body into an equally sensible dressing-gown, above her sensible nightie, and crept out of her room, along the corridor and down the main stairs.

Once, she thought that she had heard a noise below, and stopped halfway down the broad flight . . .but. . .nothing. She was imagining things. Fortunately the library door was closely adjacent to the bottom of the grand stairway, and she made for it confidently; the whole house seemed to be wrapped in sleep.

She opened the door. The library was bathed in silver moonlight and she moved forward into it, closing the door carefully behind her. The shelves of modern novels were on the right, just beyond the slightly enclosed area which made up the study and a large fireplace, where, earlier, a fire had burned because the room had been prepared for her father to work in.

Thea walked in quietly, but perhaps not quietly enough, for she had disturbed someone, a someone who stood before Hector's desk, and who turned on her entry, a someone who was a tall man, whose face was hidden by a strange mask, his hair by a black beret, and at whose sight she stood stock-still, thrusting her hands over her mouth to suppress a scream, for she was fearful of what he might do to her if she called for help, to reveal that there was a

robber in the house. . .for robber he must surely
be. . .

Gis Havilland's reconnaissance had paid off. He had
left Padworth in his Sunbeam tourer shortly after
two in the morning and had entered Mereside
through a window in the library which he had noted
as a possible weakness to be exploited—it was—
and found that his judgement as to where Hector's
safe might be hidden, was correct. Pushing aside an
eighteenth-century landscape painting, a Richard
Wilson he thought, badly in need of restoration, he
found what he had expected, and grinned when he
saw that it was a simple safe to crack.

He slipped the glove off his left hand, and began
to manipulate the lock, remembering as he did so
who had shown him how to crack safes. His father's
secretary had lost the keys to the safe in Sir
Richard's study, and his uncle Gerard had offered
to try to open it for him. He had been twelve years
old at the time, and had entered the study to watch
Gerard at work. The safe had been opened in a trice
and Gerard had grinned at his wife, who had come
in not many minutes after Gis.

And then he had given her a wink, and said,
'Brings back memories, Torry, my love,' and Aunt
Torry had blushed and the two of them had laughed,
and Gis's intuition had told him that Uncle Gerard
had cracked safes before, and that once Aunt Torry
had been present. . .and something odd had happened; he wondered what it could be. Gerard had
seen Gis watching, and had said to him, 'Want me
to show you how to do it, Gis? With your permission, Richard, of course.'

'Oh, please,' he had said, and he had proved an apt pupil, which surprised nobody; what would have surprised them was that Gis couldn't do anything to which he had put his mind.

Reminiscing while he manoeuvred the lock had helped to keep his hand steady, and the safe door swung open. . . It was full of legal papers, of deeds, of worthless, tarnished jewellery, of old letters — but none of them was Sophie's. Gis sighed. It was possible that they were at Hector's London home, but he didn't think so. He straightened up, looked at the big desk in the corner of the room, went over, and forced the lock, a simple matter.

And there, in plain sight in one of the pigeon-holes, was the little bundle of Sophie's letters, tied with pink ribbon. Perhaps, reflected Gis, rifling through the other pigeonholes to see if there were any more of Sophie's letters hidden away, Hector was sharper than he looked. Perhaps like the man in Edgar Allan Poe's story, 'The Purloined Letter' he had decided to deceive the world by putting them somewhere obvious where no one would look — if he had thought at all, that was.

Gis held them in his hand, meditated a moment. Then he walked to the hearth where the dying embers of a fire lay, pulled a box of Swan Vesta matches from his pocket, and, placing the letters on the ashy coals, he set fire to them. Sophie, he reasoned, could not want them back, and best — in the unlikely event that he was discovered — that he was found with nothing on him.

The letters burned rapidly, fell into a heap of ash, indistinguishable from that around them, the last evidence of Sophie's folly quite gone. He thought again, then walked to the desk, to try to lock it, and it was at that point that he heard the library door open behind him, and turned to see a young woman facing him.

A young woman — no, it was a girl, a thin, pale, plain thing, except for a pair of brilliant green eyes. Her chestnut hair hung in two unfashionable plaits, and she had stuffed her hands over her mouth, presumably to stifle a scream — which was sensible of her, and fortunate for him.

He walked towards her. He must, somehow, prevent her from giving the alarm which would trap him, and finish him for good. One part of him was amused at the thought, the other, the more sensible part, told him that he must do everything he could, foul or fair, to avoid discovery and ruin.

Thea, seeing him come towards her, stepped back, took her hands from her mouth, said, faintly at first, and then her voice gaining strength, 'No, don't come near me. Who are you? And what are you doing here? I shall give the alarm,' and she made for the bell pull by the hearth.

Gis was upon her in an instant, so near that she could see the details of his mask, an odd one, which fitted the top half of his face, disappearing into his hair. The mask even had a rudimentary nose, almost like a bird's beak, only not so long. Through the eyeholes a pair of blue eyes glittered, and when he spoke at last she saw that he had excellent teeth — which was something of a surprise.

'No,' he said, in a hoarse voice — quite unlike his own — standing between her and the bell. 'I think not.'

'Then,' said Thea firmly, astonished at her own

coolness, which, she realised afterwards, was partly because the intruder was so cool, 'I shall scream, and I warn you, I shall cry rape — which should bring everybody running.'

'It would indeed,' replied Gis, keeping his voice hoarse and unidentifiable. He was annoyed that he should be caught at the very point of leaving, by accident apparently, and by Hector's dowd, of all people. 'But I warn you that, should you succeed, and I am compelled to unmask, I shall claim that you invited me here for a secret rendezvous, and no one will believe you!'

'Oh!' Thea was furious. Who and what did he think she was? 'How dare you?' she said, 'My reputation is spotless, I'll have you know. No one would believe that I would make a secret rendezvous with anyone!'

'Now, that,' said Gis nastily, 'is quite plain to see,' and he let his voice dwell on the word plain, 'but my reputation isn't, and you must admit that here we should both be, downstairs in the middle of the night, you half dressed, and I shall have disposed of my mask, my beret and my shirt, and made sure that we are both. . .dishevelled — shall we say? — before anyone arrives. The odds are against you being believed, you must admit. The whole world knows that I have never needed to rape any woman to get what I want.'

Thea almost danced with rage. Any fear which she might have felt had disappeared in a blaze of anger at his implied insults. Was she so plain that even a thief in the night might mock at her? 'You are a thief,' she almost began to shout, then lowered her voice, for, alas, he might be telling the truth, and she dared not test his assumption that to be found in her nightwear alone with a man at dead of night could admit of only one explanation.

'On the contrary,' he said coolly, 'I have taken nothing. You may search me, if you like. I was about to leave when you came in. Why are you here, by the way? Are you expecting a lover, after all? I must admit that the library is a strange place for a rendezvous, but I have known worse. Come to that, if this is a rendezvous, and the fortunate fellow has not yet turned up, or doesn't intend to, it would be a pity for me not to try to convince you that we could be lovers,' and, before she could stop him, he had bent his head, taken her in his arms, and was beginning to kiss her on the lips.

Thea was almost incandescent between frustration and outrage. The wretch! The vile wretch, whoever he was, and he did mean to attack her, after all! She tried to hold her mouth firm, to resist him, but he put one hand up to brush back a lock of errant hair, took his mouth away for a moment, gave a low laugh, said, 'Come, you might even enjoy this,' and as she opened her own mouth to call for help, come what may, he put his own on hers, and it was a real kiss this time, and Thea, hardly aware of who or where she was, found herself co-operating, returning his kiss, drowning in it, aware of the male scent of him, of something which held a hint of lemon.

She was lax against him when he finally pulled away from her, said, reprovingly, 'Look at you now. No one, but no one, would believe that you had not invited me here,' and he took her right hand in his left and lifted it to kiss it mockingly.

As he did so, Thea saw two things, the first that not only was his left hand ungloved, but it was shapely, and he wore a strange small ring on his little finger, and the second, that tendrils of fair hair had escaped from his mask.

'Goodbye,' he said, as he relinquished her hand. 'You see how difficult it would be to betray me. Why not let sleeping dogs lie? I promise you I am not really a thief. Nothing of value has gone.'

'I came for a book,' Thea stammered, dazed. And why she said that she did not know; it was quite irrelevant.

'How very improving of you,' he mocked, as he reached the window. 'Or was it simply a novel—something for a young girl to enjoy? But I was much better for you than fantasy, do admit.' And now he was leaving by the window, and why she did nothing to stop him, and made no effort to give the alarm, Thea didn't know.

He gave her one last white smile as he disappeared into the dark, and she was still standing dazed, her body beginning to lose its feeling of having been struck by lightning, when she heard a car start up in the distance, and then an owl hoot.

Thea shook herself. She must have dreamed it, but the evidence of his recent presence was all about her, and particularly inside Thea herself where two passions warred.

The first was a flaming feeling of revolt and fury that he had considered her to be nothing, a plain chit to be teased, and the second that from the moment he had laid hands on her, something had begun to happen to poor unawakened Thea Dunstan. Oh, shameful, that an unknown man, whose face she had not even seen, could cause her to tremble and quiver as she had done, so that for the first time not only was she aware that she had a body, but that that body could give her pleasure!

She went to bed, but not to sleep: could hardly wait for the morning to find out what the bold robber had taken, but he had taken nothing; true, the safe, as she had seen, had been broken into, and Hector had sent for the police. What was puzzling was that one might have thought him gratified by the failed robbery — but he seemed to be in the worst of moods when one might have expected him to have been in the best.

Neither Thea, nor the rest of his guests were to know that Hector, after the police had departed, had disovered that Sophie Moreton's letters had gone from his desk! The worst of it was that he couldn't report their disappearance, and he couldn't, for the life of him, think of who might have taken them. The why was a different matter.

Consequently the visit which Lady Edith thought might have been productive of an offer was productive of nothing at all. The Dunstans left for their next stop, Padworth, without any offer being made. Hector, far from pursuing Thea the harder, seeing that he had lost any chance of getting at Sophie's supposed wealth, found the prospect of marrying such a plain, cold piece as Dorothea Dunstan even more depressing than before. What he really needed was to go up to town and drown his sorrows at Kate Merrick's, not waste his time entertaining bores.

In private Lady Edith might storm at Thea for not being forthcoming, but she was all graciousness in public. Padworth was where she did not want to go, despite an invitation there being something of a prize. The professor had corresponded with Lord Longthorne who, although he was a Yankee, had a strong interest in eighteenth-century realist philosophers, dear also to Theodore Dunstan's heart, and possessed a splendid and unique library of books and manuscripts centred on them. The professor had written asking Lord Longthorne if he might visit and inspect it.

Gerard's answer, saying yes, and also inviting the professor and his family to visit Padworth, delighted his scholar's heart. He was not to know that Gerard, matchmaking in his turn, invited him because of Thea. Perhaps, thought Gerard drily, a clever girl, which the professor's daughter was supposed to be, might attract young Gis, even if she were plain.

The Dunstans arrived there in the early afternoon, and after helping Harvey, her maid, to unpack, Thea went downstairs on her own to find occupation. Her father, she knew, would have made straight for the library. Lady Edith had said in a solemn voice that she must rest, the ten miles between Mereside and Padworth having apparently exhausted her.

Thea made her way down a grand staircase to the ground floor. They had arrived earlier in the afternoon than expected, having made excellent time on the road, and Lady Longthorne and her sister-in-law, Lady Havilland, were out visiting. Lord Longthorne had greeted them, and he had been something of a surprise to Thea. His urbanity nonplussed her. From her mother's frequent complaints about 'rich and vulgar Yankees taking society over; at least the King does not favour them as his father did, although, goodness knows, the Prince of Wales is mad on them,' she had expected someone quite different from the deeply civilised person Gerard appeared to be.

He had apologised for the absence of his family. His wife and sister would be in for tea — the time at which the Dunstans had been expected — his eldest son, young Gerard, had been badly wounded in the war, had had an operation and was now convalescing in the South of France with his wife, and Thea already knew that both his daughters were married.

'Young Gis Havilland is somewhere about,' he had said helpfully. 'I suppose you know him. He's just finished his second year at your father's college. He first went to Oxford in 1913, did one year there, and then the War came and interrupted things. . .'

No, Thea didn't know Gis Havilland, although she had heard all about him, and the imp observed, How cross Mother will be. We have spent the whole year dodging him, and here he is, waiting for us at Father's Mecca. She avoided meeting Lady Edith's eye while their host rang for servants to take them to their rooms, where coffee and biscuits would be sent up to them.

Thea had drunk her coffee with pleasure, had closed her ears while her mother, before retiring, had told her that she was by no means to encourage young Havilland in any way, 'Although,' she added tartly, 'it would be just like you to do so, while refusing to be more than civil to poor Hector!'

The words rang in her ears as she wandered along Padworth's winding corridors. Someone, somewhere was playing a paino, and playing it well, and she followed the music to a pair of double doors, which she opened to find herself in a light and airy drawing room, filled with flowers, a large grand piano at one end beside glass doors opening on to a garden and the strains of Debussy's 'Clair de Lune' in her ears.

The pianist, a young man, had his back to her, and she entered as quietly as she could, so as not to disturb him, and thought that she had done so, until he said, without turning his head, 'Do sit down, if you wish. I never mind an audience.'

She did so, wondering how he had known that she was there. Gis, not allowing her entrance to disturb his concentration, had seen her appear in a large and splendid Venetian glass mirror on the wall beyond the piano, and had thought, Ah, yes, I was right at Mereside. It *was* Hector's dowd who caught me, for he knew that the only persons expected at Padworth that day were the Dusntans.

Thea was wearing a dress of cream lawn with some fine lace inserts. Her hair was plainly dressed in two plaits wound around her head, Lady Edith did not approve of the new fashion of bobbing the hair, which was a pity, Thea thought, since it would have suited her. Altogether she looked extremely ladylike — and extremely dull.

Debussy over, Gis began on Brahms. It was typical of him, she later found, that although his manners were usually excellent, when he was engaged on some task which engrossed him, everything had to wait until it was completed. Thea did not recognise the music, and her effort to try to place it showed on her face. Gis, mind-reading, said, over his shoulder, 'It's Brahms, a movement from one of the string quartets adapted for piano.'

He dropped his hands on the keys when the short piece came to an end, and, swinging round on the stool, offered, 'My mother says I'm always being a mannerless oaf; I should have greeted you properly earlier. I am Gis Havilland and you must be Thea Dunstan,' and he half rose from the piano stool, to bow to her.

'Not at all,' Thea returned, 'I would much rather you continue playing. You play beautifully,' which he did. She was speaking with as much composure as she could muster, for her first full sight of him had shocked her.

She had heard so much about him, his brilliance, his womanising, the practical jokes which he played, the fact that he was something of a bounder who had bolted back to America the moment the war had started, only to reappear again when it was over, not having had the grace to enlist in the American Army, even though it was rumoured that Kate Havilland, an American, was his mother.

What no one had told her of were his extraordinary good looks. From the top of his golden head to the toes of his light shoes he was not only the most handsome and athletic-looking man she had ever seen, but he was also perfectly turned out. And he played the piano like an angel.

'You like Brahms,' he said, spinning round again, and, putting his hands on the keys, asked her, 'Do you like this?' and he began to play ragtime, his hands flying along the keyboard, and the tune was, improbably, 'Alexander's Ragtime Band'. He sang it as well, in a pleasant baritone, ending by cocking his head on one side, and winking at her, so that cool Miss Dorothea Dunstan disappeared as she broke into a fit of the giggles.

Gis got up in one lithe and graceful movement to walk over to the chair opposite the sofa on which she sat, and said approvingly, 'There, I knew I could make you smile, but neither Debussy nor Brahms would have done the trick,' and his own smile was so warm that Thea found the ice around her heart dissolving, and her own grew broader as she said softly,

'Was it essential that I should smile, then?' which was the kind of flirtatious offering which she never normally made, but he seemed to be expecting it.

Gis thought that when the serious and clever Miss Dunstan, for such was her reputation in Oxford, smiled, her whole face was transformed.

He looked serious himself, clasped his hands together beneath his chin in imitation of every don in Oxford questioning a student, and said portentously, 'Now, you know as well as I do, Miss Dunstan, that every young woman when she first meets a strange young man is expected to offer him a smile of welcome. Now, mark me, young miss, the smile must be carefully calculated; too wide and cheerful, and her reputation is gone, not to smile at all brands her as proud, so it must be just so, like this —' and he unclasped his hands and gave her a shy simper, screwing up his eyes a little, so that he looked exactly like Cousin Lilian on meeting a handsome young man — which was the sort of thing which her mother always wanted her to do. . .and which she never did.

'Do you think,' she said, stifling even more giggles — she had always despised gigglers, 'that you

could give me lessons? You do that so much better
than I can.'

Gis returned his face to normal, wondering why
it pleased him to embark on such a childish flirtation
with a young woman of such marked lack of obvious
attractions. Pity, perhaps? Or was it that he must do
everything in his power to be as different as possible
from the sexual pirate and robber whom she had
surprised at Mereside?

'Why not practise a little now?' he suggested. 'We
are alone. Any mistakes which you make will go
unnoticed. Pretend I am, say, the curate from the
church at Longthorne come to visit. He has no
money, and is of good family. Offer me the sort of
welcome which would be suitable in such a case.'
And he immediately looked quite solemn, as though
ready to read the collect on Sunday at any moment.

Thea just managed to smile after a fashion which
suggested friendliness, but no real warmth, when
the giggles overcame her again—whatever is the
matter with me? she thought. Behave yourself, said
the imp, severely. He will think you a fool.

If he did, he gave no sign of it. 'Not bad,' he said
critically. 'Perhaps a little warmer than his wealth
and status deserves. If he had a suitable compe-
tence, now, I would suggest even more warmth.'

'At what point,' enquired Thea sweetly, 'would
one break into hearty laughter? If I were introduced
to a royal duke, perhaps, say York, or his brother,
Prince Henry, or at that point would one not smile
at all?' The game was beginning to amuse her, and
she was also beginning to wonder why her mother
had been so determined that they should not meet.

Why, he's nice, she thought, and then, Perhaps

he's charming to everyone, and he's only being
charming to me because there's no one else about.
Not a happy thought, that.

'And what,' said Gis shrewdly, 'is worrying you,
Miss Dunstan? The question of how to greet the
monarch?'

She could not tell him the truth, said airily, 'I was
wondering where Father was, and whether I ought
to go and look for him.'

'Not at all,' said Gis. 'He's with my uncle in the
library. They were disputing over the relationship
between Isaac Newton in the seventeenth century
and Deism in the eighteenth. I much prefer
"Alexander's Ragtime Band" to that, don't you?'

She thought that now Gis was not telling the
truth, and he, reading her a little, laughed to himself
and rose from his seat.

'Come,' he said, 'let me show you the garden,'
and he waved her to the glass doors, and, taking her
arm, led her through them.

Thea was still overwhelmed by him, but tried not
to show it. Never before had she met a man who
attracted her as Gis Havilland did. It was not just
his good looks — she had met good-looking men
before — it was everything about him. The slight
laugh in his voice, the ease with which he spoke to
her, so that she, poor, plain Thea Dunstan, felt
herself at one with all the other beauties whom he
was reputed to know.

Once in the garden, her entrancement continued.
He led her along where the branches of the trees
had been pleached — intertwined so that they were
walking in shade, stopping to show her an antique
bronze nymph, fleeing from Apollo, already turning

into a tree to escape the God's charms. Should she try to turn into a small bush to escape Gis Havilland? the imp queried her wickedly. The thought made her smile. Finally they reached a herb garden, bordered on all sides by hedges cut into fantastic shapes: a swan, an eagle, something which looked like a bear. In the warmth of the August afternoon the scent which arose from the plants laid out before her added to Thea's enchantment.

'Oh,' she said, 'how beautiful,' and Gis, bending down, nipped a small sprig from one of the plants and handed it to her quoting gravely, '"There's rosemary, that's for remembrance; pray love, remember. . .",' and he cocked an eye at her, so that she answered him with Ophelia's next words, *Hamlet* being a play she had both read and seen at Stratford.

'"There's fennel for you, and columbine and. . ." What was next? Rue, I think. "O! You must wear your rue with a difference".' And her eyes sparkled, and her whole face shone with the pleasure of speaking to someone who could play at allusions with her, and not look as though she had taken leave of her senses if she did.

Gis laughed, and plucked a sprig of basil, saying, 'I refuse to quote Keats to you, when I offer you basil, Miss Thea Dunstan. I heard that Professor Dunstan's daughter was clever, and, for once, rumour did not lie.'

The compliment, as was usual with compliments, undid Thea. She went an embarrassed red, said hastily, swallowing her words a little, 'Oh, I am not really very clever. I never went to a girls' public school, nor to one of the new women's colleges. . .'

and then she stopped dead, for she feared that she was telling him something about herself which she had told no one else.

Oh, but she was, for Gis looked at her, said softly, 'But you would have liked to go to Girton or Somerville, wouldn't you? Did your learned papa educate you?'

'Yes.' Thea was suddenly breathless, and again, surprisingly, told him more about herself — how was he managing to extract such confidences from her? 'He wanted a boy, you see. But all he got was me, and so he treated me as though I were a boy, but Mother wouldn't allow me to go to school or to college. It wasn't fitting, she said, for I shall never need to earn a living.'

Animated, her small face was not beautiful, but its eagerness interested the handsome young man who was passing an idle hour by charming a girl at whom he would not normally have looked.

'So, Miss Thea Dunstan?' he asked her gently. 'What did he teach you? Greek, Latin, and philosophy? Enough to get you a double first, perhaps?'

Thea swallowed again, said, steadily, 'Yes. He made no concessions to my female mind. He said that he had neither the time nor the patience for that.' She didn't tell Gis, and she didn't need to, that Lady Edith had instructed her, again and again, that she was not to let any young man whom she met — or any older one, for that matter — know that she was a mistress of such unwomanly arts.

'So,' said Gis, beckoning her to a small rustic seat, nothing artistic, but suited to the place in which they found themselves, 'if I wish to be ready to engage with your formidable papa next term, I perhaps ought to have a small tutorial with his daughter first. How do you recommend that I approach him? All agog, or would he be more pleased with a casual air which implies that I am ready to joust with him on equal terms?'

Thea began to laugh. 'Are you never serious?' she exclaimed.

'Not often,' he said, one eyebrow rising — Thea found herself charting his every expression. 'Now you, I think, are serious all the time. Wouldn't it be a good idea if we changed places, that I become serious, and bequeath my frivolity to you? We should both please our mothers a little more if we did so.'

He knows about Mother, then, and what her opinion is of my charmlessness, thought Thea, swallowing a little, but she said brightly, 'Suppose we each gave the other a little of what most engages us, then we should keep our own identity, but surrender just enough to allow us to please others a little more.'

'A female Solomon,' pronounced Gis. 'Now you must answer my question about your papa. I see that your advice would be most apt.'

'High seriousness would be best,' she advised. She hesitated. 'Papa doesn't possess a great sense of humour, and distrusts people who do.'

'Does he distrust you, then?' queried Gis shrewdly.

'He doesn't know that I have one,' she replied simply.

Gis suddenly felt an enormous pity for the girl to whom he was talking, and, at the same time, felt a little ashamed of his own rather lordly patronage of

her. He was well aware that he was doing her no
favour if he encouraged her to fall in love with him,
and, without being conceited, he knew that he could
charm Miss Thea Dunstan into worshipping him, if
he took the trouble.

But he was really only showing such interest in
her to dispel any suspicion she might have that he
was the midnight intruder of Mereside, by being so
charmingly civilised that such a suspicion would be
absurd.

She had a good mind, though, and possessed the
sense of humour which she complained her father
lacked, and which he knew Lady Edith also did.
Lady Edith was famous in Oxford for her managing
ways, and had been nicknamed 'the professoress'
for them. Thea, he had heard, was plain and dull.
Well, she wasn't dull, but he must go carefully.

Going carefully did not prevent him from continuing to entertain her. Presently they renewed their
stroll aound the garden, and were laughing together
about Gis's description and impersonation of the
comedian, George Robey, whom he had seen on a
recent visit to London, when Lady Longthorne,
with Lady Havilland and Lady Edith in tow, found
them in the garden.

'Good,' said Torry, a pleased expression on her
face. 'I see that you have been entertaining our
guest for me, Gis. I came to tell you that tea is being
served on the lawn at the back of the house, and to
offer you my apologies, Miss Dunstan, that I was
not present when you arrived. I believe that you do
not know Lady Havilland, Gis's mother.'

Lady Havilland was not at all like Gis, being small
and dark, with a witty face full of character. Like

Lady Longthorne she was beautifully turned out,
and made Lady Edith look over-upholstered, the
imp told Thea critically. Lady Havilland was wearing a frock of the most delicate but flaming beauty,
which Thea later found was by Fortuny, the great
Venetian dress designer.

She was aware that her mother was furious that
she had been found alone in the gardens with the
undesirable Gis Havilland, and Lady Edith, for one,
was determined not to be charmed by someone who
would never be charmed by her.

Her look for Thea was pure poison, but she was
compelled to be civil by the presence of the creature's mother. Some instinct to be contrary kept
Thea by Gis's side, and when he assisted her into a
basket chair on the lawn and was assiduous in plying
her with paper-thin cucumber sandwiches and tiny
cakes, and all the goodies brought out to console
the visitors between early lunch and late dinner,
Thea was suddenly sure that part of his courtly care
for her was there as much to annoy Lady Edith as
to please herself!

How she knew this was a mystery, for such
insights had rarely been granted her before, and it
was odd to find that she had such a psychic com-
munication with a young man whom she had only
just met, and whom she could not believe that she
had charmed—however much he charmed her!

So many internal exclamation marks were beginning to overwhelm the imp, who warned her tartly,
Be careful, now, Thea, my girl. A dashing creature
like Gis Havilland cannot be for you. Burned
fingers, at the very least, will result from warming
your hands before such a fire.

Oh, do be quiet, do, she almost said aloud, I am enjoying myself, and, looking up, she saw Gis's eye on her, and out of sight of the others he leaned forward to hand her a plate of chocolate biscuits, breathed, 'Indulge yourself, Miss Thea, I beg of you,' and gave her a meaningful wink when he saw her hesitate.

I have had no practice at this, was Thea's dazed internal response. Aloud, she said, 'I do believe I will. I am a little tired of being good all the time,' and she ate her biscuit with gusto, trying not to catch his eye, but she did, and, while Lady Edith was loudly deploring the manners of the modern young, he whispered to her,

'Bravo, have another,' so she did, with the imp saying sternly, You will pay for this later, since Lady Edith was looking daggers at the pair of them, little escaping her eagle eye.

'So,' she said awfully, to a preoccupied Thea, having made a special visit to her room while she was dressing for dinner, 'I see that you have nothing better to do than to make sheep's eyes at Ghysbrecht Havilland, and after I had told you to stay away from him, too. I could wish that you would be half as civil to poor Hector Dashwood. What can be the attraction, I wonder?'

'Perhaps because he is rich, Gis Havilland, and he amuses me,' replied Thea, pertly for her, slipping on a beige coatee over her extremely dull beige dress, wondering what on earth Gis Havilland would make of such a very dowdy ensemble. Between her mother's desire for her to be always dressed as a perfect lady, and her own desire not to attract

attention to her plain face, she seemed to be
doomed to appear middle-aged before her time. She
had never before resented this, but meeting Gis
Havilland had changed her perspective on life.

Perhaps, suggested the imp slyly, one way to
attract him might be to adopt the eccentric mode,
since being fashionable won't answer. A green and
gold silk Egyptian trouser suit, perhaps, and an
ebony cigarette holder eighteen inches long might
do for starters.

This notion so entranced Thea that she lost track
of what her mother was saying.

'Now, do pay attention to me, Dorothea. . .your
mind is wandering again.'

Her mother's scolding voice rose an octave, so
that her father, coming in, remarked mildly to his
wife, 'Here you are, then, my dear, but what has
Dorothea been doing to deserve such a roasting?'

'And how should you know, Mr Dunstan,' said
Lady Edith, more exasperated than ever, 'since you
have spent the whole afternoon closeted in the
library with Lord Longthorne? If it were left to you
I do believe that Dorothea would end up marrying
the milkman, and you would not even notice.'

'Seeing that the milkman is at least sixty and a
grandfather,' Thea could not help remarking; the
devil — or was it Gis Havilland? — seemed to have
got into her since she had arrived at Padworth, 'I
am sure that even Father would notice when he led
me to the altar, with his wife crying bigamy behind
him.'

Both parents stared at her, and, 'If this is what
exposure to that young roué does to you,' began her
mother, and her father, more mildly,

'Dorothea, my dear, hardly a proper thing for a young girl to say. . .'

The imp, for the first time, took over, and spoke aloud in Dorothea's voice. 'You amaze me, Mother, and Father, too. Why is it perfectly proper for a penniless *old* roué to make unpleasant overtures to me in private for the money he supposes I shall inherit, while a conversation in public with a rich *young* roué is considered improper? So far as you are concerned, Father, I would expect you to understand that such a proposition cannot be logically expressed, even if the concept is beyond my mother.'

There was the most dreadful and appalled silence, as both her parents stared at her again. Lady Edith in horror, Mr Dunstan with his mouth twitching in an effort to avoid an involuntary smile. Thea had not raised her voice; her manner was as calm as though she were demanding an extra cup of tea. Lady Edith, who did not quite grasp her daughter's insult, was, however, well aware that she had been insulted. 'Mr Dunstan,' she began, 'are you going to allow this. . .'

To which he replied, 'What do you suggest, my dear? Thea is a little old for a spanking, however salutary such an act might be. I could suggest that you might dock her dress allowance, but somehow I think that would not trouble Thea over-much. Putting her in the corner for the next hour would mean that she could not go down to dinner with us, and explaining her absence would be tiresome, to say the least.'

Faced by rebellion from her two erstwhile slaves, Lady Edith threatened to turn on the waterworks.

She lifted her handkerchief to her eyes, announced, 'So! This is what I get from my efforts to settle your daughter in life, Mr Dunstan. Were I not of stronger metal I would give up, instanter, but no, nothing, I tell you, nothing, will stand in the way of my intentions to arrange a good marriage for your only child. And you see how right I was to try to keep her away from creatures like Gis Havilland. Two hours in his company and she forgets herself completely.'

Oh, if only I could, Mother, was Thea's inward thought, if only I could. She looked at the tragedy queen Lady Edith had turned into, shrugged her shoulders, walked over to her, said, in an effort to placate, 'I'm sorry that I was rude to you, Mother, but you did provoke me. I'll try to be more patient in future,' and was rewarded by an approving smile from her father.

But I shall talk to Gis Havilland as often as I like, and as long as I like, was her rebellious inward comment as she walked downstairs to dinner.

Dinner was as good as might be expected, and Thea was seated next to Gis, who kept up an interesting flow of conversation. They discovered that they both liked the same reading matter. At least Gis confessed a taste for Stanley Weyman and Rafael Sabatini without letting Thea know that their romances had been enjoyed by him when he was twelve years old, precocity being his middle name.

He liked Charlie Chaplin, too, a taste in Thea deplored by Lady Edith as low. She had been horrified when she discovered that Thea's governess had been taking her to the cinema to enjoy such a common Yankee entertainment, and the poor governess had been sacked on the spot, not even Thea's father being able to save her. Thea would have liked to tell Gis of this, but with Lady Edith's eye on her she dared not.

What she did dare was to talk as animatedly to him as she could, delightedly aware that there was nothing Lady Edith could do about it — as long as dinner lasted. She swept out with the ladies, leaving Gis amused by what he had correctly identified as her small rebellion. He had seen — and read — the glances which she kept shooting in her mother's direction. He knew from what his mother and aunt Torry had said that Lady Edith was pursuing Hector for her daughter, and shuddered at what Thea's fate might be if she married such a brute.

Why it should matter to him he couldn't understand. Only, having met her, she seemed such a small helpless creature to be so sacrificed, and he had been amused by the brave spirit she had shown when speaking to him, so much at odds with her mild appearance.

But am I doing her a favour to set her against such a formidable mother? he asked himself, only to let the thought die as he joined in the conversation struck up between the professor, his father and his uncle, about the new German Republic of Weimar, and its chances of success in the post-war world. His elders were optimistic, but Gis, surprisingly for one so young, was of the opinion that the Germans would never be satisfied until they had reversed the defeat of 1918.

The conversation then moved on to the perennial problems of Ireland and the activities of Sinn Fein,

and how to counteract them. More optimism was
expressed and again Gis found himself in a minority.

Discussing the fate of nations, he forgot the fate
of Thea Dunstan.

plum. Don't run away, Thea. I've nearly finished.
And when I have, I'll give you a guided tour of
Padworth's treasures, just as still a moment, there's
a good gift.'

Thea considered . . . [illegible] up she said, 'Why
not? Nothing can happen in the library, can it? So

CHAPTER THREE

THEA walked into the library to escape everyone.
She couldn't seem to please her mother, and she
was distressed that her relationship with her father
had changed since the days when he had seen her as
a substitute son — now that she was a woman he left
her more and more to her mother. Gis Havilland
she most definitely didn't want to see.

And why not? Her sensations when she was near
to him were beginning to frighten her, cancelling
out the pleasure she felt in talking to him. Besides,
she knew how little she meant to him. That morning
her mother had told her in some triumph, 'Well,
you won't have young Havilland to pursue after
lunch today. He's off to Poyns to spend time with
Diana Troy, and we all know what *that* means!'

She hadn't answered her mother, simply made for
the library to find a refuge there.

But it wasn't a refuge. Gis Havilland sat at the
big table before the hearth, several books before
him, a look of acute concentration on his face. He
was writing at a speed which she found incredible,
his hand travelling rapidly across the page. She
turned to go, to find somewhere where she might be
alone, and not be tormented by everyone she met.

Concentrating he might be, but, as in the drawing-
room on that first afternoon, he apparently knew
she was there, for without slackening speed, or
lifting his head, he said, the laugh in his voice quite

plain, 'Don't run away, Thea. I've nearly finished.
And when I have, I'll give you a guided tour of
Padworth's treasures. Just sit still a moment, there's
a good girl.'

Thea considered bolting, but the imp said, Why
not? Nothing can happen in the library, can it? So
she sat down, and after a few more minutes Gis
gave a great 'Oof' of a sigh, put down his pen, and
swung towards her, smiling.

The imp, for once, was wrong. Something *had*
happened in the library. A something which hit
Thea hard in an unmentionable place, there, just
below the pit of her stomach. A place no lady
owned or acknowledged existed. And the sensation
told her, beyond a doubt, that she had done the most
foolish of all things, and worse, that Lady Edith was
right. She had fallen in love with Gis Havilland.

Did it always happen like that? A thunderclap
and then one vast ache. The world swung about her,
like a kaleidoscope being shaken, and a new pattern
was before her, a pattern in which the man opposite
to her, whom she had only known for forty-eight
hours, had assumed an importance which he would
never lose. Of all people to choose to fall in love
with, it had to be the Golden Boy — for Thea knew
of his nickname — who could never ever fall in love
with Professor Dunstan's plain and dowdy daughter.

'Ready?' he said, and then, looking at her white
face, and his intuition failing him for once, he
misread its meaning, thought that she was feeling
faint, needed air, said, 'No, let us go outdoors, into
the garden. There's a walk I know you have not
taken, with a view of the lake and the woods
beyond, which more than one painter has thought

worth recording. The library can wait until I come back from Poyns.'

'I shall be gone by then,' offered Thea.

'I think not,' he said, smiling again, so that her heart turned over. 'I'm only going there for two nights. Moidore is off abroad at the weekend, and wants to wind up his party in style. He has a guest he want me to meet. A Danish philosopher, no less.'

So, it wasn't only Diana Troy who was the attraction. Thea immediately felt better.

They both rose. 'Come,' he said, and put out a hand to take hers. What made Thea look so closely at the offered hand she never knew. Perhaps it was only to check whether the hand was as beautiful and shapely as the rest of him — which it was. Perhaps it was to avoid the splendid blue eyes, his beautiful mouth, his whole overwhelming self which was causing her heart to jump out of her breast. No wonder Diana Troy — and all the others — pursued him with such vigour.

And thinking this she looked at his outstretched hand — and nearly froze. It was not only the double of the shapely hand which had belonged to the unknown robber who she had disturbed at Mereside, but there, on its little finger, was the small strange ring which the robber had worn. . .

Suddenly icy-cold, from being burning hot, torn between the first desires of her newly awakened body and the significance of what she was seeing, Thea looked up at Gis. She looked at the perfect profile, at the tendrils of golden hair which clustered around his head like the hair on the statue of Antinous which she had seen in one of the Oxford colleges. . . .and she remembered the golden strand which had strayed from beneath the mask that night. . .

Improbable though it might seem, Ghysbrecht Havilland, charming, rich and clever, was the night-time intruder whom she had disturbed in the library at Mereside and who had so ruthlessly plundered her mouth!

The imp's teeth chattered, not hers, so that Gis heard nothing. He was talking in his light and pleasant voice, telling her of Padworth's history, of the family who had owned it since the Middle Ages, and from whom his uncle Gerard had bought it some twenty years ago. Was it possible that the hoarse and threatening voice which she had heard at Lancing was also one which Gis Havilland could assume? And why? Why should he be burgling Mereside? He had been there for some time before she had arrived, she was sure of that, but Hector had been firm that the intruder had taken nothing.

Was it a bet? A dare such as she had heard that the Bright Young Things of London society went in for now that all constraints had been loosened by wartime? Somehow, she didn't think so.

'Yes,' she said in answer to a question from him, astonished at her ability to do two things at once, analyse the Mereside episode and carry on a casual conversation with him, a faculty which she shared, although she did not know it yet, with her companion. 'Yes, I have visited Poyns, and yes, the gardens there are beautiful, too.'

Such inanity, when she was considering whether it was an impossibility that Gis could have been the burglar — except that memory told her that she was mistaken neither over the ring nor the hand. There could not be two such. What was she to do? Did he — could he? — know that she had recognised him? Oh, said the imp, but reflect. *He* must have recognised you — and that is why he has been flirting with you, and charming you with such assiduity — despite your lack of charms!

Desolation swept over her, as he gently guided her along a gravelled path, across a lawn, through another set of hedges decorated with some remarkable topiary work — could that really be a phoenix ready to fly, or was it merely a peacock? Why would her mind not stop wandering when she wished to concentrate? No, she didn't wish to concentrate, to think, because she knew that she was nothing to him, and yes, as his beautiful voice ran on, there was mirth underlying it, and what a marvellous instrument it was, and how cleverly and heartlessly he was using it to further his own wicked interests.

Despite the warmth of the day Thea found herself shivering. What was she to do? There was no one to whom she could turn. The thought of confiding in either her mother or her father was ridiculous. Not only would she have to claim that she had recognised Ghysbrecht Havilland as a thief and a liar, but she would also have to explain why she had not given the alarm when she had surprised him at Mereside.

By now they had reached the promised view. The tall hedge was behind them, before them the ground fell away towards a small lake with woods in the background, green near to, mauve in the distance. The sky was a perfect Mediterranean blue, the scene

before them such that normally she would have felt
only the gravest and purest delight at the sight of it.

And now he was showing her a small white
temple, with two columns only, and inside the
temple's rotunda a small marble bench and table.
'Henry James's corner,' he said. 'He used to stay at
Padworth before the War, and rumour says that he
wrote part of *The Wings of the Dove* here. If so, it
must have pleased my parents, for Venice figures in
it, and they first met in Venice.'

Thea knew that *The Wings of the Dove* was all
about treachery between men and women in love,
and thought how apt it was that he should speak of
it now, when she had discovered his treachery, and
that all his seducing charm had been directed
towards her for his own ends, with the result that
she had fallen deeply and hopelessly in love with
someone who was not worthy of the affection she
felt for him. Someone who was a liar, a coward —
remembering his lack of war-service — and last of all
he was a thief, for, despite what Hector had said —
and why he had lied about it she didn't know — she
was as certain as she was of anything that Gis *had*
broken into Mereside to steal something, and all she
could find to say to him, in a little girl's voice, was,
'How interesting,' when in reality she was wandering through the Sahara, alone, as usual.

Gis had no idea of what Thea was thinking. She
had retained her calm expression and even calmer
manner. But he knew that something was wrong.
Looking down at her from his greater height he was
astonished by the emotion which swept over him —
it was such a new one.

Ever since he had discovered at the age of sixteen

that his supposed foster-parents were his real ones, and that he had been conceived eight years before their marriage, he had been a hard man. His experiences during the war had made him even harder. His cynicism was absolute, but was cloaked beneath a massive charm, exploding outwards only at intervals, and usually at those he considered cruel frauds.

Love, for him, was a matter of pleasure, although lately the pleasure had begun to pall, and he was not looking forward to going over to entertain Diana with the same enthusiasm which he had once done.

But Thea Dunstan was quite another thing. She was like a small shy animal in her contained quietness, with a hint of fierceness underneath. She had faced him at Mereside with little sign of the fear which she must have been experiencing, and had endured his explicit sexual onslaught after a fashion which had left him feeling ashamed.

Quiet beside him, listening to him talk, making the occasional pointed and relevant comment, she gave off her own aura of pleasant control, together with a scent of wild flowers—a scent which he had first noticed when he had taken her in his arms at Mereside.

An overwhelming surge of something, protectiveness, perhaps, laced with the merest tinge of sexual desire passed over him, bewildering him a little for nothing he had experienced told him how he ought to cope with it. Why protective? he asked himself. She has a father, a mother and a fortune, will make what the world will call a 'good marriage'.

But the mother is appalling, Gis thought savagely, and the father, outside his scholastic preoccupation, is ineffectual and has resigned her to the predatory mother. Her fortune cannot help her for her mother is using it to buy a title whose owner is disgusting, and who will misuse her in every way. . . Even if her fortune is tied up so that he cannot squander it . . .particularly if her fortune is tied up, he will punish her for that, forgetting that it will repair Mereside's roof, restore the house to its former glory and settle new tenantry on the neglected land. . . She will be a reproach and a millstone.

Still talking lightly, and, like Thea, thinking of other things while he spoke, he mocked himself. Why worry about this one small girl? The world was full of small girls whose fate was far worse than that which faced Thea.

Ah, but I do not know them. He almost flung away from her. He didn't want to pity her, to be compelled to do something to save her. Thank God for Poyns and Diana where he could lose himself in sensation, and forget the resurgent conscience which he'd thought that he had strangled long ago.

'When I come back from Poyns,' he heard himself saying, with some surprise, 'I shall take you for a spin, and we can visit the small wood which you can see over there,' and he pointed into the blue distance. 'You would like that. There are animals there, and orchids, wild ones, far more delicate and beautiful than the cultivated ones worn in ballrooms.'

Thea's face lit up. She forgot, momentarily, that he was Mereside's thief, and the dilemma which that knowledge had placed her in.

'Oh, yes, I should like that very much,' she replied eagerly. 'I have always been interested in wild flowers. The governess whom Mother dismissed because she took me to the cinema without permission taught me about them, and how to press them, and I have never forgotten — even though I think pressed flowers are dismal things — they seem so dead and gone.'

'Like fossils in the rocks,' suggestd Gis. 'But they have the power to remind us of our past. What did your governess take you to see, Thea?'

'That was when I saw Charlie Chaplin. She took me six times before Mother found out,' replied Thea wistfully. 'He was so funny, and I have never seen him since. Mother doesn't approve of the cinema.'

Gis said, surprising himself again. 'Perhaps, then, instead of visiting Birley Wood, we could go to the cinema together.'

Thea clasped her hands, forgot the moral problem Gis presented, forgot that she hated him for pretending to like her, said painfully, 'Mother would never allow. . .'

'Need she know?' murmured Gis naughtily.

This reminded Thea all over again of his deceit — and that she hated him.

'I could never do anything of which Mother might disapprove,' she announced loftily.

'Nothing?' Gis was naughtier than ever, bent down, and, without touching her in any other way, bestowed a butterfly kiss on her parted lips, lips which had parted so eagerly at the thought of a visit to the forbidden cinema. 'Not that, for instance?' he asked, pulling away only to return again, the kiss still light, as though he were a bee gently sipping the nectar from the flower, not pillaging it in any way.

Thea's senses reeled. Oh, he was wicked, wicked! First he broke into Mereside, and then he kissed her, hard, to keep her quiet, and now here he was, kissing her again! The mild flirtations in which even well-brought-up young girls indulged had never been part of her life.

He pulled away. Thea involuntarily gave a little wailing, 'Oh.'

'You liked that?' Gis was beginning to wonder at himself. The scent of honey which her hair exuded, the delicacy of her, even the plain face delicate, but the green eyes in it larger than ever as she received her first lesson in light lovemaking, were beginning to have a surprising effect on him. 'Do you think that you would like this, even if Mother disapproved?' And he put both hands about her face, drawing her gently towards him, and now the kiss was deeper, roved about her face, but was still innocent, nothing to frighten the shy untouched thing that she was.

She liked it. Oh, yes, she liked it. But she shouldn't and the warring emotions inside Thea — pleasure at being so deftly handled, and rage at him for deceiving her — were now so mixed that she hardly knew how to react. It was her turn to pull away, face flushed, her hands gathered into fists at her side.

She said, breathlessly, 'I didn't give you permission to do that.'

Gis put his head on one side, breathed a gentle, 'No? Then why don't you? Give me permission, I mean.'

'Because you do it to all the girls. I know you do.'

'Not like that I don't.' He was naughtier than

ever, thinking of the wild way in which he and
Diana made love, and the touching innocence of the
young girl before him, which he had respected by
handling her so delicately.

Now what could he mean by that? Perhaps if she
had been more often to the wicked cinema, or had
been allowed to play with her Dunstan boy cousins
when she and they were younger, she might know
what he was talking about. As it was, Thea felt her
sexual ignorance keenly. She went an unlovely red,
muttered, 'I want to go back to the house, please,
and no, I won't go anywhere alone with you. You
might do all that again.'

'Do admit that you liked "all that" a little,' urged
Gis, a little distressed by her distress. He had tried
not to go too quickly with her—but why was he
going with her at all, even slowly?

He had to admit that his behaviour to her was
more than a desire to deceive her, to make her
forget the night-time bandit. He was doing this for
her. For Thea, not out of deviousness nor to amuse
himself. On the contrary, it was to please and
entertain the pleasant child that she was.

Thea's head went up. She couldn't confess that
'all that' was new to her. He would think her a fool.
Yes, she was a fool, compared with all the other
girls she knew. She knew that they laughed at her
because she was so completly underneath Lady
Edith's thumb—but how to wriggle out from under
it? If it were not for what she knew of him, she
thought that Gis might be a means of escape, but
no. . .

'I want you to behave yourself properly when you

are with me.' Her voice, she was pleased to hear, was quite firm and determined.

'As a point to discuss,' offered Gis, taking her by the elbow, and beginning to return her towards the house—and safety, 'my behaving properly to you, might constitute, in my terms, kissing you.'

'Not in mine.' Thea was firm again.

'You're quite sure?' Gis stopped. 'You wouldn't like me to give you another demonstration so that you could be certain in your own mind that you wouldn't wish to do a little more of "all that" with me?'

'Mother wouldn't approve.'

'Oh, I'm not kissing Mother.' His voice was lazy. 'The demonstration was for you, not her.'

It was no good. Robber, liar, cheat, womaniser and coward he might be, she couldn't help it. Thea began to laugh. Not a ladylike laugh, half behind one's hand, head slightly averted, but a joyous one.

'You are quite ridiculous, Gis Havilland.' Her voice was as frank and free, as devoid of all the constraints which being her mother's daughter had placed upon her as it could be.

'I aim to please,' was his only reply, with a slight bow, and now the green eyes on him were telling him a story of which their owner was not aware, so that he bent down, and gave her another kiss, on the slightly turned-up nose. Why, the child was not so dreadfully plain, after all, and he capped the kiss by saying, 'You don't mind if I practise a little, do you? It has been some time since I carried on a flirtation in the open air. I don't want to grow rusty.'

So that's what they were doing, flirting, and he was practising on her! How dared he? And then she

heard herself saying — or was it the imp? — quite
disgracefully, 'I could perhaps do with a little practise myself. We both seem to be in need of it when
we are together.'

And, even more disgracefully, she lifted her face
towards him, crossing her fingers behind her back,
defying her mother, her father, God and the devil,
and St Michael and all angels as well.

'Oh, then, I'm quite ready to oblige. And I agree
with you, we seem to do a lot of practising together,
don't we?' And he turned her towards him, put his
right hand round her shoulders, tipped up her chin
with the betraying left one, the sun catching the ring
on his little finger, but what of that? For now she
was drowning in the first real kiss anyone had ever
given her, for the one at Mereside really didn't
count, even if it had been exciting in the extreme.

At first Thea was quite passive, let him do the
work, let him pull down the stiff plaits which were
arranged around her head, like the ones on the
medieval statue in Padworth church, let him kiss her
eyelids, and then when he whispered in her ear,
'Don't I deserve being practised on, too?' she kissed
him back, first on the cheek, and, when his mouth
reached hers, it suddenly became a passionate, fire-
raising thing, quite unlike the play of a moment ago.

As at Mereside, only more so, she felt that she
was beginning to dissolve, felt that only his hands
were holding her up, and Gis, suddenly and acutely
aware that he had roused her — and, what was
worse, was rousing himself — and that would never
do, was the first to pull away, saying, hoarsely,
'Practice over. I think that the pupil is coming on a

little too fast. The simpler exercises need more time spending on them, I fear.'

Thea didn't know whether she was glad or sorry. She had forgotten everything during the few short minutes when they were on the verge of making genuine love. Confused thoughts ran through her mind.

Will he think me fast — or loose? Common-sense said, I don't think we really did anything very dreadful, but, at the same time, a certain desolate feeling, associated with being Thea Dunstan, was beginning to overwhelm her. He had been amusing himself, quite heartlessly, probably; she mustn't forget that. No one would wish to make serious love to Thea Dunstan, surely.

Nor must she forget to pin up her plaits.

Gis said, suddenly and abruptly, in tones quite unlike the gentle ones he had been using with her since the start of their walk, 'Why don't you wear your hair loose, or have it bobbed? That severe style doesn't become you.'

'Mother. . .' Thea began.

'Doesn't wish you to wear it loose, or have it bobbed,' he finished for her wearily. 'I suppose she chooses your clothes, too.'

He didn't know why he was being so harsh with her. Perhaps it was her touching vulnerability, and the knowledge that there was really nothing he could do to rescue her — complicated as their situation was by the circumstances of their first meeting, and her mother's disapproval of him.

They had reached the glass doors again, were being observed, and so were perfectly proper. Seen from the outside, the handsome young man escorting the plain, shy girl so formally, no one could have guessed that Thea Dunstan had just been given her first lesson in sexual intrigue — and had enjoyed it.

But, after making some fevered excuse, Thea had retired to her room to sit on her bed. The heady effect of her walk with Gis had worn off. What did she think she had been doing, and what ought she to do?

Thank goodness that he was going to Poyns. It would give her time to think about her problem dispassionately, as though it were simply a problem in logic. And perhaps she could think about *him* dispassionately. She loved and hated him at the same time.

And when he came back, what then?

And when he was at Poyns, what would he be doing with Diana Troy?

And what a stupid question that was. She knew perfectly well what he was going to do with Diana Troy, and for the first time in her life she thought of a man and a woman together — and wondered what it would be like — and knew that the only man that she could contemplate doing *that* with, was Gis Havilland.

Which meant that she would have to refuse Hector. For the mere idea of going to bed with Hector made her feel so physically sick that she actually rose and rushed into the little cloakroom to lean over the sink and have the dry heaves at the mere idea.

She lifted her face, to stare at it, ashen, in the mirror. The sense of being alone had never been so strong in her. If only she could believe that she

could accept this morning's flirtation at its face
value, that he was attracted to her.

But oh, he was devious! She knew that as no one
else did. Yes, they knew that he was clever — it
shone out of him — but she knew that he was more
than that. . .he was the devil, wrapped up in a
shining carapace of charm and good looks. And the
devil was tempting Thea Dunstan, but she would
resist him, yes, she would. And the next time he
exercised his charm on her she would be cool and
distant and send him away with a flea in his ear.

But she knew that she wouldn't. . .

'Oh, damn you, Havilland, you have the luck of the
devil! If it is luck.'

Gis's hand, about to rake in his poker winnings,
froze in mid-air. He stared at Hector Dashwood
with his father's expression on his face, the
expression that Sir Richard used with the presump-
tuous. Gis would have been annoyed to learn how
like his father he was at times.

'And what, precisely, do you mean by that,
Hector?'

'What you like,' said Hector offensively. He was
half cut, sprawled in his chair, and no man who was
half cut should ever get into a poker game with Gis
Havilland, as half the men around the table could
have told him, Tom Moidore for one.

Tom intervened. 'Drink talking, Dashwood,' he
said cheerfully. 'You should know by now not to
take liberties with Gis at the card table. Memory
man himself, ain't he? Mathematical wizard, too.'

'If that's all,' pursued Hector doggedly and
unluckily, staring at the blond boy opposite to him.

He possessed no great intellect, or powers of reasoning, but it had become inescapably clear to him who had probably stolen Sophie Moreton's letters; Gis Havilland had visited him not forty-eight hours earlier, and had been sneaking around the library, too.

'Lucky devil, ain't you, Havilland?' He was worrying away at Gis like a dog with a bone. 'Missed the war, didn't you? Nice to have a bolt-hole in America to go to. Some of us weren't so lucky.'

Gis began to laugh, although what he found amusing about Hector's offensiveness Tom Moidore couldn't imagine. He tried to think of a way to end the game before the whole thing blew up beyond retrieval.

The men of the Poyns house-party had embarked on an evening's all-male gambling, with the reluctant agreement of their women. Diana had wanted to play, and then had tried to get Gis to cry off and join them in the drawing-room, only to have Tom say, 'But Gis is particularly needed, my dear. We all want a shot at him, to try to win a little back for a change.'

She had given way with an ill grace, thinking that she would have him all to herself later. Her husband, nearly as sodden as Hector, but holding his drink better, had watched the fracas with a little amusement. Wouldn't harm young Havilland to run into a spot of bother. Perhaps teach him not to be so offensively clever, and so attractive to other men's wives.

'Come on, Hector,' Gis said, drawing his hand back from the mixed pile of notes and coins which made up the pot he had won. 'Shuffle and deal again, eh?' He didn't feel like a run-in with the drunken fool before him, because, for once, he was not sure of retaining his own composure. The thought that Lady Edith had chosen this ill-conditioned swine for poor young Thea was making him feel quite sick.

Damn Thea Dunstan, he thought savagely. Why in God's name does she persist in walking through my mind?

'Unpleasant bastard, aren't you,' leered Hector, 'as well as a coward? Not surprising you're a card-sharp. Think I'll take my money back,' and he placed a predatory hand on the pile of moeny.

Gis's temper did not so much snap as implode. Face unchanged, he put out his right hand, to grasp Hector's and pin it to the table.

Hector tried to pull his hand away, but couldn't, and gradually Gis began to squeeze it cruelly, his own face remaining as calm and good-natured as ever.

'Let it be, Hector,' he said, coolly. 'It's my money, not yours. I'll give you a chance to win it back. Pax, eh?' And he flung this contemptuously at Hector, as though they were schoolboys together, fighting over conkers. 'You take back what you said, I'll let you have your hand back, and we'll deal again.'

Hector began to struggle, rose from his chair to try to recover his hand from that of the brute opposite.

'No. And damn you, Havilland, let go!'

Tom Moidore intervened again. 'Come on, Gis. Let him go. We all say what we don't mean when we're drunk.'

'Do we?' said Gis coolly, still increasing his grip. 'Perhaps that's why I never get drunk. So that everyone knows that when I'm offensive, I mean it. You're a poor loser, Hector, at cards and at life. Say pax, and I'll give you your hand back, and all's forgiven.'

'No, by God,' roared Hector, his face turning purple. 'And I meant what I said, Havilland, you're a bastard, and the whole world knows it. Bastard and coward, damn you, bastard and card-sharp.'

Gis rose, pulled Hector towards him, put his splayed left hand over Hector's enraged face, pulled his right hand away from the table, and, using his considerable strength, shoved Hector back, so that he was sent shouting and howling to hit the wall, hard, slither down it and land sitting on the floor.

'Bastard I undoubtedly am, so I forgive you that because you were simply telling the truth. Card-sharp I am not; coward I might be. Deal me out, Tom, I've better things to do with my time than play against an offensive oaf. I apologise to you for what has happened.'

Tom Moidore put up a hand and walked towards the pair of them, separated by the card table, the watching men ready to hold either of them back if the fracas continued further. Scandal was the last thing which he wanted, particularly a scandal which might damage young Havilland. He wasn't worried about Hector Dashwood; nothing could damage Hector, he was too damaged already. But he owed several debts of gratitude both to young Havilland's father and to his uncle, and now was the time to pay them.

After all, young Gis's status was equivocal enough, without its being further compromised.

His voice was the voice of the peacemaker. 'Come,' he said easily, 'neither of you wish to do anything you would permanently regret. Dashwood. . .' He turned to Hector who was being helped to his feet. 'I am sure, that, on reflection, you will take back what you said to Havilland, and Gis, I am sure that you will agree, that although it was understandable you perhaps. . .over-reacted a little to what was said. Shake hands, I beg of you, and Gis, stay a little longer in the game. No hard feelings, eh?'

He thought for a moment that scandal was not going to be avoided. Gis's expression changed. His blue eyes had been as hard and remote as an Arctic sea, the pleasant charm which he always showed the world quite gone. He had been, for a moment, a different man, one Tom Moidore and the others had never seen before, someone formidable—a blond and beautiful Gerard Schuyler, perhaps.

What no one in the room knew was that the moment he had put his hand on Hector's face, thinking of Thea as he had done so, a raging red berserker rage had consumed Gis. He had known it before, and when it was on him he had the utmost difficulty in controlling himself. He knew, and had proved to himself, that he could kill when he was in its grip.

He had first known that he possessed it when he had been taunted at Eton by the boy who had informed him that all the world knew he was a bastard. The other boys had had to drag him off his tormentor for fear that he might kill him. He had been consumed by it again when he had seen his friend shot down in flames over the western front, and had pursued the man who had done it, until he, too, had dropped from the sky, a flaming torch.

The rage might be red, but its possessor was icy calm. Slowly, Gis felt the cold fire die down, said, almost indifferently to Moidore, who had always been his friend, 'As you will, Tom,' and put out his hand to Hector, although it was the last thing he wished to do.

Hector stared at it, stared at Moidore, who said, still easy, 'Unwise to refuse, I think, Dashwood,' and Hector was not so far gone that he did not hear the warning note. If Moidore cut him, refused to receive him, few in society would. He was one of society's great arbiters, and he might drop out of everything if he incurred Tom's displeasure.

Grudgingly he put out his hand to meet Gis's. The hands touched. Just. It was enough; a collective sigh went round the room. Gis sat down, as did Hector, and the game began again. The red mist had departed, but Gis was in a frightening mood which sometimes succeeded it. The world had become distant, and the people in it unimportant. He chose to let his superb memory, his knowledge of the odds, his understanding of the men around him, lead him to lose, not to win. It almost became a point of honour that he took no money from the table, other than which he had originally put in the pot.

That achieved, he rose and made his excuses to the company. Moidore chose to halt the game for a moment. Something about young Havilland worried him. Such perfect self-control in one so young was almost frightening, and he was aware, if no one else was, that Gis had, cunningly it was true, thrown his winnings away.

'Time for a rest,' Moidore announced, and rang for coffee. 'Black and plenty of it,' he added, before walking casually to the door. 'Gis,' he said, as the door closed behind them, 'sorry about that, but you bring some of it on yourself, you know.'

Gis's shapely brows rose. 'Yes?' He was cool. 'By existing, I suppose.'

'Oh, more than that. I meant the accusation of cowardice.'

'I notice that you left bastardy out,' was Gis's only reply, 'but then, I can hardly take the blame for that. As for the other. . .' and he shrugged.

Moidore laughed. 'You're a cold-blooded devil,' he said admiringly. 'No, you have only to speak, and that *canard*, cowardice, would not be muttered behind people's hands.'

'Better that than to my face. My business, Tom. And what busybody told you? My esteemed father, my loving mother, or my worthy uncle?'

'I found you for your parents,' was the blunt reply to that.

'Oh, congratulations.' Gis was sardonic. 'Hadn't you enough to do running the war, without looking for one poor byblow who chose to go his own way?'

Moidore refused to be put out.

'Self-pity,' he said cheerfully. 'Not a pretty emotion in an adult.'

'Self-pity.' Gis began to laugh, the perfect control almost leaving him. 'No, Tom, realism. And I didn't manhandle Hector because of anything he said to me about my supposed misdemeanours. I pushed his face in for quite another reason, and one I am not necessarily proud of.' He thought fleetingly of Thea for a moment. 'And I promise to behave myself in future. I'd better go. Diana will be waiting, and her patience is fraying a little these days.'

Moidore was blunt again. 'Old age,' he said, 'doesn't improve the disposition. When are you going to marry, Gis?'

Gis chose to misunderstand him. 'Diana? I can't marry Diana. She's already married.'

'You should be a politician,' was Moidore's only answer to that. 'As a master of misdirection you would end up as Prime Minister.'

'God forbid.' Gis was cheerful at last, Moidore was pleased to see. 'I've quite another end in mind,' he said, but he wasn't telling what it was, and Moidore didn't ask.

And if I thought that that little *brouhaha*, coupled with Tom Moidore's implicit warning, would silence Hector, then I thought wrongly, was Gis's conclusion, driving back to Padworth and Thea. For he had gone down early to breakfast the next day, hoping to avoid Hector, only to find him in the dining-room, and on his own, as well, which some unkind God must have arranged.

Gis's, 'Good morning,' was as cool as he could make it. He collected his breakfast, a large one, noted that Hector's was mostly black coffee, and sat down to eat it, while Hector picked up *The Times*, but not to read it.

He sat down opposite to Gis, said, 'I only shook hands last night to keep Moidore quiet.'

'Oh, good,' was Gis's cheerful reply to that. 'We're quits, then; so did I.'

'Think yourself damned clever, don't you, Havilland?'

'No,' said Gis, forking up scrambled egs with a gusto which had Hector wincing. 'I don't think so, Hector, I know.'

'You're a conceited bastard, Havilland. I do know that.'

'I wonder why my legitimacy should be of such concern to you, Hector?' Gis was disgustingly cheerful. 'Yours doesn't trouble me.'

'You trouble me, Havilland. As well as everything else, you're a thief. I know who broke into my home, but I can't prove it. And I know why you broke in.'

So, Hector had at last worked out who was the only person who would have troubled to steal Sophie's letters. Which certainly wasn't difficult, didn't need Einstein, thought Gis irreverently, seeing that it couldn't be Sophie herself, nor George, and it certainly wasn't Mother or Father!

'Been robbed, have you?' he enquired politely. 'My commiserations.'

'Damn your commiserations, Havilland, I'll make you pay for taking Sophie's letters, if only to make up for what I lost by your theft of them. If I had any hard evidence, I'd hand you over to the police.'

Gis was getting tired of this. 'But you haven't, have you?' he said kindly. 'You know what, Hector, you're tedious, damned tedious. And all you can think of is to blame me for your carelessness in losing your possessions. You'd do better to save your breath and buy a few good locks for Mereside.'

He thought that Hector was about to burst with ire, wondered exactly why Hector disliked him so,

not being aware that Hector had made a dead set
for Diana Troy before he had arrived at Poyns and
had been sent away with a frank comparison of his
lack of charm, compared to Gis's, which, added to
Hector's suspicion of Gis's thieving, put the tin lid
on it, as far as he was concerned. He would have
been even more irate if he had known that Gis had
rung Sophie from Poyns and told her, guardedly, in
case any one might overhear them, that the small
problem of which she had spoken to him was solved,
and that she should expect to hear nothing further.

'Must be off. Letters to write,' Gis said carelessly.
'You'll have to entertain yourself, I'm afraid. Not
much in *The Times* today.' And he strolled out of
the room, Hector's baleful stare following him all
the way.

Of course, the letters were imaginary, but the
writing was not. He had had a splendid idea about
the nature of truth, which had come to him while
reading Bertrand Russell's *Principia Mathematica*,
and he wanted to confront old Dunstan with it in
writing when term started.

CHAPTER FOUR

'ARE you listening to me, Thea? I don't want you
wandering about the gardens alone with young
Havilland when he comes back this afternoon.
Thea!'

'Yes, Mother,' replied Thea wearily, 'I heard you.
I am not to wander around the gardens on my own
with Gis. I promise you I won't.'

'Not that I disapprove of his mama,' said Lady
Edith expansively. 'He must be a great trial to her —
I never did agree with adoption.'

Thea, dressed rather more elegantly than she
usually was, her hair slightly looser than Lady Edith
really considered proper, picked up her parasol,
and, her mother's admonitions in her ears, walked
down the main staircase, across the hall, into the
drawing-room, where, instead of waiting for Lady
Edith, she calmly crossed to the glass doors, stepped
through them, then took her way along the terrace,
down the wide stone steps, taking the path to the
stables — or rather to the garages, where Gis might
be expected to arrive at any moment.

Earlier questioning of Haines, the Longthornes'
chauffeur, had elicited the information that young
Mr Havilland was expected back around two
o'clock, thus confirming what Gis's mother had
announced at breakfast.

The stables and the garage were always busy, and
were not places where ladylike young creatures

ought to spend time. Thea put up her parasol, and mooned across the broad expanse of the yard under Haines's somewhat sardonic eye. At the far end was an arch, through which several of the Longthorne stable were being walked to exercise. Gerard was not a racing owner, but he liked to ride, as did his wife. Kate's attitude to horses was equivocal since her first husband, Justin, Earl of Otmoor, had been killed out hunting. Her second husband, Sir Richard Havilland, rode, as he did everything, extremely well.

Thea followed them out, to find herself in the kitchen garden, a lush place, walled on three sides. Two gardeners were engaged in picking salad stuffs, presumably for their evening meal. They looked up briefly as she wandered down the gravel path, admiring the cordons of peaches, the fruit ripening in the sun. She thought that she had never seen a country house and gardens which were as well run as Padworth.

Her musings were interrupted by the sound of a car arriving in the stable yard. She had been listening for it, was sure that it was Gis, hot from Poyns — and Diana Troy's arms presumably — but what of that? She turned around and made her way rapidly through the arch to see that the car was drawn up in front of one of the garages and that Gis Havilland, wearing grey flannels, a cream silk shirt, and a pair of cream and coffee coloured light shoes, was removing his panama hat, while one of the footmen was engaged in lifting his bags from the car's boot.

'Hello,' he said, 'well met. Inspecting the kitchen gardens, were you? Everything in order?'

Thea inclined her head graciously. At least he

had not brought Diana back with him, something
over which Kate Havilland and Torry Schuyler had
debated.

'Very nice,' she said, almost pertly, for what did
Thea Dunstan know of kitchen gardens? 'I thought
that I might find you here.'

'Did you, indeed?' Gis swung round, said to the
footman who was carrying his bags, 'Tell Lady
Longthorne and my mother that I am back, would
you?' and then he swung towards Thea again,
smiling. 'Now, I wonder why you were waiting for
me? You were waiting for me, weren't you?'

The imp spoke aloud, even more pertly. 'Questions, questions,' Thea said, surprising herself;
where was all this coming from? 'But yes, I was. I
thought that if you were not too tired after your
journey from Poyns you might like to drive me to
the woods which you spoke of the other day.'

Gis's eyes first narrowed then widened. He
walked away from the car to close the distance
between them.

'I thought that you had turned down that offer,
Miss Thea.'

'I did. But I've changed my mind.' Thea offered
him no explanation. She didn't even know why she
was doing this—except, perhaps, to annoy Lady
Edith. No, that wasn't it. Ever since he had gone,
she had dreamed of him coming back, and of the
conversations she would have with him. In one, she
behaved as she imagined Diana Troy might, and
flirted madly with him. In another, she reproached
him forcibly for all his wickedness—particularly to
her. Breaking into Mereside, pretending to like her;
he really deserved to be thoroughly set down, left in

the lurch himself, to prove that everyone was not charmed witless by him.

Instead, she was behaving in the most forward manner, asking a young man to take her for a drive — alone, of all things.

'Well?' she said imperiously.

'Would your mother approve?' Gis asked, amused by the whole fighting stance — for that was the one she had assumed, whether she knew it or not. Who was she defying? Him — or her mother? Perhaps it was the pair of them. He had been right about the hidden spirit. He decided to reward it even as Thea said, repressively, 'No, but I am not going to ask her permission. You might, but I warn you that she'll say no.'

'In that case,' responded Gis, with his best grin. 'I shan't ask her, and yes, I will take you for a spin. Give me five minutes to make myself presentable — there's a bench in the kitchen garden, well out of sight of the house, and I'll come for you in a moment.'

Thea lifted a hand in assent, 'Very well,' and she wandered off, her parasol above the chestnut hair which he saw had been much more softly dressed than usual — she had obviously taken note of his advice.

She sat on the bench in the warm, afternoon sun, watching the gardeners, who were now bringing pot plants from the hothouses at the far end of the garden, and placing them on a large wheelbarrow before taking them into the house. Lord Longthorne was giving a dinner for his friends and neighbours, and the dining-room must be suitably decorated. It occurred to her, not for the first time, that a whole

life went on around her, about which she knew
nothing, and that her idleness, of which she was
acutely conscious, was the product of that life.

For a moment Thea daydreamed of a life in which
she had gone to university, and had been properly
trained afterwards, to do something useful. She
thought that she might have liked to try to be a
journalist—she kept a secret diary in which she
wrote down her impressions of the life around her.
It was one of her greatest fears that Lady Edith
might find it.

'Thea?' It was Gis. He had changed his shirt for a
pale blue one, which matched his astonishing eyes.
'Wake up, your steed awaits you.'

Thea was confused, said, 'Steed?' to have him
reply,

'Metaphorically speaking, yes. Though it's a steed
which won't raise a hoof for you—I mean the
Sunbeam.'

He put out a hand to her, and walked her through
the arch to the open tourer which a mechanic, under
Haines's superior eyes, was running a rag over.

At the last moment Thea was suddenly aware of
the enormity of what she was doing, but it was too
late. She was handed in. The mechanic was starting
the car, and they were roaring out of the yard, along
another sweep, and then were travelling in front of
the house, its noble Georgian façade gleaming in
the sun, past assorted stone gods and goddesses,
but, worst of all, past a group of ladies, parasols up,
enjoying the afternoon sun, among them Lady
Edith, whose face was a picture of rage and fury as
Gis raised a hand to them all before disappearing
through the iron gates at the end of the drive, and

turning into the road which ran round the house and
its grounds.

Thea, wickedly, had almost thought of giving a
wave herself, but they had swept by too quickly for
her to add that last act of defiance to the list of her
misdeeds.

Gis shot a look at her, and was amused by the
expression on her face, of glee and misgiving combined. He picked up speed as they ran along the
metalled road, then he slowed again as he left that
to travel along a minor one which threw up white
dust around them, so that Thea choked a little, and
understood why, in the early days of motoring,
ladies had worn veils against the dust.

'Soon be off this,' said Gis, and they were,
climbing, now, on a road which was little more than
a farm track, its soil baked hard by the sun. And
then the sun was gone, and they were in the woods,
still climbing, until the track petered out into something little larger than a lane up which two might
walk, side by side.

Gis stopped the car, and helped Thea out. He
took the parasol firmly from her, saying, 'You won't
need that here,' for the sun, Thea saw, showed only
in patches and blobs as it slid through the branches
of the trees to lie, dappled, on the ground.

He took her hand, and side by side they walked
along the track, through the trees. Thea's heart was
bumping. She had never before been alone with a
man, so far from home, away from her mother's
eye. And what a man to be alone with! Gis was as
notorious in Oxford as he was in London, for what
Lady Edith called 'his goings on of all kinds'—

which included womanising and driving the dons and the bulldogs mad.

They were in the dark now. The branches overhead were so thick that they were in a kind of blue-black aquarium. Silence was absolute, and Gis did not speak, nor was Thea inclined to. Suddenly, they reached a clearing where broken logs and the occasional stump showed that some of the trees had been felled. In the distance, a bird sang, and then was quiet.

'There should be an altar,' said Thea, and was not aware that she had spoken until Gis answered her.

'There probably was, once. They used to hold sacred rites in such places as these, but I suspect that the only visitors now are the foresters who look after the woods for my uncle.'

'He owns this?' Thea was still speaking quietly, as though the deity who ruled the place might appear at any moment and rebuke them for their presence.

'Yes.' Gis gestured at one of the tree trunks. 'We might as well sit down, and you can do your communing with comfort.'

'With nature, you mean?'

'Exactly. If we sit here, quietly, we might, I say might, see some small animals. You would like that.'

Thea, seating herself, nodded. He sat beside her, his eyes on the plain face which slowly assumed a look of infinite peace. She took him at his word and said nothing, her hands lightly clasped in her lap.

Plain face? Gis thought of Diana Troy. She had been demanding last night, and he had not wanted to be demanded. He had known for some time that his *affaire* with her was over, dead, and he thought that Diana knew so, too, but she would not let it lie down and be buried. For the first time, at the age of nearly forty, she was becoming aware that her days as an imperious beauty were over, and where once she would have given Gis his *congé*, without a thought, and moved on to another, now she was clinging to him, and for all his internal protestations of hard-heartedness he was finding it difficult to break with her. Her eyes gave too much away.

They had agreed long ago, that neither had any claims on the other. . .a bird was hopping towards them, and Thea's expression was a wonder, lips slightly parted, eyes shining, and the softness of her hair, which was beginning to escape its moorings, added to her look of charming innocence. Anything less like Diana Troy's hard, sophisticated beauty he could not imagine. The thought of Hector laying hands on her. . .was not endurable. He moved slightly in his effort to dismiss these unwanted thoughts — and the bird clapped its wings and flew away.

'Thea, I'm sorry,' he said, and the words burst from him. She turned, green eyes sparkling, and he saw for the first time that she was a late developer, and that although she would never be a beauty she would, if treated properly, have a face full of character.

What surged inside him, Gis did not know. Was it protectiveness, or some emotion which he had never felt before? He guessed that Thea was inexperienced, unsure of herself, but was beginning to be aware that she was a woman.

'Not your fault,' she said, and then stopped speaking, for he could not prevent himself from pulling her towards him, putting his arms around her and kissing her, gently at first, on the tender lips.

For Thea, this was why she had come with him. She knew that the moment he began to make love to her. And this time she responded immediately, not thrusting him away, but offering herself, her body moulding into his, as though she had come home. She felt no fear of him, for she trusted him, even though she knew what he was, what he had done, even more than Lady Edith did.

This time, her hair came loose immediately, for him to stroke his hands through it, and, growing bold, Thea ran her hands through his blond locks. Passion suddenly flared between them. Gis pulled away, said, 'No, Thea. We. . .shouldn't. We're proving Lady Edith right.'

Thea looked firmly at him. Near to, she could see herself in his eyes, a miniature Thea, stars in her own eyes. It was as though the gloom of the woods had stripped her of her fear, of herself and him, as well as of her inhibitions. 'I would like to practise flirtation a little more,' she said hesitantly, 'and you are the only person whom I can ask. I. . .can't imagine myself asking Hector.'

This remark lightened the atmosphere between them, which had grown heavy. 'Amen to that,' said Gis. 'But I don't think you know what you're asking, Thea. I shouldn't take advantage of you, and that is what will happen if we go on.'

'But I asked you,' replied Thea truthfully. She wanted him to kiss her again. The sensations which she felt when he did both excited and exhilarated her. Perhaps he had been misjudged, perhaps she had misjudged him, and he was not wicked, after all.

Gis knew something of what was passing through her mind. Two furrows had appeared on her brow, and she looked so charmingly worried, that he began to laugh, said, 'Just a little more then,' and began where he had left off.

The trouble was, both of them thought together, that after the early pleasure of exchanging fairly innocent kisses they rapidly wanted more. The difference between them was that Gis knew what that more was, and Thea didn't.

Gis's hands, despite all his brave resolutions were misbehaving; they ran down from Thea's face, to her bosom, where one of them, from long practice, found itself stroking Thea's right breast through the fine lawn of her dress. The other began to unbutton the dress at the neck, so that his mouth could find the warm skin below the dress's neckline. . .

Thea was in heaven. She thought as before that she was going to dissolve. She had never known such pleasure as Gis's hands and lips were giving her, and then. . .and then. . .it was as though a fire-bell went off in her head, as the last button gave way, and his mouth found her breast. . .

God knew, Gis had not meant to begin to seduce her, and even as his mouth found what it wanted the fire-bell went off in his head as well, and they both drew away together, to sit looking at one another, eyes wide.

'No!' They spoke simultaneously, and then Gis said, buttoning up her dress rapidly to remove temptation,

'Oh, Thea, I never meant to do that. I should have had more sense than to lead you on.'

Thea found herself shivering. One part of her wished that they had not stopped; the other part was relieved that they had. 'I led *you* on,' she said dismally. 'Perhaps Mother was right. I shouldn't walk out with you alone.'

Even at this sad point, Gis could not help saying, 'As a matter of accuracy, we were sitting down at the time.'

'Oh, you know what I mean, what Mother means.' Thea's eyes filled with tears. 'I suppose that this proves that I am no better than I should be.'

'On the contrary,' Gis found himself saying, to reassure her. 'What we did was most natural.'

'That's the trouble, though.' Thea's expression was nearly as gloomy as the wood, and she had begun to try to pin up her hair. 'Being natural, I mean. Not the way to behave at all.'

'Don't blame yourself.' Gis was humble. 'Entirely my fault, I assure you. I lost my head.'

'I didn't exactly keep mine on, did I?' Thea was even humbler.

Gis decided to be a trifle pompous. 'As the elder, and more experienced, I knew what I was doing; you didn't.'

'But I shall never know unless I practise,' sighed Thea mournfully. 'But I am begining to see that practice is dangerous.' And she looked wickedly at Gis from beneath her eyelashes. What native coquetry compelled her to do this she never knew.

It lightened the atmosphere wonderfully. Gis began to laugh, bent down and gave her a brotherly sexless kiss on the cheek, pulling her to her feet at the same time.

'Let's go home. The woods are dangerous. Satyrs catch nymphs in them. I should have remembered that.'

Tension gone, they walked back to the car, to drive home. . .to Lady Edith.

'After all I said to you,' snorted Lady Edith. 'And then you go off with him in his car, without asking me for permission, which I should never have given you.'

'You told me not to wander alone with him in the gardens,' retorted Thea wickedly. 'You didn't say anything about me going out alone with him in his car.'

'Oh. . .' Lady Edith was outraged. 'You wicked thing! You are asking him, yes, asking him, to take advantage of your innocence.'

'Well, he didn't.' Thea was provoked beyond belief. She crossed her fingers behind her back. 'Unfortunately, he behaved perfectly.'

'Unfortunately! Whatever can you mean?'

'Well, Mother, you do go on about the horrid fate which awaits me if I encourage anyone but Hector Dashwood, and there are times when I want to find out exactly what that horrid fate is! It's not pleasant being kept in the dark.'

'If you were three years younger, Dorothea Dunstan, and we weren't staying at Padworth, I would send you to your room without your tea, or your dinner. . .' Lady Edith was puce.

'Do you think Hector Dashwood would behave perfectly if I were left alone with him?' enquired

Thea, whose imp seemed to have broken loose and be taking over her conversation.

'There is no talking to you,' announced Lady Edith tragically. 'I shall inform your father of your behaviour, and we shall see what he says.'

'Very little, I dare say,' was Thea's reply to that, which, seeing that it was the truth, left Lady Edith with no move to make, and all in all, thought Thea, inspecting her boring toilette in the mirror, we might as well call that Mate to me, although I dare say Mother will find some means of bringing me to heel, once we have left Padworth. Having to behave in front of the Schuyler family does seem to cramp her style.

It was not only Lady Edith's style which was cramped. The day before the Dunstans were due to leave, Kate Havilland sent for her son. She waited for him in the suite of rooms which Torry always gave her. The little salon which served as a sitting-room overlooked Padworth's park, laid out two hundred years ago and only now coming to its full beauty; the family which had owned Padworth had planned for its future — which its own heirs were never to see.

Gis came in. He was as elegant as he usually was and looked more like his father than ever. His whole appearance took Kate back nearly twenty-five years, to the time when she had first met Richard, when all the world had seemed young, and there had been no dreadful war to change things forever.

'You wanted me?'

Kate nodded. 'I think we need to talk a little, Gis.'

He nodded, wondering what was coming. No, he didn't, he knew.

'I think you know what I mean,' said his mother, reading him correctly, for once, for Gis had the power to deceive her, as he deceived others, but today he was leaving himself open to her, and she wondered why.

'It's about Thea Dunstan, Gis. Are you being kind?' Kate had not meant to be quite so abrupt, but something about Gis daunted her. Had, if she were honest with herself, daunted her ever since he had discovered the truth: that she and Richard were his true father and mother and he had been born out of wedlock. She had lost him then, lost the open, loving boy he had been, and the man he was now she hardly knew.

'Kind?' murmured Gis. 'I don't quite follow. What is kind?'

'You may save logic-chopping for your tutorials at William and Mary,' replied his mother sharply. 'You know perfectly well what I mean. I have seen the way she looks at you, and the way in which you look at her and encourage her to think that you may be serious. It is not kind, Gis, to raise hope in such a pathetic creature, bullied by her mother, from whom she has no chance of escape. Once they leave Padworth her mother will punish her in a thousand ways for the manner in which you are encouraging her to behave here.'

Gis said coldly. 'Have you finished, Mother?'

'There is more I could say, but I won't.' Kate was as cold as he was. 'Just this. You're not a very nice

person to know these days, Gis. Encouraging Thea
Dunstan to think that you might love her, and to
defy her mother into the bargain is the act of a. . .'
She paused for a moment; could a mother be
frightened of her own son?

'Cad?' Gis finished for her. 'Is that what you think
of me? Useful to know, Mother. Don't worry, I've
no intention of hurting Thea Dunstan; I leave that
to others.' He turned away from her, then checked
himself. 'Diana Troy and her husband are expected
here for the afternoon, I understand, on the way
home. And when they leave tomorrow morning I
shall go as well, not with them, you will be relieved
to hear, but first to London and then to Barton
Dene. I need to do some reading before term starts.
After that, who knows? You may write to my
London flat if you need to communicate with me. I
shall arrange for letters to be sent on.'

He did not like himself very much when he saw
his mother's face contract with pain, but he would
not be controlled and managed, and what he felt, or
did not feel, for Thea Dunstan was his business, no
one else's. The sharp intelligence which ruled him
was warning him that for Thea pain and distress lay
ahead, and there was little that he could do to help
her. And his mother thought that he was about the
easy game of making her fall in love with him. . .

God knows, he thought bitterly, that if I had
wanted to seduce her she would have been mine by
now. The truth is much more complex than *that*,
Mother, dear, but give a dog a bad name and hang
him.

He carried the memory of his mother's stricken
face, as he kissed her coldly on the cheek, down-

stairs with him, to look for Thea. Since the ride to
the woods he had enjoyed himself childishly with
her; it was like being a boy again. They had played
croquet on the lawn, he had taught her to play
tennis, he had shown her the treasures in the library
as he had earlier promised. They had walked in the
grounds, all under the disapproving eyes of Lady
Edith. In the evening he had played the piano for
her, and she had sung with him: she had a pleasant
light soprano voice, which had been well trained, he
granted Lady Edith that.

And he found that beneath the quiet exterior she
had a keen intelligence. He already knew that she
had a witty tongue. And if more than once they had
each longed to put their arms around the other,
both had acted with restraint. Instead, they practised lovemaking through speech, for that was what
it was, he thought, each striking sparks off the
other.

Love-making, true. But what of love? Gis shied
away from that thought; he didn't love anyone, least
of all little Thea, he told himself firmly. She troubled
him by her helplessness, that was all.

Nevertheless, when he found her in the morning-
room, reading letters, Lady Edith, for once, not
hovering, he knew that there was something he had
to say to her, and quickly, before Diana Troy, and
the world, arrived. His mother's attempted repri-
mand had concentrated his mind wonderfully.

'Thea,' he said, 'let us go to the lake again. A
walk before fresh guests arrive.'

She looked up at him, smiling; shyness and her
fear of him had both disappeared in the glamour of
his company. She was wearing a pretty pale blue

dress, with inserts of white ribbon, a little childish
for her years, but kinder to her than the outfits she
usually wore. The loosened hair she had adopted
became her, although Lady Edith grumbled about
it.

'Yes.' Her reply to him was frank. Since losing
her fear of him, she was always frank, like an ardent
boy, nothing coquettish about her. The flirtatious
arts which the other girls he knew had learned in
order to attract men were foreign to her.

They had reached the view of the lake and the
woods before Gis said to Thea what was in his mind.
She wondered a little at his silence. He was usually
talkative, amusing, made her laugh, so that her
rather strained face softened.

'Thea.' He was as abrupt as his mother had been
with him, he thought ruefully. No diplomatic piff-
paff such as his father used here. 'There is something I must say to you. If you ever need a friend,
or help, of any kind, you can always turn to me.
You do know that. You trust me, I think.'

She looked at him steadily, and then told him
what he did not know.

'Yes,' she said, 'despite what you did at Mereside.
Breaking in, I mean. Kissing me, to keep me quiet.'

She had surprised him at last.

He began to laugh, almost helplessly. The innocent child before him had kept to herself for the last
fortnight the knowledge that it was he whom she
had surprised in the library, and he had not had the
slightest inkling that she had recognised him. His
respect for her grew, and his determination that she
should have one friend in the world was enhanced.
'You knew. When did you find out — and how?'

Thea told him, watching him as she did so, watching the play of light and shade on his mobile features, in the knowledge that whatever he was, whatever he did, she loved him. It was like having a secret treasure which only she might know and visit.

He looked ruefully at the small ring on his little finger, said, reprovingly to himself, 'Oh, careless, careless,' and then wondering a little, 'And you registered that, in the middle of your fear.'

She nodded, wondering what the disclosure would do to their strange relationship.

'Don't you want to know why I was there?'

Thea shook her head vigorously. 'No. That's your business, not mine. I don't think. . .' She hesitated. 'I may be mistaken, but. . . I don't think that you were doing anything wrong. . .'

Gis laughed shortly. 'I wasn't, if you don't call theft wrong, that is. But I had my reasons.'

'I have come to know you,' was all she said, and the simple words wrung his heart.

'And now, I must tell you, Thea, that what I said earlier, about being a friend, should you need one, was not mere idle words.' He took a piece of paper from the pocket of the blazer he was wearing, gay with William and Mary's colours of purple and gold. 'I have a small cottage at Barton Dene, ten miles out of Oxford. It's a. . .kind of hideaway, that few know about, where I go when I want to be alone, or to work. If you want help, you can always go there. And if I'm not there,' and he fished in his pocket again, and brought out a key, 'that will let you in.'

Thea took the paper and the key, said wonderingly, 'I can't imagine that I should ever need to do such a thing, but thank you, Gis, for offering such a kindness.'

'Can't you?' he said, almost roughly to the first part of her answer. 'Oh, Thea, "We know what we are, but know not what we may be", Hamlet said, and it applies to us as well as to him. I know it applied to me.' And he thought of his anguish when he learned the truth about himself, Gis Havilland, who had no real name.

'I shall look after them,' she said gravely, examining the key and the paper, before slipping them into the pocket of her dress, 'and yes if I need you, I shall come.'

'In the cottage,' he went on, 'you will find a telephone, and by the telephone a book which will give you the addresses and telephone numbers where I might be found, if I'm not there. Promise me, Thea, promise me, you will take this offer seriously.'

Why he was so troubled Gis did not know. Only that once or twice in his life, he had had feelings — premonitions, call them what you will; perhaps they were only the result of his ability to read people correctly — which had come true, often in unexpected ways. He had this feeling with Thea. Symbolically, it was as though a cloud hung over her, and the only way to dispel the cloud was by the intervention of himself.

'Don't tell anyone,' he said feverishly. 'It is our secret.' He wanted to take her in his arms, to kiss the troubled little face, surprised that he should be so wary for her, but something stopped him, and so shocked were they both, Gis by the strange feelings which overcame him whenever he was with Thea, and Thea because she was so surprised by his worry for her, that on the way back to the house they were silent.

Just before they reached it, he spoke, the words wrung from him. 'Diana Troy will be coming here this afternoon, to see me, but it doesn't mean anything, Thea.'

'It must have done once,' she said, surprising him by her shrewdness.

'Yes, it did. But not now. I think that we both know that.'

Thea nodded, and that was that.

Watching from a window, angry eyes on them, Lady Edith saw Gis take her daughter's hand, lift it and kiss it gently, and a shudder went over her at the sight, and her manner to Thea for the rest of the day was as harsh as she could make it.

Not that she was so in public. Diana Troy arrived that afternoon. She had rung Torry Schuyler and in her prettiest voice had asked her if she and Bernard might stay overnight on their way down to their home, Trewarden, in the South-West. Bernard was a back-bench MP, voting fodder, nothing more, not always that, but it paid to keep him happy, and Gerard as one of the leaders of the failing Liberal party was bound not to antagonise him.

'I dislike the woman intensely, but I have to do Gerard's political duty for him,' Torry said frankly to Kate, who was also preparing to leave on the following Sunday. She and Richard had been away quite long enough from young Richie and the girls, who had been staying at Frinton with some Schuyler cousins, and were due home at the weekend. 'Richard doesn't draw the line at many things,' she said to Torry, 'but he refuses to play with a bucket and spade on the sands! He's such a good father in so many other ways that we have to humour him in that.'

So Diana Troy arrived, trailing Parisian chic and triumphant sex, which was the comment of Thea's imp, not made aloud. She had to admit that she would probably have been jealous of Diana even if she and Gis had not shared such a long. . .involvement. As it was, Thea was drinking tea, far away from Gis, who had been cornered by his mother, while Gerard Schuyler had chosen to come and sit by her.

Thea was a little afraid of Gerard. Despite his being Gis's uncle, the two men bore no resemblance to one another — physically, that was — but when he spoke to her Thea, who was beginning to register more and more of such nuances, could hear an echo of Gis in him. They seemed to share the same mordant wit. But Gerard was dark and almost ugly compared with Gis's golden beauty. She couldn't help shooting glances at him as he sat talking to his mother.

Their parting that morning had, she knew, been a signing-off for both of them — so that he could take up with Diana again, for all his fine words and promises, the imp commented bitterly.

Diana was wearing a Fortuny model, extravagant where the ones worn by Kate Havilland were discreet. She was smoking, waving a long ivory cigarette holder about as she talked.

'And when are you coming to Trewarden, Gis?' she drawled almost before she was settled with a cup of tea, 'No milk, lemon please, and no, no sugar,' frowning when he looked up smiled, and answered her.

'Not sure, Diana. Some of us have to work. Must catch up with my reading. I'm told that Professor Dunstan here is a hard taskmaster.' And he smiled engagingly at Thea's father, who was quietly drinking his tea and conversing with another of Padworth's many guests from the political world.

Gerard's entertaining at his country home was so famous that those who visited him were sometimes called 'the Padworth set' and given an importance which the amused Gerard knew that they didn't deserve.

'Mustn't overdo things,' murmured Professor Dunstan in answer to Gis's comment, 'but I am happy to hear that you are taking your studies seriously. We have had occasion to wonder,' and he gave a mild chuckle to indicate that he was making a joke.

'There,' said Diana triumphantly. 'No reason why you shouldn't come. You can study just as well at Trewarden as at. . . .wherever. Why not change your plans and come with us.'

Gis. Study? At Trewarden. With Diana. What at? clipped the imp curtly, while Thea ate bread and butter with an angelic expression on her face. Diana's frantic and rather public blackmail was beginning to amuse her.

It didn't amuse Gis, but he didn't let it show. He said, for Diana's question deserved an answer., 'Sorry, plans already made, I'm off to London this evening — an appointment I can't break. Some other time perhaps.'

To the horror of most of the company who had

been listening to this desperate and public inquisition, Diana opened her mouth again, only for her husband to take over for once.

Improbably, thought the fascinated Thea, he was as annoyed at Gis's refusal to accomodate his wife as Diana was. 'Some other time, then,' he offered. 'mustn't forget how young Gis is, my dear. Want to paint London red with a few of your friends, eh, Gis. Take your Oxford hi-jinks there. I remember how I was at his age,' he finished, making Gis sound about fourteen.

Which didn't appear to trouble Gis, and a more general conversation ensued, Diana, dropping out of it, sulking behind her cigarette holder, mannerlessly continuing to smoke throughout tea, giving off angry puffs — rather like an out of control railway locomotive, remarked the imp.

And then the party was breaking up. Diana managed to have a word alone with Gis before he left, but with no more success than she had had at tea. He had told her at Poyns that their *affaire* was over, and she knew in her heart that it was, for her as well as for him, but she didn't like to lose her long-time admirer.

The Dunstans were driving to London, to their house in Hampstead. Deprived of most of the London season by the Professor's academic duties and responsibilities, Lady Edith made up for it by going there in August. It was not the same, of course, but she could shop, and visit the Royal Academy and the theatres and introduce Thea to a wider society than that which she met at Oxford. Thea was also going to meet Hector Dashwood again, although she didn't know this, Hector having

lost so much money at Poyns and elsewhere that he
had decided that he must offer for Thea Dunstan as
soon as possible, and Lady Edith had carefully
informed him that the Dunstans' destination after
Padworth was London, and given him their address
as well.

If Thea's heart was utterly and irrevocably given
to that unsatisfactory creature, Gis Havilland —
Lady Edith's words — Gis, driving to London, more
admonitions from his mother in his ears, and a final
enigmatic message of, 'Be careful, Gis,' from his
Uncle Gerard to speed him on his way, possessed a
more divided mind. For the first time in his life he
had no clear knowledge of where he was heading,
what he was to do. The straightforward and selfish
path through life which he had devised for himself
since he was sixteen years old, of which a principal
element was that he would never love anyone again,
had suddenly become obscure, had taken an unpre-
meditated twist. Standing in his way, a melancholy
look on her face, a look which she assumed when
she thought that no one was watching her, was Thea
Dunstan.

CHAPTER FIVE

'DEAR GIS'. . . . Thea stared out of her bedroom window at Hampstead Heath before continuing with her letter.

> I do hope that you're not growing bored with what Papa would call my daily budget. I couldn't help thinking this morning about our walk in the woods. That landscape is so different from the one which I can see when I write. Yes, it is Hampstead Heath before me, but I agree with Papa when he says it is only the country in the town: 'Mere *rus in urbe*,' to quote him, which is not at all the same thing as the country is.
>
> Yesterday, remembering our conversations in the library about the war poets, and your recommendations that I read some others beside Rupert Brooke, I bought the little book of Wilfred Owen's which you told me about. Needless to say, I did this behind Mother's back — she would definitely not approve. Reading them proves how wise I am to be deceitful.

Thea bit her pen again. There was something which she wanted to say to Gis, which she did not like to put down on paper, so she continued writing lightly to him.

> I cannot say that I enjoy being in London. There is so much which I would like to do, but of

which Mother does not approve. I know that I am wrong to write this to you, but I am sure that you will understand. Mother has her way of thinking; I have mine. I do so miss our talks at Padworth. Last night Mother played for me and I sang—we had company—but that was not like Padworth either. This is not so cheerful a letter as the ones I have been writing to you, but then, the time since I last saw you is growing longer.

She was never quite sure how to sign off, so she simply put, 'Thea', then, biting her pen again, wrote,

P.S. Hector proposed last night, and I refused him, so I am confined to my room today. Mama is most enormously cross with me, but I can't marry Hector, I can't.

And then, boldly, 'Your Thea'.

Thea looked at the page in front of her, and heaved a tremendous sigh. She then closed her diary, in which she had been writing a daily letter to Gis, instead of recording the happenings of her uneventful life. She had written of his offer to help, but had been careful not to put in it anything about the key and the address of his cottage in case her mother might find it. She went over to her small dressing case, unlocked it, and hid the book carefully inside it, before locking it again.

She had been writing daily to Gis ever since she had left Padworth. She had no address, other than the cottage, to which she could send her letters, but, in any case, fear of Lady Edith kept her from a true clandestine correspondence. She walked over to the

window and looked out of it again, and tried to put
out of her mind what had happened the previous
evening, but couldn't. . . .

Afterwards, she told herself that she might have
known that Lady Edith was, in the words of her
own maid, Harvey, 'up to something'. She had come
into Thea's room while Harvey was helping her to
dress, and had taken a scathing look at the elegant,
rather severe, but becoming deep bluey-green dress,
which did things for Thea's eyes and hair—she had
bought it the other day from a small but exclusive
dress shop because Gis had told her that it was the
colour which she ought to wear.

'Not that,' she said decisively, 'most unsuitable,
something sweetly pretty, I think.' She went over to
the big oak wardrobe, and fished out a something in
pink, which would have been delightful on the
blonde beauty whom she wished that she had produced, but which was guaranteed to kill Thea's only
beauties, the astonishing green eyes, and the chestnut hair, stone dead.

'Oh, no, Mother,' wailed Thea, holding on to the
beautiful frock which she had bought with such
eagerness, thinking that if Gis were there when she
wore it, he might see something better than an
inappropriately dressed dowd.

'Nonsense, child, that is not at all the thing. It
resembles something Diana Troy might wear,' said
Lady Edith ruthlessly, wrenching it from Thea's
hands, tearing it in the process, and throwing it on
the bed. 'I suppose,' she sneered perceptively, 'you
were thinking that it might tempt her lover, but I
wish you to please a gentleman tonight, not a
dubious Yankee nobody like Gis Havilland.'

Why does she hate Gis so? Thea asked herself. After all, he is filthy rich, stands to be richer, and is a member of two families whose social credentials are impeccable, even if his are odd. I might have thought that she would have thrown me at him, rather than run round him warning me off. And then, looking at her mother, the appalling truth overcame her. Why, she's jealous of Diana — who is, after all, not so much younger than she is — because she has had an affair with him. She hates Gis because he fascinates her, and she knows that she could never attract him, never be his lover, so she will not let me have him.

This unwanted knowledge made her feel so faint that she ceased protesting altogether, and, shivering a little, allowed Harvey to dress her in the unsuitable pink frock, and style her hair in a way, which, however ladylike her mother thought it, wrecked her last chance of appearing other than a plain fright.

It's Hector, said the imp, it's Hector she's dressing you for. What's the betting that he will be at dinner tonight, and she will be throwing you at him?

Be quiet, snarled Thea at the imp, life's hard enough without you making it worse, and, of course, when the guests came, one by one, Hector's arrival, just before dinner was served, confirmed all Thea's worst expectations.

He was reasonably sober, for once. He had met Thea several times since she had returned to London, had sat in the Dunstans' box at the opera, and had chattered his way emptily through it to Thea, spoiling both the occasion and the music for her. For Hector, the opera was merely something

where you went to see and be seen, and the pity was
that he would have to be seen with, and tie himself
to such a wet rag as the Dunstan's dowd. But needs
must. . .

Thea knew exactly what he was thinking, and he
could not dislike more the idea of marrying her than
she disliked the idea of marrying him. But he had,
in his way, tried to charm her, and had continued
the process at dinner, even while he thought, Good
God, what sort of rag is *that* to dress a plain girl in?
Thea was perversely pleased that she was not looking her best, and relieved when the ladies withdrew
at the end of dinner, and she could escape through
the French windows, to sit on the terrace.

Not, she afterwards thought, a good idea. For
Hector, leaving the other men early, to do his
unpleasant duty, followed her there, to sit by her
and to praise the embroidery which she was doing,
a tapestry-work cushion kneeler for the church
where the Dunstan family worshipped.

'Pretty, hey!' he offered, staring at the fleur de
lys, which Thea was so carefully working. 'But what
about a little relief from it? Mustn't strain your eyes.
How about a turn around the garden?'

It was impossible for Thea to refuse him without
causing offence. She rose, put down her work and
he took her arm. Instinctively, she shuddered at his
touch. She wondered why. He was quite a handsome man, although his face was beginning to show
the effects of hard living, and when he was Gis's age
must have been his equal in looks and charm.

But he frightened her, and she could tell quite
plainly that he despised her, and that her sole
attraction for him was the money which she would

inherit from Lady Edith. She knew that he was a distant, very distant cousin, and also knew that part of the reason for Lady Edith's determination to have her marry him was that the family title, which was more ancient than Hector's, might be revived, and her own line continued.

It might be 1920 and the whole of aristocratic privilege might be under threat, but Lady Edith took no note of that; she was still living in the world of her youth and was determined that Thea should live there, too.

They walked down the garden path. Hector didn't have at all the same scent as Gis. He reeked of drink and of tobacco. Gis was rare among young men in that he didn't smoke, and although she knew that he occasionally drank, and drank hard, it was not an everyday thing with him as it was with Hector and his kind.

He was talking to her, the sort of nonsense which a hard-living man might talk to a pretty and innocent girl whom he wished to impress, praising her looks — she knew that he was lying, he thought nothing of her looks — asking her if she had been to the theatre to see *Chu Chin Chow* and when she said yes, asked her what she thought of it, but Thea could tell that he was not really interested.

They had reached the two small hothouses at the garden's end. There was a rustic bench and a table set out on a small lawn. Hector handed her on to the bench, remained standing himself, said, one hand behind his back, in the dandy's stance, 'You must surely know, my dear Thea, why I have brought you here, and what I mean to say.'

Thea wanted to reply sharply, 'No, not at all, and

there is nothing which you could say which would interest me,' but she kept quiet; that sort of thing was reserved for the imp — one didn't say it aloud.

Hector must have taken her silence for assent, for he pushed on, 'And that being, so my dear, and knowing that your father and mother look upon me with favour, I have the hope that your answer will prove to be as pleasing to me as my proposal will be pleasing to you.'

There is no way, Thea thought, that I can stop him, no way in which my refusal will come as anything but as a shock to him and to Mother. What Father thinks about all this is beyond me. Perhaps he doesn't think about me at all; I am an irrelevance, compared with his books and papers. And then she thought, I really must pay attention to what Hector is saying.

Which was, in effect, that he was smitten by her charms, and wished her to be his wife, his Countess. 'It would,' he said; he had stopped short of going on one knee, but only just, for the lawn was damp, 'be the joy of my life to be settled at last, and with such a charming creature as yourself. Thea, my dear, please say yes, and make me the happiest of men.'

Wildly, although nothing in her manner showed how distressed she truly was, Thea stared at him. Could she believe a single word that he was saying? She knew quite well what her fate would be if she married him. She was not so innocent as to be unaware that his sexual reputation was of the most unpleasant. And she was to share his bed so that he might get his hands on Lady Edith's money.

The thought of defying her mother over this made her feel quite faint; the thought of 'doing that' with

Hector made her feel fainter still. Which was strange, because she knew that if it were Gis Havilland who had been proposing to her, dreadful reputation and all, she would have been as quick to accept him, as she was slow in answering Hector. She became aware that he was waiting for her to speak.

'Oh,' she said, as pleasantly and ruefully as she could, 'I am aware of the honour which you do me by asking me to be your Countess,' she was quite proud of her coolness as she said this, 'but, Lord Dashwood, Hector, I must tell you, that although I am pleased and flattered by your attention——' which was a lie; she wasn't '—I don't feel for you what a girl ought to feel for her future husband— liking is not enough—and so I must regretfully decline the honour which you have offered me.'

For a moment Hector Dashwood hardly registered what Thea had said. Lady Edith had assured him that Thea would accept him, and without that assurance he would never have proposed, never have risked a refusal. His vanity, his *amour propre*, which were inordinately strong, were both offended by her.

'Refuse me,' he almost spluttered, and then, 'But your mother?'

'You are not proposing to my mother.' Thea's control had slipped a little and this flew out, willy-nilly. 'And my mother knows perfectly well that I'm not willing to become your wife.'

Hector's face was ugly. 'That was not what she said to me, and I assure you, young woman, that she will not be best pleased when she hears of the answer which you have given me.'

And that is putting it mildly, was Thea's inward response. But she cannot kill me, or even imprison me, or thrash me, as happened to girls in my position a hundred years ago, but all the same something inside her cringed and shuddered at the prospect of Lady Edith's wrath and what she might do.

'For your own sake,' he almost snarled, 'you will, I trust, reconsider, and allow me to take to your mother the answer which she expects to hear, and the one which I consider I ought to have heard from you, in view of the encouragement which I have been given.'

'Encouragement?' exclaimed Thea. 'If being coolly civil to you is encouragement, then I have been encouraging! You are quite mistaken, my lord. I have never had the slightest intention of encouraging you, and you are old enough and experienced enough to know that this is true.'

To have his antiquity and his known reputation flung at him by this plain chit who seemed totally unaware of what an extraordinary concession he was making to propose to her at all was almost too much for Hector. He advanced on the dowd, remembering that Lady Edith had hinted that strong tactics might be needed to persuade her to accept him. He had not believed her — but he did now.

'Come, Miss Dunstan,' he began, 'let us see if you can be persuaded to change your mind.'

Thea gave a little shriek and dodged away from him, to disappear from sight by running around the back of the hothouses, to take a winding path back to the house, in the hope that, alone in the half-dark in a strange place, Hector might not at first grasp where she had gone.

She was lucky at first, not so lucky later. She reached the terrace and the safety of the house, could hear Hector blundering after her, calling her name, rendered desperate at the thought of all those pounds, shillings, pence, stocks, shares, lands and foreign investments, disappearing before him.

Lady Edith met her as she entered the drawing-room by the French windows. 'Well?' she said, smiling, and then, before her guests, seeing by Thea's white face, and her appearing without Hector, that all had not gone to plan, she took Thea by the arm, and dragged her from the room, along the corridor, and into the small breakfast-room where she could carry out her inquisition without being overheard.

'Never say that you have refused him,' she roared at her daughter.

'I can't marry him, I can't, don't ask me, Mother,' panted Thea, trying to pull her arm away.

Lady Edith's response was a violent box on the ear which flung Thea against the opposite wall, knocking her over a small stool on the way.

She leaned forward, pulled the half-stunned Thea to her feet, and gave her a second blow, harder than the first, which left Thea dazed, her head ringing. 'You will go back to him, at once,' she ordered, 'and tell him that you have changed your mind.'

'No, I shall not,' panted Thea, waiting for the next blow, for Lady Edith had raised her hand again. 'You may beat me senseless, but I won't say yes. I won't, ever.'

Lady Edith looked at the daughter whom she had

thought spiritless, and knew that, for the moment at least, direct violence would not work. Something more subtle might have to be tried. Let the child think that she might have got away with this.

'Go to your room at once,' she said slowly. 'I shall see Hector and tell him that when you have had time to think you may be in a more amenable frame of mind.'

'After what I said to him, he won't believe you,' asserted Thea determinedly.

'Be quiet,' ordered Lady Edith, 'and go to your room. Don't think that this is the end of the matter, Dorothea Dunstan, because it isn't. You may not come down until I tell you.'

There was nothing more to be said. Thea took herself, her head still ringing from the two cruel blows, upstairs. Her mother had frequently struck her in the past, but never before with such brutal force. Gis Havilland had told her that he would help her, and she might have to keep him to that promise, but how he could help her and what the result would be was a mystery.

Lady Edith was a bit of a mystery as well, because the following lunchtime she allowed Thea to come down, and all seemed to have been forgotten, Hector's name and Thea's refusal not being mentioned, so asking Gis to help her wouldn't apparently be necessary after all; her mother must have changed her mind.

Gis Havilland was not writing unposted letters to Thea Dunstan, but he was thinking about her. Mostly, now that they were apart, he was thinking how ridiculous he had been to imagine that she was in some sort of danger.

He could only conclude that the brief and innocent idyll which the days he had spent with her at Padworth had been had in some way deprived him of common sense. Or it was parting from Diana Troy after so many years? Yes, that was it. After breaking with Diana he had wanted something else to occupy him, and he had found that occupation in Thea.

That was in the day. He had banished her from his conscious thoughts, by the process of reasoning—the power by which he ruled his life—but he could not erase her from his subconscious. At night, his dreams were disturbing, and Thea ran through them. Fear dominated them, so that he awoke, sweating and shaking, unable to remember exactly what had caused the fear. He had an impression of trying to escape from something—only he was not the one escaping. That was Thea.

Years before, when he was a child, he had been kidnapped, and then rescued by the man whom he had not then known as his father. Before the kidnap he had had premonitions, connected not with himself, but with the doll which he had loved. Named General Lee, it was dressed as a Confederate general, and the dreams had centred around the doll's despoliation, destruction and loss.

During the kidnap he had stripped the doll of its distinguishing dress, hat, sword, boots and epaulettes, throwing them away as clues in the hope that someone would trace him. But in doing so the child he had been had effectively killed General Lee, and the loss in his dreams had become the loss of reality.

Gis had read Freud's work on dreams, and what

he had found there had helped him, but only a little.
Freud might suggest, and he might agree, that the
General was himself, and that he had feared for
himself, but that did not explain why the General
had ended up in life as he had done in the dream.
Not exactly, it was true; in the dream the General's
death had been gory, but it was the General who
had perished, not Gis.

And why should he identify himself with Thea?
But, even more strangely, why, after meeting her,
should he fear for her to the extent that, having
banished her from his conscious mind, she should
run, terror-stricken, through his dreams? It was all
nonsense, and he must try to forget her—but he
could not forget that he had given her the address
of his secret hideaway and its door-key.

Three days after Thea had been proposed to by
Hector, Gis was invited to dinner in Chelsea by an
old friend of the Havilland family who had discovered that he was in town, and was hopeful of
interesting the rich and handsome young man in his
daughter. Lady Edith's attitude to Gis's dubious
origins was not shared by everyone in society.

So much for his resolution not to think about
Thea Dunstan, he thought wryly, for the first person
he saw when he entered the Robertsons' drawing-
room was Lady Edith, and the second was Thea.
And all his strange feelings flooded back in an
instant. For she looked ill. There were purple
smudges beneath the beautiful green eyes, and a
quiver to the small mouth. If he had ever seen a
hunted creature, it was Thea Dunstan.

She was doing her best, he saw, not to reveal

distress, but the distress was there, so real that it was a live thing which he could almost touch.

Could no one else see it? Apparently not. He went up to her, said, 'Thea?' in a questioning voice, and when she saw him he thought that she was about to burst into tears, or cry out.

'That's a charming gown you're wearing.' He had lied about the cocoa-coloured thing in order to have her look at him, her face showing him not grief, but a wry amusement.

'No, it isn't, Gis. It's horrid, and you know it. I bought the bluey-green which you said would suit me in the style you recommended, But Mother. . .' For a moment her voice almost broke. 'Mother threw it away. She didn't like it.'

It was General Lee all over again. The sense of impending loss was so strong in him that it was as though passing bells were tolling in his head.

'Never mind,' he said. 'One day. . .'

'Pigs might fly,' riposted Thea more cheerfully, even managing a smile. The very sight of him made her feel happy, that, and the spectacle of Lady Edith, hovering, annoyed at his presence, and that they were talking together.

She was even more annoyed at dinner. Gis had been given Mary Robertson, a pretty girl who held no attraction for him at all, to take in, but he found himself at table with Mary on one side, Thea on the other. Presumably they were not at all worried that Thea would provide any competition for Mary's bright, if conventional looks.

Lady Edith, across the table, glared at Thea; her father gave her small encouraging smiles. He thought that his daughter looked a little peaky these

days, although she seemed to have cheered up
wonderfully since arriving at the Robertsons'.

Gis did his duty by Mary, to the degree that her
hopeful parents thought that he might be genuinely
interested in her. But it was Thea to whom he said
softly, between the fillet of beef and the sorbet
which followed, 'Do you ever go out alone, Thea?
Does Lady Edith allow it?'

Thea picked up her spoon, said, 'No — why?'

'I thought that you might like to meet me one
day, say this Friday, and we could go to the National
Gallery together, or the zoo.'

Thea considered her sorbet as though it were the
most interesting thing in the world. She could feel
her mother's eyes on her. She thought of Hector, of
Gis, of how wicked she would be to do what he
said, looked at Gis and murmured, 'I am due to
spend the day with Monica James on Friday. Mother
will not be going. Monica is a little fast, but her
family is good. I think that I could persuade her to
let Mother think I was with her, and I could meet
you, instead. I won't tell Monica who you are, just
that you're a friend. She's always telling me that I
let Mother walk all over me, and that I ought to do
what I want for a change. I don't think that she
would say so much, if she had to live with Mother.'

Gis began to laugh under his breath. 'I'm corrupt-
ing you,' he said softly, so that no one could
overhear. 'Now I'm going to talk to Mary again,
and then I shall turn to you and suggest where we
might meet.'

The rest of dinner passed in a haze for Thea.
When Mother's not about, I'll ring Monica, she
decided when she and Gis had arranged matters to

their satisfaction, and ask her to cover for me. I'm sure she will. Sneaking off to see Gis would mean that she would have to take a tube train—on her own; the mere idea was frightening, and liberating, to someone who lived in a world of limousines, cabs and her mother's chaperonage.

Gis might have corrupted Thea, but Monica James was already corrupted.

'Oh!' she exclaimed over the telephone, Thea ringing her up when her mother was engaged in the kitchen. 'You've given me a splendid idea. I shall ask Mother if we can both go up to London for the day, and when we get there we can separate, I can persuade Clive Temple to take me out, and you can meet your mystery man. What a dark horse you are, after all, Thea Dunstan! Why can't you tell me who he is? Is he unsuitable?'

'Sort of,' replied Thea truthfully, 'but he's madly rich—which is something.'

She felt a bit of a traitor saying this, because his wealth had nothing to do with why she had agreed to meet Gis, but she knew that such a confession would excite Monica.

'Lucky you!' Monica carolled down the phone. 'Now Clive's dirt-poor, which is why I've agreed to meeting him secretly. I'm surprised your mother isn't happy about you taking up with someone rich.'

'Wrong sort of rich,' said Thea briefly, and then, hearing her mother coming into the hall, she said hastily, 'That's all right, then, Monica, see you on Friday—lovely.'

'Ringing up Monica, were you?' said Lady Edith, giving Thea a look of approval for once. 'Now, there's what I call a sensible girl. She does what her mother tells her, and always looks sweetly pretty, too.'

It took all Thea's moral strength not to inform her deluded parent that far from being biddable Monica was going out in secret with a young man her family considered undesirable, and Monica had even talked dreamily to Thea about the possibility of going 'all the way' with him. 'He says that he knows how not to give me a baby,' she had told a wide-eyed Thea.

Any hint of 'all that' to Lady Edith and she would never have been allowed to meet Monica again.

'Going all the way,' indeed, Thea had thought, and then with a strange excitement, Does Gis want me to go all the way with him? *That's* what he was worried about in the woods, that he might, I suppose. And was he worrying for me — or for himself? for, unknown to Lady Edith, despite her innocent and timid appearance, Thea was extremely hard-headed, as an amused Gis was beginning to find out.

'Now,' he said to her, on Friday morning as the clocks around Oxford Circus were chiming eleven, 'where would you like to go?'

Thea had been in an inward lather of excitement all the way to her destination. She had not, after all, had to undertake most of her journey alone. Monica had come with her as far as Oxford Circus, but was joining Clive at the next station.

Even when she had reached Oxford Circus and was going up on the escalator — on her own! — she was worried that Gis might not be there. Suppose that it was all a bad joke, his whole involvement with her, she thought, her poor heart bouncing and

fluttering with fear so that when she saw him waiting
for her, exactly where he had said that he would be,
she had the greatest difficulty in not throwing herself
at him.

Her mother's daughter in her determination, if
nothing else, she mastered herself and walked
towards him. She was wearing the light blue cotton
dress which she had worn at Padworth and which
she was well aware was kinder to her than most of
her unsuitable clothes. She was also wearing a rather
old-fashioned wide-brimmed straw hat, trimmed
with daisies and poppies, but nothing to that; she
knew that it suited her better than the more fashionable smaller hats which were coming in.

But she couldn't compete with Gis. He was head-
turning in his William and Mary blazer, cream
flannels, light shoes, and a straw boater with more
of the William and Mary colours around it. Before
Thea's arrival he had already been accosted and had
refused the pretty lady who had been attracted by
his whole appearance of perfect looks combined
with athleticism and wealth, and she had even
smiled through her disappointment when he had
said cheerfully to her, 'Not now, darling, waiting for
my girl, you see. Better luck next time.'

His smile was mostly for Thea today, and when
he had taken off his boater and kissed her on the
cheek, which surprised her so much that she put her
hand up to caress the favoured spot, she was in a
daze of happiness, and said to him, 'Oh, you choose.
You know so much more about all this than I do.'

'Well, then,' he said, taking her arm, and walking
her along, 'I propose that first of all we have a
pleasant walk to Soho, via Liberty's, where they

have some splendid fashions for you to look at. . .'
for Gis was sure that Lady Edith would not approve
of Liberty's but thought that Thea might, which she
did.

He had never expected to find his pleasure from
looking at the play of expression on a rather unre-
markable girl's face, but Thea's innocent delight in
all that she was seeing enchanted him.

'How do you know so much about this sort of
thing?' she asked him wonderingly as he walked her
around Liberty's, taking her into the showrooms
where exquisite ceramics were on display, as well as
allowing her to admire the dresses and accessories
which were arranged around the main hall. She was
surprised that such a masculine man should know so
much about what she had always thought of as
feminine things.

'Oh,' he said. 'I don't really know much. I'm a
sort of parrot, you see, I have this odd knack of not
forgetting anything I have seen or heard. And I
have been round here before with. . .others, and
I'm telling you what I heard then.'

With Diana, thought Thea with a pang, but he's
not here with her, now. He's with me.

They left Liberty's and walked slowly along
Regent Street, and then Gis said, 'Would you like a
light lunch now, Thea? While we're eating it, we
can decide what to do with our day. I know a little
place in Soho, very private, no one we know is
likely to see us there, and the *patron* is a friend of
mine from. . .' He hesitated, then stopped.

Soho! Go to Soho, another place which Lady
Edith spoke of as though it were situated in the

suburbs of hell. 'Oh, yes,' she breathed, 'I should like that very much.'

It was so very different from the bored acquiescence of most of the girls and women whom he had escorted that Thea's pleasure became Gis's.

He walked her along Wardour Street and down an alley, where a sign over a small and dark doorway announced that they were at the House of the Golden Snail.

'Snails.' Thea's eyes were huge. 'Do you expect me to eat snails?' And then, bravely, 'If you do, I shall try to like them, I can't promise that I will like them, but I can promise that I shall say I do,' and her small face, whose expression had been growing in amusement since she had met him at Oxford Circus, was alight with happiness, at him, at her unexpected day, and at her own response to it all.

The *patron* did know Gis. They hurled rapid French at one another, the *patron* kissed Thea's hand, brought her a glass of *citron pressé* himself, and Gis a Dubonnet, so that they could have something to drink while they chose from the menu.

'Not too much,' Gis announced to the *patron* in English. 'We don't want to be too full of food to enjoy whatever *mademoiselle* here decides we are going to do this afternoon.' He looked across at Thea, whose face had now assumed a look of fierce concentration as she tackled the menu with nothing but an arsenal of schoolgirl French. Gis's fluency had awed her; was there nothing he couldn't do?

She looked back at Gis, said, 'I wish that you would help me. You choose — nothing heavy, please.'

'Very well. A light soup, I see that there is a

consommé. An omelette *aux fine herbes*, a green
salad and fruit to follow. Do you think that you
would like that, Thea? Oh, and Georges, a glass of
white wine for us both. Open a bottle of your best
Chardonnay, and drink the remainder yourself.'

Thea nodded her agreement, almost too full of
what was happening to her to take in everything
around her. One thing over which she had previously agonised was solved for her by Gis's tact.
While they waited for the soup—the *patron* had
already brought them French bread and country
butter—he leaned forward and said, 'Perhaps you
would like to powder your nose. There is a ladies'
room over there.'

Of course she would, so that was one worry
solved. Powder her nose! She never used powder;
Lady Edith did not approve of that—one more
thing on her list—but what a useful phrase it was;
she must remember it when next nature called. She
giggled at herself in the mirror and decided that she
didn't look half bad, as Monica's schoolboy brother
had once said of the American film star, Theda
Bara.

The meal was both delicate and remarkable, and
Thea enjoyed it heartily. Gis called for a coffee
when it was over, and it came in small cups, black
and scalding.

It was while they were drinking it, after deciding
that a visit to the zoo would be the thing, the day
being too fine to be spent indoors, and Lady Edith
having never allowed Thea to go to the zoo, that
the odd thing happened.

A young man, slightly older than Gis, came in, a
pretty girl, who proved to be his wife, in tow. The

patron went to meet them, and walked them by Gis's table. Thea saw Gis's face change as the young man approached, a strange expression on it, and the young man must have seen Gis at almost the same moment. He stopped, said 'Excuse me,' to the *patron*, and spoke to Gis.

'Gil, Gil Schuyler! What a piece of luck to see you! I thought that we should never meet again. You disappeared as quickly after demob as you had arrived. Lucy,' he turned to the girl with him, 'this is Gil Schuyler, about whom I never stop talking, and Gil, this is my wife Lucy,' and now he addressed Thea, 'Forgive me, I have no manners, but then, Gil never had any either.'

'Harry Marlowe, by all that's holy,' said Gis quietly, standing up and taking the offered hand. 'And what are you doing these days?'

Thea knew immediately that the encounter was disturbing him, although nothing showed; he was as cool and pleasant as ever.

'Not as well as you, I'll be bound,' retorted Harry frankly. 'Come into money, have you? You never looked as splendid as that on the squadron.' He turned to his wife and to Thea. 'He was the biggest scruff you ever saw, Gil was, and got into the most trouble, but no one could fly a crate like him. Still driving everyone mad, Gil? But it seems to have paid off, looking at you. Married, are you?' And he smiled at an entranced Thea.

'My turn for introductions,' said Gis smoothly. 'This is my friend, Miss Thea Dunstan, Mr and Mrs Harry Marlowe, and yes, I came into money.'

'Pity you didn't earlier,' said Harry, candid again. 'You could have done with some more in France.

We all thought you'd stay in the RAF when the big
flap ended. I thought about it, but decided against
it. Helping my father to run the family business
now.'

He hesitated, said, 'I see you're at the end of your
meal, or I'd have suggested we ate it together so
that we could talk about old times. Remember the
day when you downed that Boche over Abbeville
after he damned near downed you? We all thought
Gil had had it,' he explained to Thea, who was
beginning to grasp that Gis had known this young
man when he was serving in the RAF.

Serving in the RAF? The Royal Air Force, down-
ing Germans over Abbeville? He couldn't have
done. She remembered the snide comments about
his sitting out the war in the United States, and tried
not to look at him as he turned his charm on the
Marlowes, exchanged addresses, giving them, Thea
noticed, not his London one, but that of the cottage
whose key he had given her.

Trailing clouds of reminiscences, Harry Marlowe
was quite unaware that he had dropped a mortar
bomb on Gis Havilland's table, and added one more
mysterious piece to the puzzle which made up Gis.

After he had gone, Gis drank up his remaining
coffee before smiling wryly at Thea. 'Say something,
Thea. You must be bursting with curiosity after
those revelations.'

'Your business, not mine,' she said primly,
although he was right, she *was* bursting with
curiosity.

'I forgot that I used to come here with Harry,' he
said, 'on leave, in the war,' offering no explanations
at all, and then, 'You're a clam, Thea, I know that

from your response to what happened at Mereside. I promise you that later on, when you have seen the animals, I'll explain to you what that was all about. I know you won't talk. Can you be patient, and forget this until later? I don't want it to spoil this afternoon for you.'

'It won't,' said Thea truthfully, and he could tell that she meant it, and their leaving the restaurant was nearly as triumphant as their entry had been, and next stop the zoo, Gis said portentously, once they were out in the street again, fed and watered and ready to tackle lions, tigers, rhinos and giraffes.

Being at the zoo with Gis was all and more than she had expected. The same might have been said of Gis. To go to the zoo might seem a childish occupation for a young man of his intellect, sophistication and experience, but somehow, with Thea, he found himself a child again, the child he had never really been.

Everything entranced her. Before the giraffes she stood, awestruck. The nicest thing about her, was that she never chattered. She possessed the art of silence, an art she had learned in order to endure her mother, he suspected. But her silences were companionable. Once, she slipped her hand in his when they were looking at the elephants, majestic creatures, 'Sailing around their enclosure like great lumbering galleons,' she surprised him by saying.

Thea liked the birds, too, and the open spaces where one could sit, and watch some of the minor animals in their small enclosures.

'Do they mind,' she said once to him, 'that they're behind bars? I can't help thinking that they must dislike it very much,' and she heaved a great sigh.

She liked being with Gis. He didn't trouble her with a torrent of comments, which surprised her a little, for the Gis she had so far encountered had been voluble, amusingly so, it was true, but with her he was silent.

She worried a little, at first, that he found her boring, and she turned to him once, and said, a little awkwardly, 'This isn't really your sort of place, is it? It's somewhere you take children to.'

Gis looked down at her from his great height, said slowly, 'I like animals, Thea. They don't waste time thinking and talking about their immortal souls, or worrying about the correct clothes to wear. Like you, I worry a little that they're behind bars, I don't like to think about anyone being caged, but that sort of thinking is part of the unnecessary nonsense we surround ourselves with. They may suffer, but they don't enlarge it by being self-conscious about it. Among them, I can forget myself a little. Now you may call me unfeeling, but don't forget that in the wild most of the animals you have seen would have been dead long ago. Their true world is a cruel one.'

Without knowing how, Thea knew immediately that this was not the kind of confidence Gis usually offered people, and she thought about what he had said, her face assuming an expression so serious that this time it was Gis who took her hand, saying, 'Don't worry, Thea, about me or the animals; there's nothing you can do for either of us,' and he led her to a bench where they could sit and enjoy the afternoon sun.

Let's pretend, said Thea's imp, that he's your young man, who has taken you out for the afternoon, out of passion, not pity. The thought made her smile, and Gis, looking at her reflective face, noting the small hands clasped in her lap, was aware that for Thea quiet resignation to her lot was a way of life, and the thought appalled him.

To dispel it, and because he genuinely wanted to confide in her, to touch the inner strength which he knew that she possessed, he said slowly, 'I told you at the Golden Snail that I would explain the little scene with Harry Marlowe, because I know that you would tell no one else of what I am about to reveal.' He paused and Thea looked at him, eyes wide.

'I never tell anyone anything,' she replied seriously.

'I know that, too, after Mereside.' And he gave a small strange laugh. 'You trusted me, and I am going to trust you.' He looked away and was silent while he wondered how much he could burden her with, she had so many troubles of her own.

'You must know,' he said at last, 'of the gossip about my birth. No details, but it's all true. I am illegitimate; the reasons for it don't matter much, even to me. But my parents never told me. I think, now, that they thought to spare me, but they were mistaken. What was worse, or better, perhaps, is that I was a distressingly precocious child, and I don't think that the revelation would have troubled me then. I found out about my birth when I was sixteen, at public school. I was precocious there as well, I was several forms ahead of my age, and it was arranged that I should go to Oxford a year early, at seventeen — I was ready for it at sixteen.'

He paused, wondering how to tell her tactfully of the next step in his pathetic saga, as he usually

savagely named it to himself. 'There was a boy
there, two years older than I was, who wanted. . .
to be my great friend. . . I didn't like him. . .and
didn't want his friendship. One day I had to. . .
rebuff him rather strongly. He took his revenge by
informing me, publicly, that I was a bastard, that
everyone knew about it, and laughed behind my
back.

'I suppose that I was a conceited child, and what
he said hit me harder than it should have done. My
idea of myself, of my. . .father and my mother, was
in ruins. I could tell by the other boys' reactions
that what he said was true. I went for him, I was big
for my age, as big as he was, and I half killed him
before they pulled me off.' He stopped again. 'I'm
not proud of how I behaved after that, Thea. I went
a little mad, I hated everyone, particularly my
mother and my father. I felt that everyone was
laughing at me, had done for years, that my life had
been lived in public, and I had known nothing of
it—you see what I mean about the animals. I went
to Oxford in a cloud of hate, my poor mother and
father hardly knew me. I had been a clinging and
affectionate child, very biddable, but now I was as
rude and unkind to them as I could be.

'I had been at Oxford a year when the War came.
I wasn't happy. I'd thrown myself into hard work to
try to forget what I was. I was nearly eighteen and
I'd always been interested in flying, I'd read H G
Wells's *The War in the Air*, and kept up with all the
advances in aeronautics. It was in the long vacation.
I wrote a letter to my tutor telling him that I was
leaving Oxford for the duration of the war, and
when it was over I would finish my degree, and

without saying anything to my parents I went off and enlisted in the ranks of the Royal Flying Corps, the RFC as it was then, which is the RAF now.

'I wanted to be like the animals, not clever and remarkable Gis Havilland, expected to get a double first before he was twenty. I was a private and lived off my pay. They trained me as a mechanic; I was the lowest form of life, an erk. It was a hard life and strange, I was a fish out of water at first, but I came to enjoy it, and finally I became a pilot and went on active service. My poor father and mother must have gone mad when they received my letter saying that I had enlisted—but giving them no details. My father's friend, Lord Moidore, had a post in the government, connected with the war office, and he started a search for me, and finally tracked me down. I had changed my name to Schuyler, which, if I am entitled to a name, is the one I ought to own. I called myself Gil, not Gis, because that was more ordinary, and by the time I was a pilot I was thoroughly accepted as one of the lads, as you probably gathered from Harry.

'So, I went home again, in 1916, on leave, and the prodigal was forgiven and cried over, but I only went back on one condition, that no one should be told what I had done, that the story that my parents had put about to explain my disappearance, that I had gone to the States, should be adhered to. Do you understand why I did that, Thea? They couldn't, my father and mother, but I think that Uncle Gerard does, although he never says anything.'

Thea had remained silent while Gis was speaking, looking carefully away from him. When he asked his question she turned towards him and said in her quiet voice, 'Oh, yes, Gis, I think I do. It was something of your own, wasn't it? Something private that no one could tear to pieces with either their spite or their praise. Oh, yes, I understand you,' and she put out her small hand and took his large one and stroked it gently.

Gis sat quite still, said in a stifled voice, 'But you can't condone what I did to my father and mother,' he said at last.

'Oh, no, not at all, but that's not the same thing as understanding why you did it, and why you still let people think the worst of you about the War. It's something all of your own.'

Gis took the stroking hand, lifted it to his lips and kissed it. 'Yes, you extraordinary child, you do understand, and I do believe that you will say nothing. Do you have your own private world, Thea, which no one is allowed to enter, which shields you from life's harshnesses? No, don't answer if you don't want to.'

'Yes,' said Thea simply, 'nothing like yours, though. My affairs are small and rather silly.'

It was no longer than ten minutes before Gis was to ask himself whether Thea was being entirely truthful, but at the time he felt a certain sense of relief. Probably his forebodings about her were baseless after all, that it was himself he was dreaming of. He felt that a load had been lifted from his back, now that he had confided in her.

'Enough,' he said, rising. 'Let us emulate the animals and not scratch our wounds over and over again. Only I'm sorry for what I did, for the love and trust between me and my parents was destroyed by my actions and mine alone, and I broke a bond of love that I don't think can ever be renewed.'

Thea made no answer. She felt that she had nothing useful to say, so said nothing. Gis was grateful for that, and led her across the grass to their last port of call, the rhinos.

'They're so much bigger than I expected,' said Thea, awed by them. 'Oh, I have enjoyed today. I can't thank you enough. Oh, I do hope that Mother doesn't find out. It would quite spoil everything.'

'Perhaps we can do it again, soon,' murmured Gis, who had enjoyed his day far more than he had expected to. She was really quite pretty after all, he thought, when she was enjoying herself. Animation improved her, although he liked her look of calm meditation, particularly when there was no aura of worry around it, as there had been at Padworth, or whenever she was with her appalling mother.

He thought Lady Edith even more appalling a few minutes later. Unknown to Thea a bee had begun to circle her hat, perhaps mistaking her poppies and daisies for real ones. It finally began to settle near her eyes, and Gis saying, 'One moment, Thea,' put up his hand rather suddenly to brush it away.

To Thea, this unexpected movement brought back an unwanted memory. Lady Edith's blows had been traumatic ones, and his hand, rising up towards her head, had her putting her hands over her ears and cowering away from him, stammering, 'N-n-no, please, don't,' before she remembered where she was and that she was with Gis, who wouldn't hurt her. All the colour had fled from her face.

'I'm sorry,' she said, trying not to shiver, 'I'm

sorry.' Her ear still hurt her a little, and the memory of what Lady Edith had done seemed to have brought the hurt back again.

Gis had gone white. He realised at once that she had thought that, improbably, he was about to strike her. The berserker anger rose in him; he controlled it with difficulty, said, his voice quiet, but Thea could sense the rage which lay behind it, 'What is it, Thea? I was only going to knock a bee away, and. . . Who hit you, Thea, and why?'

She did begin to shake then, and the contrast between the happy child whom she had been a moment ago and the frightened creature before him fuelled the rage.

'Tell me,' he asked, still quiet, all his worst forebodings about her returning in full force.

'It was your mother, wasn't it?' he said. 'Why, Thea, why?'

'I can't tell you,' she said, but he knew that he had guessed the truth. 'Oh, Gis, don't let's talk about it. My day has been so happy. Don't let my stupidity spoil it for us.'

'Your stupidity!' Gis turned away from her, to master himself. They were by the wall of the bird house, and he struck his fist, hard, against it, angered by his own impotence, his inability to do anything to protect her. The feelings which were overwhelming him were so new and strange that he could hardly cope with them. The world grew far away, as it did when the rage struck him, particularly when he could not give vent to it in action.

'Gis, what is it?' And now Thea was alarmed by him, which wouldn't do at all.

'Nothing,' he said, and smiled at her. 'It's

nothing, just. . . Thea, you still have the address I gave you, and the key?'

'Yes,' she said. 'But, there's nothing to worry about. I think that Mother has changed her mind.'

It was over Hector Dashwood, of course, and the old baggage who had once given him the glad eye — Gis could think of no name bad enough for Lady Edith — was determined to make Thea accept him.

'You refused Hector Dashwood,' he managed to get out.

'Yes.' Thea was startled. 'How did you know?'

'Magic,' said Gis starkly. 'No, Thea, everyone knows that your mother wants Hector to marry you.'

Gis leaned forward and kissed Thea gently on the cheek. He wanted to do rather more than that, but there was always another day, and he didn't want to frighten her more than he need. She reminded him of a stricken bird, but there was nothing feeble about her. After her involuntary display of fear, she had mastered herself, and tried to put it behind her.

Already her colour was returning, and her eyes had begun to sparkle again. Her gallantry shamed him, particularly when he thought of his own spoiled reaction to his troubles, which seemed minor compared with the regime of sadistic bullying which he suspected Thea was enduring. His own parents had shown him nothing but love — and how had he behaved the first time anything had disturbed his lordly life? He examined himself, and found himself wanting, not a pleasant experience, if salutary.

'You're right,' he said, 'we mustn't spoil the afternoon. It's time we left the zoo, anyway. I thought that you might like to go to a Lyons tea-

shop for afternoon tea before I take you to the tube.
Where and when are you meeting that forward
young friend of yours?'

'Monica?' Relieved that the atmosphere had lightened, and that their happy day had not been ruined,
Thea began to laugh. 'Yes, she is forward. We
arranged to meet at Oxford Circus, at five o'clock,
and then go to her home. I'm to stay for an informal
dinner with Monica. Mother will be sending the
chauffeur for me at half-past ten.'

'Off to Joe Lyons, then,' smiled Gis, and had the
pleasure of explaining who Joe Lyons was, before
sitting by Thea on the tube as they returned to
Oxford Street, and when he took her hand to hold
it she said nothing, only squeezed his gently.

She loved the tea shop, another new experience,
smiling at the nippies, as Gis told her the waitresses
were called, running to and fro. 'Don't their feet get
tired?' she asked him.

'I expect so,' was his answer to that. It occurred
to him that Thea's depths were greater than he had
imagined, but she ate cream cakes and drank tea
like a healthy schoolboy on holiday.

Thea was lost in thought, seated by Monica, who
prattled merrily all the way back to Hampstead, via
tube and cab, outlining the mythical day which she
and Thea had spent together so that neither her
mother nor Lady Edith should suspect that their
daughters had spent the day alone in wicked London
with equally wicked young men.

'And he wants to meet you again, a week from
now,' said Monica. 'Oh, splendid. We'll keep to the
same arrangements as today, shall we?'

'So long as Mother doesn't know we went to

London,' commented Thea, 'let alone that we parted.

'Oh, my mother won't say anything,' replied Monica largely. 'She thinks your mother is far too strict, and that it's about time you had a bit of fun. You did have fun today, Thea, didn't you? Oh, do say you had fun.'

'Oh, yes,' agreed Thea, 'I had fun,' and she went to sleep that night while trying to decide which bit of the day had been the most fun of all.

CHAPTER SIX

'To what do I owe the honour, sir?'

Gis had arrived home. His flat was in Half Moon Street. He lived alone, employing no valet or man, either there or at his Oxfordshire cottage; a daily woman came in. He did his own cooking. He had learned self-sufficiency in the RAF and shared his life with no one.

He had hardly had time to throw off his blazer; in any case he was once again preoccupied with the problem of Thea Dunstan so that, when the doorbell rang, he answered it with a small frown on his face.

It was his father. He stared at him a moment, then said, 'Come in,' a little dismissively. Ever since Gis had secretly enlisted in the RAF his relationship with him had been purely formal, and after his talk with Thea this afternoon he found that the thought pained him. He had re-opened a wound he had thought healed. The cold question which followed the knowledge of this was thrown out to help him restore his equilibrium.

Sir Richard Havilland had learned tact and forbearance in a hard school. He was a senior diplomat, had been an ambassador, and was now between duties, acting as an adviser to the Foreign Office. If he felt pain at his cold reception, he did not show it, merely entered, put down his hat and stick and looked around his son's home, a home

which he had not visited before, so far apart had
they grown.

The room surprised him a little. It was, he saw,
as much a workroom as a place to live. Two walls
were filled with books, and a large desk stood before
the window; it was covered with paper and books.
Beside the desk was another, a draughtsman's high
table to which was pinned a technical drawing. It
was apparent that Gis had been working on something — but what?

There were easy-chairs at one end before a small,
circular, brass table. A side-table held a tray with
bottles and glasses on it. On the third wall was an
array of paintings of the Far West in America and a
few sketches and photographs of aeroplanes in flight
and on the ground.

There was nothing to suggest that the room's
owner possessed friends or relatives; there were no
family or personal photographs. The only warmth
in the room was a copper jar standing in the empty
fireplace, filled with early chrysanthemums, flaming
scarlet and gold. It was a strangely ascetic abode for
a young man best known for the gregarious life
which he lived in Oxford and elsewhere.

'I have never visited you here,' said his father in
the beautiful voice which Gis had always admired,
and which he knew that his father had passed on to
him, but not to his legitimate son, Richie. That, and
the brilliant looks they shared — although Gis's gold
was now his father's silver — was a bond between
them which neither now acknowledged. Richie
looked like his mother's family, the Schuylers, being
stocky and dark, which was ironic, because he was
nothing like them in temperament, which Gis was.

'I was in the neighbourhood and thought I would look in, I. . .we don't see enough of you these days, Gis.'

It was said simply without asking for sympathy, without reminding Gis that there had been a time when his father had been his hero and his pride, and probably, thought Gis, looking at him, that was why the knowledge of who and what I was hit me so hard.

But he said nothing of that, merely, 'Take a seat, Father. May I offer you a drink?'

His father sat in one of the large armchairs, said, 'A Scotch if you have one. Neat, not a double.'

'It was never a double, sir, as I remember.' Gis poured his father and himself a tot, handed one of the glasses to his father, and sat down opposite to him.

'*Slainte,*' he said, lifting the glass in a grave salute. 'You look well, sir. And my mother?'

His father acknowledged the salute, drank, put down his glass, and considered his wayward son. The son, who had, for the first sixteen years, been a model of what a son ought to be, but afterwards. . . and now they sat here, talking like strangers.

'Well, as always,' replied his father, 'energetic. She and your aunt Torry are always busying themselves with something. It's this project of flats for poor working girls now.'

Gis smiled, affectionately, thinking of his vital little mother. He remembered what he had said to Thea, about his sorrow over the division between him and his family, and his regret that he had caused it.

And now his father had come to see him, voluntarily. He opened his mouth to apologise for the last seven years, for his own over-strong reaction to the news of his illegitimacy, for the unkind way in which he had disappeared at the beginning of the war, but his father forestalled him, was saying, in his grave and measured way, 'Actually, Gis, it's partly over your mother that I have come to see you.'

The apology, the desire to be reconciled, died on Gis's lips. He took a long swallow of whisky, said 'Yes?', and the word was a question, but his father was continuing as though he had not spoken.

'She's worried about you — oh,' he said, raising an almost dismissive hand in response to the wry expression on his son's face, 'I know that's nothing new, she's worried about you ever since you were born, and particularly since. . .' He let the sentence die, went on, 'She's worried about your involvement with Thea Dunstan, and, I must say, so am I. She's not like the girls you usually run around with, Gis. She can be easily hurt. And your mother understands from Lady Edith that she is already half promised to Hector Dashwood. I can't say that I care much for him, but that's beside the point. It's not right to raise expectations in a girl which you have no intention of fulfilling, particularly if that might spoil any relationship that she's already undertaken.'

Sir Richard's usually smooth and balanced mode of speech seemed to have deserted him in the face of the expression which his son had assumed. He stopped.

'Yes?' drawled Gis on a rising note, all intentions of offering reconciliation and love having been destroyed by his father's warnings and the suppo-

sition that he was toying with Thea and intended to
harm her. 'Yes? And? I'm sure that there's more to
come. Don't hesitate, Father, spit it all out!'

If Gis had begun his last remarks in a cool voice,
the last phrase was flung at his father with an almost
unparalleled savagery. He put his whisky glass
down, jumped to his feet and strode to the window,
to lean against it staring blindly down at the street.
For some odd reason, the warning bell which rang
occasionally in his mind when he thought of Thea
was ringing louder than ever, and he couldn't face
his father and remain civil to him.

His father gazed ruefully at Gis's back. Long
practice kept him sitting in his chair, kept his voice
even and steady. He might have expected this, he
thought, but Kate had been insistent. He must speak
to Gis, someone must try to check him. He might
be twenty-four years old, independent, and, thanks
to the trust she had settled on him at birth, he might
be able to go his way without thought of financial
worries, but *someone* ought occasionally to point
out to him the error of his ways, stop him from
committing the unforgivable.

'I must say that you worry me, too,' said Sir
Richard at last. 'This business of not letting people
know what a good War you had. That you were
decorated for your heroism. I understand that
Hector Dashwood has been going around blackguarding you about that, and has also had the
impudence to describe you as a thief, God knows
why. He couldn't possibly say such things if you
allowed what you did to be known.'

'Very true.' The voice was Gis at his most sardonic, his father noticed miserably. 'And this is the

man whom you, Lady Edith and my energetic mother prefer for Thea Dunstan, while I am to be rebuked for speaking to her at all. I must say that you all seem to have an odd set of values.'

'Regardless of that,' answered Sir Richard, stung at last, 'I understand that Dashwood's intentions towards the girl are honourable. He wishes to marry her. What are yours, one wonders, in view of your known reputation?'

Gis, his control quite restored, swung round to confront his father with an almost savage good humour.

'Bad, of course,' he said cheerfully. 'They must be, seeing that I hold them — and considering "my known reputation". No business of yours, either, seeing that I am, as you have just admitted, well over twenty-one, am a free agent, and what I choose to say about my war service is for me to decide, and for you to respect.'

'You have gone your own way since you were sixteen,' said his father.

'True,' replied Gis, 'and, may I remind you, for the four war years, without asking you for any support, financial or otherwise or taking any money from my trust fund? I accept the money from the trust fund only until I am able to make my own way. I think I deserve to finish my education at my mother's expense, don't you? After that, I shall make other arrangements.'

This was all dismally far from what he had intended to say to his father, but the whole question of Hector and Thea Dunstan flicked him on the raw. Impossible to tell his father of his almost psychic misgivings over her fate, even though he knew that on several previous occasions misgivings concerning others had proved true. There was no evidence of any sort which he could offer to Sir Richard — especially in the face of his and his mother's apparent belief that his only interest in the girl was that of a callous seducer.

'Well, you'll go your own way, I expect.' Sir Richard sounded weary. 'When I look back, I think that you always did, but you were such a good and loving child. . . .' His voice trailed off. How to say to his son, who was staring at him as though he were a stranger, 'You were the product of your mother and father's deepest love, and, looking at you now, that is my deepest grief,' but the habits of a lifetime kept him from saying anything. And Gis, in this mood, was impenetrable.

He looked around the room, at the evidence before him of a man who had interests and tastes of which he knew nothing, and with whom he could share nothing. He knew nothing of Gis's wartime service, nothing of the wishes and desires which ruled Gis's life, outside his social life — of which he knew too much.

'I wish,' he said quietly, 'that you would at least think about the matters of which I have spoken.'

'Oh, I will,' Gis was nastily cheerful, 'and thank Mother for her continued interest in my affairs, will you?' Gis knew that he was being hateful, but he couldn't stop himself.

Once his father had gone, he sank down into the chair before his desk and rested his head in his hands. He had not meant to speak and behave as he had done, but the sense of rejection was strong in him, and if part of the reason for his rejection was his own fault then that made things worse, not better.

Presently he sat up, picked up a pencil and began to draw perfect circles on the piece of blank paper in front of him. So, Hector Dashwood was going around blackguarding him, and was hinting, or more than hinting at theft. He had better warn Sophie that Hector was going out of control, was behaving like a loose cannon, bounding about the deck of an old warship, wrecking whatever he came into contact with—and they wanted him to marry Thea! Well, he, Gis Havilland, might have something to say about that.

Gis and Thea arranged to meet secretly again, enthusiastically aided and abetted by Monica, who had her own reasons for wanting to go up west without her mother knowing that she and Thea separated at Oxford Circus.

Thea thought that perhaps the second forbidden trip might be less exciting and happy than the first one, but no such thing. True, the weather was bad, so that she had to wear a Burberry and a rain hat, and a pair of stout shoes, but what of that? And Gis, when she met him, was suitably dressed for bad weather, and looked even more handsome in his trench coat and slouch hat than he had done in his blazer.

He immediately rushed her into a Lyons to be out of the weather, to drink coffee and discuss what they might do with the afternoon.

'What a good thing we went to the zoo last week, when the weather was fine,' Thea said to him. 'Impossible to have gone today.' And she watched the rain stream down the glass windows before which they were sitting.

'Would you like to go to a matinée this afternoon?' Gis asked her. 'We could go to the Golden Snail again, and you could sample some more of its excellent cuisine, and after that move on to the theatre.'

Anything which he suggested would have pleased Thea, and to go to the theatre to sit with him, in the dark, perhaps to hold hands, sounded like an ideal arrangement. Monica had told her that when she and Clive went to the theatre or the cinema they always held hands, 'And cuddled,' she had finished with a shriek. 'Mother would have fits if she knew what Clive and I get up to. You won't tell her, will you?'

No, Thea wouldn't tell her. She couldn't imagine herself telling Monica's mother anything, let alone what Monica got up to with Clive. She avoided thinking of what her own mother would say or do if she discovered that she was slipping off to spend the day with Gis.

He decided that he would take her to see the new thriller, *At the Villa Rose*, which had been adapted by A. E. W. Mason from the novel he had written, introducing his French detective, Inspector Hanaud, to the world.

'They say it's worth seeing,' he informed Thea. He had already discovered that she had been taken by her mother to see *Chu Chin Chow* or he would have taken her to that.

Lunch together was as exciting and intimate as it had been the week before. Gis introduced Thea to *moules marinière* and she ate the little mussels with great enjoyment after some initial inward reservations. When Gis suggested *cassoulet*, telling the *patron* that if they chose it their portions must be small, she also wondered a little at a dish based on beans, but when it came ate it with gusto, and drank the glass of powerful red *Corbières* which Gis ordered with it, also with more appreciation than she had expected.

Whether it was the wine, or the increasing pleasure she found in his company, Thea didn't know, but she discovered that she was confiding in him more than ever—which was only fair, since he had confided in her so much.

'Father's going to Paris tomorrow, to the Sorbonne,' she told him, 'first to take part in some sort of seminar, next to stay on to do some research there, almost until term opens. He would be much happier without Mother and myself. . .there was no question that he might ever take us with him, and Mother wouldn't want to go.'

She put her glass down, looked at Gis, said earnestly, 'Since I met you, I seem to be thinking a lot, seeing things I never saw before. I don't think Mother would ever have married him if she had known that the War would kill all my uncles and that she would inherit everything. As it was, I suppose that she was lucky to marry Father. She told me once that it was not her family's custom to give their daughters large dowries on marriage.'

Gis knew that Thea needed no answer to all this. She was working life out for herself, growing up in front of him, putting her good mind to bear on her life, as her father had taught her to do with her studies.

Crème caramel followed. Thea ate it slowly, and, in response to a question from Gis, repeated what she had told him earlier, 'Oh, no, my father never talks to me about my studies now. I believe I told you that he handed me over to Mother at eighteen. . . If I had been a boy, now, it would have been different, but I'm not. . .' She let her sentence trail off, and ate her dessert, a slightly melancholy look on her face.

'Fortunately,' murmured Gis, a wicked look in his eye.

'What?' queried Thea, surprised, looking up at him with wide eyes. He should have remembered that flirtatious games were not her style, and neither had she been trained in them.

'Fortunately you're not a boy. You make a very nice girl, Thea.'

'Do I?' she said doubtfully. 'Mother doesn't think so, and I can't believe that Hector is very enthusiastic about me, either.'

'Ah,' said Gis, still wicked, 'but, as judges of such things go, would you call them reliable?'

Thea began to laugh. 'Well, you'd have to call Mother reliable, in other ways, that is, but Hector, he hardly knows the word exists,' and then she was a little wicked herself, 'Are *you* reliable, Gis?'

This surprised him. He had finished his own *crème caramel*, and was taking his pleasure by watching her.

'With you, yes,' he answered her slowly. 'Whatever else I may be — and God knows, I'm not very proud of most things I do — I *am* reliable where you are concerned.'

He felt ninety years old, and the desire to protect

her was changing even as he spoke, and was beginning to turn into something different. Or rather, the protectiveness remained, but another ingredient was being added to his feelings for her.

No! said something inside him. I don't want this. I want to go on being the cat that walks by itself, finding temporary friends, temporary mates, committing myself to nothing. I don't want to give myself to another.

But he put his hand out towards her, said, quietly, so that none might overhear. 'I wish you well, Thea — understand me. I would never willingly hurt you, and. . . I would hurt anyone who tried to hurt you.'

The Golden Snail was a strange place for such a declaration. It was almost one of love. Thea put down her spoon. The thing between them, unstated, was on the point of declaring itself openly. The word 'love', unspoken as yet, hovered in the air between them. He had not actually said it, and she had been careful to say nothing to him which might betray her true feelings — but it was there, and the more they saw of one another. . .

Her thoughts trailed off, and, to lighten the atmosphere, she said, 'Goodness, Gis, how solemn you are, but I thank you for your concern,' which was being as pompous as a solicitor's letter, but to say anything more personal would leave her in danger of betraying to him how much he had come to mean to her, and she wouldn't burden him with that if he merely saw her as a mildly entertaining younger sister whom he felt compelled to care for.

Her delicacy was not lost on Gis, and he repaid it by letting the subject drop, by talking of lighter things, so that by the time they had finished their coffee they were laughing together, but they both knew that a watershed had been reached in their relationship, and that to go on with it would lead them into country which neither of them had yet visited.

Gis's sexual experience had not provided him with either a guide-book or a map to help them on their way, so different was this from anything which he had ever known before.

Outside, the rain had slackened for a moment, so they walked on slowly, occasionally stopping to look in shop windows, admiring the paintings on display in many of them, some of them quite unlike anything which Thea had ever seen. Gis told her that they were French, of the Impressionist school, and their brilliant colours pleased her. She knew that her mother would have hated them.

It was while they were strolling along the Wardour Street that a well-dressed woman in her middle years saw them together. Her eyebrows went up at the sight. She recognised them both, and knew that Lady Edith would never have approved of such a thing, never have given Thea permission to be alone in London with such a. . .scamp as Gis Havilland was known to be.

She watched Thea look up at Gis, and laugh at something he said, and her lips compressed. She was on her husband's arm, began to phrase what she should say to him, and then stopped. Men! From comments he had made to her, he would most likely find Thea's naughtiness amusing, find it not deplorable that a young girl should so forget herself.

So she said nothing, but Lady Edith ought to

know about this, and she would make it her business to inform her of what she had seen as soon as possible. Girls these days were getting above themselves. It was the war which had done the damage. Where would it all end? She would phone Lady Edith as soon as she arrived home.

Unknowing, Gis and Thea took their way. Thea enjoyed the matinée hugely. Gis had bought them seats in the best box, and she liked sitting there — even if her view of the stage was peculiar — because she was alone with him, in the dark. She enjoyed the afternoon tea which he had ordered for the second interval, enjoyed his entertaining comments on the play and the actors.

It was so nice to talk to someone who didn't treat you as a fool, just because you were a young girl, and who asked your opinion as though he really wanted to know what you had to say. Gis made no concessions to her sex at all. He spoke to her as cheerfully and candidly as he might have spoken to another man, and when sometimes she couldn't follow what he was saying she said so, instead of rolling her eyes and pretending, and saying, 'Oh, how clever you are.'

Contrary to what her mother was always shouting at her, Gis seemed to want to talk seriously to her — not all the time, of course, but then she supposed that he always mixed banter with high seriousness.

Gis liked being with Thea even more than he had expected. He liked her stillness as well as her conversation. The more he came to know her, the happier and easier he was with her. The quality of tranquillity which so enraged Lady Edith and made

Hector sneer about her was one of the things in her which he admired the most.

After the show he took her for a walk. No Lyons tea-shop this time; they had taken tea at the theatre instead.

'Next time,' said Gis, 'I shall take you to Gunter's.' He frowned a little. 'The only thing is, that there might be someone there who knows us. I don't want to get you into more trouble than you already have with. . .'

He stopped. He was not really being tactful.

Thea was sensibly practical and downright, another plus for her, 'With Mother, you mean,' she said cheerfully. 'Well, that's a risk I run every time I meet you, and it's one I'm prepared to take. Let's not talk about her. When I'm with you I can pretend I'm someone else.'

This amused him. 'Someone else, Thea? What kind of someone else?'

She considered gravely, then looked at him, mischief on her face. 'Someone very pretty and very spoiled. Someone who has a mother who is sympathetic to her, a friend, even. Someone who shares confidences with her, and doesn't need to steal off to enjoy themselves just a little. Someone who knows how to flirt.'

'I think I prefer you to the someone,' murmured Gis. He took her arm, said, 'Let's go this way, it's quicker,' and he turned Thea down one of the mean alleys which ran between the luxurious shops which surrounded them. Halfway down they reached what had once, years before, been a grand town house. It had a portico. He manoeuvred the expectant

Thea until she had her back to the battered oak door, and they were sheltered from view.

'I wouldn't do this to the someone,' he muttered, 'only to you,' and he took her in his arms and kissed her.

Increasing knowledge of each other and propinquity had done its work. This time Thea gave a little sigh and co-operated with him enthusiastically from the beginning. Yes, this, this, was what she had always wanted. Gis was beginning to realise that the new and strange feelings which overwhelmed him with Thea, were also mixed with older ones which he had expressed before. He also understood that, whatever else, this pleasure for them both must be short, momentary, for what lay between them was not to be debased by haste on his part, for if he went too fast it would be lust, which cared nothing for the beloved object, only for the selfish gratification of his senses.

This interlude was quite different from the one in the wood. When he had begun to make love to her then, she had not meant very much to him, other than as the recipient of his careless pity — but now, everything had changed. She must not be exploited, not hurt; he must go more carefully with her than ever since she was becoming precious to him.

So it was he who broke away, said, 'Enough for now, Thea. I mustn't take advantage of your trust. I should be no better than a brute beast,' for he saw that her eyes were shining, her whole face had softened, and, whatever he felt for her, she was undoubtedly beginning to love him.

And it was new territory for her. Like him she had no guide-book, no atlas, and he must lead her slowly, and, leading her, they might both find the promised land.

First of all then, he must lead her from the alley, and temptation, and take her to Oxford Circus, to send her back to her desolate home.

Lady Edith did not immediately say anything when Thea reached home. Her friend, Margery Veryan, had rung her up and gleefully told her of Thea's goings-on, that she was in London — no, worse, in Soho — when her mother thought that she was safe with Monica and her mother. Mrs Veryan's comments, which were to rebound on poor Thea, were all the more poisonously nasty because of Lady Edith's overt criticism of the behaviour of her own daughter — she was allowed too much latitude, being Lady Edith's opinion — 'I should never permit Thea to gad about on her own.' So much for Thea Dunstan's perfect behaviour!

It was the professor's last dinner at home before he left for Southampton and the boat. Outwardly Lady Edith was pleasant, inwardly she was seething when her errant daughter arrived from the Jameses'. Over dinner she had told the professor of Margery Veryan's news and then treated him to a tirade against Gis Havilland and all his works, ending with, 'Theodore, I do hope that you understand what I have been saying to you — that his prey is Thea now. It must be stopped, Theodore, at once.'

The professor was ruminative, wiped his lips with his napkin, said slowly, 'Why are you so set against the young man, Edith? He comes of a good family — yes, I know about the rumours, but what of them? He is clever, and being a Schuyler offspring is rich enough for you, I would have thought; no one could call him a fortune-hunter. I know of his reputation, everyone knows about him and Diana Troy, but Hector Dashwood's is far worse. Havilland's wildness, of which you have often spoken, is only that of a brilliant, high-spirited young man enjoying himself. I am more troubled about Hector's, seeing that he is pursuing his escapades well into his thirties. I would have thought you would have given young Havilland's claims more mature consideration.'

'Nonsense, Professor Dunstan!' declared his wife robustly. 'First of all he cannot be serious, such as Thea are not for him — look at her — he must be amusing himself, and I have no mind to see her ruined to give him pleasure. Secondly, his background is such that I would have my doubts about anyone marrying him. Hector's wild days are behind him, he wishes to be settled, he cares for Thea, he has told me so himself, and he brings her a title and one of the oldest names in England; nothing could be more suitable.'

For once the professor did not agree with her, or rather did not say, as he usually did, 'As you wish, my dear, I'm sure that you know best.' Instead he offered slowly, 'I wonder what Thea's wishes are in this matter, Edith? Have you spoken to her of them? And is it logical to assume that Havilland's intentions must of necessity be dishonourable?'

Lady Edith stared at him as though he were mad. 'Thea's wishes? What have they to do with anything? She is a child, innocent, I have purposely kept her so, and as for his intentions being honourable, it is a measure of his villainy that he had

persuaded her to go behind my back to gad about
Soho with her alone, engaging in God knows what.
There is the proof of his lack of fitness.'

It was useless. His wife's mind was made up, and
nothing that he could say would answer. The professor poured himself a glass of red wine.

'Well, if you are determined, my dear. . . But I
beg of you to be kind to her. She is very young, a
delicate plant, sensitive, and, to be fair, young
Havilland is much nearer in age to her than Hector;
it is natural, perhaps, that she should find him more
attractive.'

'Kind!' snorted Lady Edith. 'She needs a good
talking-to, and that is what she will get. I am
surprised at you, Theodore. I had not thought to
see you sympathetic towards the general decay of
manners and morals since the War. No, Thea must
learn to do her duty to her parents and to the noble
family into which she has had the great good fortune
to be born.'

Lady Edith would go her own way; it was regret-
table that he was leaving in the morning so that he
could not protect Thea from her mother's wrath.
He suspected that Lady Edith's behaviour to Thea
would be even more severe than usual while he was
away — and in that, he thought truly.

Once she was home again, delivered this time by
the Jameses' chauffeur, all Thea's thoughts were
either of the day she had just spent with Gis, or the
day which she would spend with him in a week's
time. She had been a little fearful that she might be
boring him, but it was Gis who had said to her
before they parted, 'I hope that you can meet me

again next Friday, Thea, at Oxford Circus, as usual,' which dispelled her fears on that score, as she gave him her eager assent. The only fly in the ointment was the knowledge that if something unforeseen came up there was no way in which she could inform him. True, she now had his London address and telephone number—but how to get past Lady Edith to reach him?

But I am such a brown wren, was her conclusion when she examined herself in the mirror, tidying her hair, preparatory to going down to the drawing-room to say goodnight and goodbye to her father. And Gis is. . .an. . .eagle. The comparison came easily to her when she remembered what he had told her of his war service, on their first clandestine day together in London. Can a wren dare to fly with an eagle? and the answer came promptly. Yes, if the eagle is Gis and the wren is Thea.

Nothing of these subversive thoughts showed when she walked into the drawing-room. Her father, welcoming her, said, 'You look well these days, Thea, and happy. Being in London must suit you,' and Lady Edith, knowing the true and disgraceful reason why Thea looked so radiant, ground her teeth together. So, my lady looks radiant, does she? Let's see how radiant she looks when I confront her with her villainy!

'You won't be so occupied with your life here that you forget to write to your old father,' the professor said, kissing her on the cheek. He liked Thea's letters. She wrote wittily and well about her small life. A pity she hadn't been a boy; with that mind she would have gone far. Perhaps he was mistaken,

and she would survive marriage with Hector
Dashwood, give him a bit of stiffening.

He stifled his misgivings, and before he left the
following morning asked his wife to go easily with
Thea, a request which made her even more savagely
determined than ever to teach the girl a lesson, and
finish this business with Gis Havilland for good and
all.

It was fortunate that the professor was going to
France. A free hand while he was away would give
her the opportunity to present him with the *fait
accompli* of an agreed marriage before he returned.
Her plan would mean leaving London, and going
back to Oxford, but no matter, that was no bad
thing, for leaving London meant removing Thea
from Gis Havilland's sphere. Walking around Soho
with him, indeed! Why, at Thea's age she had hardly
been able to walk around the castle grounds at
Beauclair without a duenna, and she had been
offered no chance at all to associate with such a
handsome rapscallion as Gis Havilland, with his
good looks, his fine body and. . . Lady Edith
blinked a little at her betraying thoughts.

She could never admit to herself that part of her
hatred of Thea and Gis being attracted to each other
was her jealousy of her daughter. Jealousy because
Thea was young and she was middle-aged, and
jealousy because no one like Gis Havilland had ever
been attracted to Lady Edith Freville, even though
she had possessed twice the looks which Thea
possessed when she had been her daughter's age.

The simple goodness which gleamed like an aura
around Thea, added as it was to an acute intelligence, passed Lady Edith by, as it did most people.

Gis Havilland, empathetic to a degree which made him uncomfortable, had seen it immediately, and for him it was beginning to transcend the more obvious attractions of regular features, blue eyes and blonde hair. Such attributes would fade as time worked its ravages on them, but Thea's qualities would be more lasting.

Jealousy made Lady Edith bide her time until Thea had eaten breakfast, and been sent to her room to change into walking-dress. 'You will accompany me to the Heath, today,' she ordered untruthfully, but she didn't wait for Thea to come down; instead, she walked upstairs, and entered Thea's room without knocking.

Thea, startled, turned to see her mother enter, a black look on her handsome face. Harvey was picking up a fine deep blue crêpe two-piece preparatory to easing Thea into it.

'Leave that,' ordered Lady Edith peremptorily. 'I wish to speak to my daughter.' As Harvey left the room, Thea went to pick up the skirt, to be ordered by her mother to put it down. She was wearing only the lightest of underclothes, cotton directoire knickers, a featherweight corset, without any whalebone stiffeners, for her flat stomach didn't need disguising. Above them she wore a cotton petticoat, trimmed with fine lace having a baby-blue ribbon threaded through it.

Lady Edith saw for the first time that whilst Thea might not be a great beauty facially she had a perfect little figure, alabaster shoulders, a delicately rounded bosom, a tiny waist, gently swelling hips, and her arms and legs were long and shapely.

Another fierce pang shot through Lady Edith at the sight.

'Come here!' she said abruptly. 'At once!'

Thea began to tremble. Ever since her mother had struck her so brutally, she had been fearful that she would do so again. Something in Lady Edith's tone alerted her. What is it? What does she know? and then, of course, somehow, she has found out that I have been meeting Gis!

Her trembling threatened to redouble, but the imp said sternly, Don't let her see that you are afraid. Be brave. But oh, she answered him, I am afraid. She is so much bigger and stronger than I am, for Thea took after the women of her father's family, not her mother's, another reason for her mother's dislike of her.

'Yes, Mother, what is it?' She moved forward, but stopped at a little distance from Lady Edith.

'I said, come here!' roared her mother. 'And how dare you say to me what is it? You know perfectly well what it is. Did you think that you could gad about London, about Soho of all places, with that creature Gis Havilland, and not have someone see you? What a liar you are, Dorothea Dunstan, pretending to be with Monica James. I shall have something to say to her mother when I have finished with you.'

'I wasn't doing anything wrong, Mother,' replied Thea bravely. 'Other girls spend the day in London with their young man. We only went to the zoo, the first time, and to the theatre yesterday.'

'Nothing wrong?' Lady Edith was incandescent. 'How dare you say you were doing nothing wrong and prattle about other girls and your young man?

You are not other girls and Gis Havilland is not
your young man. You are the last of the Frevilles,
and should remember that. And to remind you of
what and who you are, take that, my girl.' And she
struck Thea again, as before across the cheek,
catching her right ear, so that she was thrown back
on to the bed, her head ringing.

Unfortunately for Thea, Lady Edith had discovered that striking her daughter gave her an
extraordinary pleasure, and, to ram the lesson
home, as she informed the shaken Thea, who had
risen dazedly to her feet, and was trying to dodge
away, she hit her again, shouting, 'Take that, as
well. I'll teach you not to walk around Soho.'

It was as well for Thea that the avoiding action
she took, caused Lady Edith's second blow to be
lighter than her first. She not only managed to
scramble away, but pulled a chair between herself
and her mother. Lady Edith's answer was to take
hold of the light cane curtain pole which stood by
the big bay window, and smack her daughter smartly
across the hands with it to make her let go of the
chair.

The pain was so strong that Thea did exactly that,
and started back, tears involuntarily coming to her
eyes. No, she would not cry, never, but Lady Edith
was now advancing on her curtain pole at the ready.
She was not quite sure what she meant to do with
it. Some remaining fragment of common sense told
her that she must not mark Thea in such a way that
she could be seen to have been beaten, so she flung
the curtain pole on the bed, and hit her daughter
several times on the head, arms and body with an
open hand, so that Thea sank down on to the floor

by the bed, her head between her hands, in an effort to protect herself — but in vain; her mother dragged her to her feet and continued to strike her.

The physical difference between the two of them and Thea's own revulsion at the idea of fighting with her mother was such that she stood no chance of defending herself against Lady Edith other than by trying to avoid her mother's blows. During the whole wretched business, she said nothing, uttered no cry. Two large tears rolled down her face, but otherwise she was stoic.

'There, my lady,' panted her mother at last. 'And now, let me tell you, we are going straight back to Oxford. No chance there for you to meet your would-be seducer. Do you think that such a peacock as he is interested in you for anything other than that? Get up, get dressed, and get ready to travel to Oxford tomorrow afternoon. Once we are back there I shall take good care that you don't sneak off again. What's more, you can make up your mind to accept Hector, and stop this nonsense of not wanting him. I've been too soft with you. Let's see what a little firmness will do to your defiance.'

She strode to the door, glared balefully at Thea before she went through it, taking the key with her, to lock Thea in. Thea had been thinking of ringing Gis, of asking for his help — and how did he know that she might need help? But her mother had left her with no opportunity to do so. She was under no illusions. Having begun to beat her, her mother had discovered that she was enjoying herself, and this would not be the last time she would suffer at her hands.

I shan't endure this any longer than is necessary,

she told herself firmly. Gis will help me, I know he will. And I don't believe her when she says that all he wants to do is to seduce me. If so, he could have done so several times already, but he hasn't. And he has always been the one to break off first, not me. Yes, I am wicked, Mother, I want to go all the way with him, but I'm not sorry. I'm only sorry that he never did make proper love to me, because, if Mother has her way, he never will.

She had sunk to the floor to lean her forehead against the bed's cool coverlet once Lady Edith had gone. After a time she rose, and walked slowly over to her dressing table to stare at herself in the mirror. This time the physical shock of what her mother had done to her was less, but her mental pain was greater.

This was not the end. As she turned her head, to discover that a large bruise was beginning to stain her cheek, she knew, beyond a doubt, that, once begun on this course, her mother would continue with it — until she gave way, promised not to see Gis again and promised to accept Hector Dashwood.

She moved towards the window, sat down on the Lloyd loom chair which stood in the bay, and looked out over the Heath. She wondered in how many homes such scenes were being enacted, and how many persecutors and their victims left them, to mix with others in the great world outside, pretending that they had never happened, showing bland, blank faces to deceive that world into thinking that all was well.

And why were they going back to Oxford? She knew that their servants were due to leave for Beauclair in a fortnight to open the wing of the great house in Northumbria, in which the Freville family had lived for generations, so that the Dunstans could pass the end of the long vacation there, after the professor's return from France.

But the worst thing of all was that she would not be meeting Gis next week. She knew that Lady Edith would give her no opportunity to telephone or to write to him, nor to send him any message via Monica — that friendship was over for good if Lady Edith had her way.

The tears threatened to fall as she thought of him waiting for her at Oxford Circus, of how he would look regretfully at the clock as the time passed and no Thea appeared, of how he would finally walk away, disappointed.

Or would he, as her mother suggested, simply shrug his shoulders because his prey was eluding him and walk away to forget her and pursue another? No! He wouldn't do that, not the Gis she was coming to know, who had told her his secrets and to whom she had told hers. He might not love her — how could he? — but he liked her and had offered her practical help if she needed it. He had been kind to her, and few people had ever been kind to Thea.

She thought a moment, went to her wardrobe to put on a light wool dress, for despite the day's warmth she felt strangely cold, then fetched her journal from her dressing case, where it had been safely locked away, and began to write in it. She began:

Dear Gis, I am so sorry to have to write to tell you that Mother has found out that we have been meeting in London. She has locked me in my room and we are going back to Oxford tomorrow, where she intends to keep me a virtual prisoner, so that I may not see you again.

She paused and shivered; even though he would never read her letter she couldn't write down that her mother had beaten her, nor tell him that writing to him was painful because the blow from the curtain pole had left a great weal across the back of both her hands.

One advantage of his never reading her letters was that she could tell him, quite simply, that she loved him. Writing these words brought him before her. The strangest thing about that was that, when she conjured him up, it was not his extraordinary good looks she pictured, but the sound of his voice, the kind tones in which he spoke to her, the gentle way in which he had taken her hand, the care he had shown for her comfort, the warmth of his body against hers when he had kissed her in the doorway, and the scent of lemon and clean man he gave off, so different from the smoky aura of stale tobacco around Hector Dashwood.

She locked the journal away again, went to her bedside table and picked up the volume of Wilfred Owen's poems which Gis had recommended to her, and began to read. After all, the men in the trenches had suffered far more than she was doing at her mother's hands, she told herself firmly, and tried to lose herself in the verse.

CHAPTER SEVEN

GIS had just returned from Oxford Circus where he
had waited for half an hour for Thea to turn up,
growing more uneasy by the minute. He had
behaved exactly as Thea had thought he would,
finally walking away, not to try to make a rendezvous with another woman, but to ponder over what
must have happened.

Somehow, Lady Edith must have discovered that
Thea had been meeting him. Otherwise he was sure
that if she had been prevented from turning up for
any other reason she would have found some means
by which to inform him, presumably by telephone
or by letter.

The matter troubled him all afternoon, prevented
him from working properly, so that the procession
of visitors who came to his rooms were almost a
welcome distraction — the 'almost' was because the
first two came either to reproach or to warn and
advise him.

His uncle Gerard meant well, Gis was sure, but
for once he was in no mood to bear his kindly
advice, plus his warnings of the slanders Hector
Dashwood was spreading about him. Gerard,
always as aware as Gis himself was when he was *de
trop*, soon left. His second visitor was Diana Troy,
who came to try to revive their affaire which she
had agreed to end — and also to warn him about
Hector. Any slight chance she might have had of

changing his mind disappeared when she began to speak in a derogatory fashion about the Dunstan chit and her ridiculous crush on him. 'How long will such a childish nonentity satisfy you, do you think?'

She knew that she had lost him when she saw his face change, was quick to try to mend matters and even wished him well before she left, saying, 'No, don't see me out. When we meet again, Gis, it will be as friends,' and the kiss which she gave him was that of a sister, not a lover. It was finally over, and he was alone again — perhaps for life.

His final visitor arrived when he had begun to work in earnest, and he sighed when the door bell rang again. This time, it was Sophie, who half ran by him into his living-room, to turn and face him when he entered behind her.

'Oh, Gis!' It was plain that she was in some distress; her mouth was trembling, her hands, which had torn off her gloves and her hat, were shaking. She couldn't stand, sank into one of the chairs.

'Soph, what is it?' For he could see that something was very wrong.

'I hardly know how to tell you. It's Hector again.'

'Again? How again? Never say that he has found some more of your letters?'

'Exactly that. He rang me yesterday, asked me to meet him, at the National Gallery of all places. I didn't know that Hector was aware that the National Gallery existed.' Sophie was almost hysterical, stopped to take a deep breath, started again. 'I went there, of course. He told me that he had found some more in an old trunk, that you hadn't stolen them all, and his price for not sending them to George has gone up —— Yes,' she said, to forestall

Gis's question, 'yes, he does have them, he showed
them to me, two—but they are all he needs. How
does he know that you stole them, Gis? Did you?
And what am I going to do? He says that he is
putting them in the bank, where even you cannot
get at them. What am I to do? You know I have no
money to give him.'

Gis considered. He felt ninety years old, with the
weight of the universe on his shoulders, the universe
which his uncle had just accused him of inhabiting
alone. 'Don't cry, Soph,' he said gently, and that
was an inadequate comment, if one were needed.
'Let me think.'

He sat down beside her, and tried to comfort her.
If Hector had done what he said, then there was no
hope of his retrieving the letters this time. After a
few moments when Sophie's sobs had lessened, he
said, his arm about her shoulders, 'There's only one
thing you can do, Soph, but you'd have to be brave,
and it might not work.'

She showed him her tear-stained face. 'Yes, Gis.
What is it?'

The look of hope which dawned had him saying,
still gentle, 'Oh, Soph, it would be an awful risk,
but the only way to stop this is for you to tell George
the truth. It would be better coming from you than
from Hector.'

Sophie let out a loud wail and pulled herself from
him. 'Oh, no, Gis. You know George. . .'

Gis put out his hand to take hers, before she
could retreat from him completely, perhaps out of
the door and to ruin.

'Think, Soph, think; unless you do, you will never
be free of him, and he could ruin you at any time,

out of spite. You will never know whether he has given them all back. I destroyed the first batch when I robbed him, because I thought that was the safest thing to do; I didn't want to be caught, red-handed, with the letters on me. Then we should both have been ruined, but I'm not sure now whether I was wise. What is wise?' he said, wryly, as once before.

'No, if you tell George, I know you risk divorce, or separation, but I don't think George would allow it to be scandalous, for his sake. And think, if Hector took your letters to the Press, he would be ruined socially, so for all that he has threatened to do so I don't think that he would. It's a risk — but what is left, other than that?'

'I have never thought to tell George, not once,' exclaimed Sophie passionately. 'Oh, I'm afraid of him, Gis. What a fool I was. He's a good husband, and kind, if strict. He wasn't so strict when we married, but the War and politics have hardened him. You don't know what you are asking of me.'

'I'm not asking anything of you,' Gis was calm, because someone must be, 'only advising you, and really, Soph, if I could think of anything else, I would. Now, no need to decide what to do at once. Let me make you some tea.'

It seemed that the world and his wife were intent on visiting Gis Havilland, to stop him from thinking what to do about Thea Dunstan. He couldn't let Sophie leave without comforting her, and pointing out to her the impossibility of letting Hector rule her life, seeing that there was no way that he, Gis, could rescue her again.

He and Sophie drank tea, and he even persuaded her to eat a toasted tea-cake. Sophie came through to the kitchen in the middle of his labours, to watch him carry out the menial tasks of ordinary living, usually performed by servants. Such a romantic-looking man to make tea! And, as Sophie discovered by questioning him, make the fire and keep his rooms clean. A charwoman came in too, he said.

And finally, she left, and he began to think about Thea, to plan what to do about her—which was little enough. He would try to discover whether the Dunstans had left London, and where they had gone, and then what? He had never felt so helpless, so little like clever Gis Havilland who had an answer for everything, even poor Sophie. He still had no answer when he went to bed, and the sense of desolation was strong in him when he went to sleep—and surfaced in his dreams.

He was being carried along, under a smelly blanket, a man's strong arms about him. He was holding a doll, General Lee, the pride of small Gis Schuyler's life. It was important that his mother and her friend Sir Richard Havilland should know that he had been kidnapped, and one way of them tracing him was to throw the General's distinctive uniform and possessions behind him.

The adult Gis knew that he was dreaming of the past, but he could not break free from the dream. The man holding little Gis was running, and Gis threw the last of the General's possessions behind him. He didn't want to, because he felt that he had violated the General, but he could not prevent himself from looking down into the doll's face, to see it white and blank, the eyes staring. The almost living companion which the doll had been to lonely Gis Havilland was dead.

In his dream, he gave a great sob, looked away, only to look back again, to scream aloud in terror, and who was screaming, the little boy Gis, or the grown man the child had become, he didn't know. And the terror was because he was not a child carrying a doll, but he was a man stumbling along in the dark, carrying a woman's body, and the face on the body was Thea's and she was as dead and mute as General Lee had been. . .and he had not saved her. . .

Gis awoke, crying out and sweating. The dream had been so detailed, so distinct, as dreams rarely were, that it was as though he had experienced it in reality. He knew that it arose from his fears for Thea, but, sitting there, he also feared that his intuition, working overtime, was telling him that Thea was in danger, and that as he might not be able to save Sophie, could not help Diana, except by betraying himself, so Thea, too, might be beyond salvation.

He wondered where Thea was, what she was doing, whether Lady Edith had struck her again, and the thought made his hands ball into fists, and increased his feelings of helplessness. Logic told him to sleep, that lying in the dark, worrying about her, was of no assistance to either of them, but for once logic and its dictates was not enough for Gis Havilland. He was learning to feel and to bleed for others.

His final decision, before he slept again, was that he would visit Hampstead, to see whether the Dunstans were still there, and if they were not he

would go to his cottage at Barton Dene, so that
Thea might find not it empty if she fled to it for
sanctuary.

Back in Oxford, Thea, on the day that Gis was
confronting his past and his present, was not in any
particular danger. Contrary to what she had
expected, since they had arrived back home her
mother had not threatened her directly again. True,
she had developed an unpleasant habit of pinching
Thea when she wish to make a point, and, what was
worse, Thea was confined to the house.

Her arms might be sore, but she hadn't been
beaten, nor had Hector's name been mentioned.
The worst thing was that when she began her letter
to her father her mother came in, snatched the
paper from her, and threw it into the waste-paper
basket.

'I shall write to your father on your behalf,' she
announced. 'I shall tell him that you have damaged
your wrist and cannot write. I'm not having you
trying to send him lies about what you and I are
doing.' And she was as good as her word.

This upset Thea more than a beating would have
done. She liked writing to her father, had no intention of complaining about her treatment by her
mother, cruel though it was, but it was plain that
her mother was intent on treating her like a
criminal.

They had not been back a week before her maid,
Harvey, had given in her notice. She disliked Lady
Edith, and was pretty sure that Thea was being
abused in private by her mother.

'I shall tell the old cat so,' she announced in the women servants' dormitory at the top of the house.

'You'll only make it worse for Miss Thea if you do,' Cook said. 'You should know Lady Edith by now. Any opposition and she goes into one of her tantrums.'

'Poor child,' said Harvey. 'Yes, I suppose you're right.'

'I know I am,' said Cook. 'The only person who can save Miss Thea is the girl herself.'

'Her father?' suggested Harvey.

'Not him,' said Cook contemptuously, 'too wrapped up in his books and his students to worry about his daughter. Best you go, if you're unhappy. Got a new post, have you? One where the missis don't beat her daughter?'

All the servants knew what Lady Edith was, and Harvey, having found her out, had set herself up, she told Cook, with a new position in Warwickshire. 'But I'll bet the old cow will make me work my notice out,' she said gloomily.

But she was wrong about that. Lady Edith took her resignation with remarkable equanimity, and, when Harvey asked if she could waive her notice, was graciousness itself. 'You may go as soon as you have packed,' she said. 'Miss Thea must learn to look after herself. Tomorrow, if you like.'

She was pleased to lose one of the servants, and that one near to Thea. She had made her plans and Harvey's going would ease them. Cook raised her eyebrows when Harvey told her jubilantly that she had been given permission to leave the next day. 'What's the old cow up to, I wonder?' she said — and then thought no more about it until two days

later Lady Edith sent for her and the housekeeper
and told them that she was sending all the servants
to Beauclair before the weekend to open the house
up for herself, Thea and the professor when he
returned from Paris.

The housekeeper demurred a little, to receive a
frosty answer from Lady Edith. 'Who's to look after
you and Miss Thea, then?' she asked.

Lady Edith refrained from saying, 'None of your
business,' but instead replied coldly, 'I am having a
temporary cook and two servants come in daily for
the week before Miss Thea and I join you. I'm not
sure exactly when the professor will be back.'

This unwonted acceptance of hardship from a
woman who always arranged everything to make
her own life easy surprised the housekeeper more
than a little, but the unpleasant glint in her mistress's eye kept her quiet.

Thea knew nothing of this arrangement until the
servants were being driven to the station, to take
the train to Alnmouth, the nearest railway station
to Beauclair, where they would be met by some of
the skeleton staff retained there to see that the
house did not fall into complete ruin.

'While the cat's away. . .' remarked the irreverent
cook complacently, as she watched the Dunstans'
home grow small behind them, before the car turned
out of the drive and headed for central Oxford and
the station. 'Wonder why she's doing this? Poor
Miss Thea.' A sentiment echoed by all the servants.

Standing in her bedroom window, Thea watched
them go in some surprise. She was not allowed
downstairs until after midday. Her mother had said
nothing of their departure, and when the new daily

came in with their ill-cooked dinner she said, in as bright a voice as she could manage, 'Have the servants gone to Beauclair, Mother? And if, so, when shall we follow?'

'Oh, not for a week,' said Lady Edith carelessly, spooning greasy consommé into her mouth.

'A week!' Thea could not prevent herself from revealing her surprise. 'And why have they all gone? You usually keep Cook, and the senior maid.'

'Well, really, what an inquisition, my girl,' replied her mother. 'Because I say so is why they have gone. You have forfeited any rights to be consulted by your behaviour.'

'What rights?' said Thea spiritedly. 'I can't remember when you ever consulted me about anything, even about my clothes or my hairstyle, let alone the running of the house.'

'You impudent baggage,' began her mother, face reddening. Thea thought, not for the first time, that when her mother reprimanded her she descended to the language of the very people whom she affected to despise. Then her mother stopped, said, with what could only be called a smirk. 'You'll find out soon enough why I have sent the servants away.'

After that she refused to speak again but drank her soup with an expression on her face which filled Thea with the direst of forebodings, and prevented her from eating very much at all.

This provoked her mother's only comment. 'Really, Thea, you look plain enough already, without starving yourself and making yourself look like a victim of an Eastern European famine. Get some food down you, my girl, or it will be the worse for you.'

Gis didn't seem to mind my plainness, was Thea's rebellious thought, but later, looking in her mirror, she could not but own that her mother was right. She had lost weight since she had returned to Oxford, and looked thinner and more gaunt than ever.

He won't want me if I look like this, was her desolate thought, and then, What did Mother mean about knowing soon why she sent the servants away? This puzzle occupied her for some time, but she could find no answer and she sat down to read, instead.

This time it was *Beltane the Smith* by Jeffrey Farnol, whom Thea usually found rather treacly, but in her unhappy, Gis-less state she found his sugary heroines and impossibly brave and beautiful heroes soothing rather than otherwise. Misery is destroying my critical sense, she thought, putting the book down.

Once a day she checked that she had the spare key to Gis's cottage, and the little map he had drawn her safely in her handbag. She had looked up Barton Dene, and found out how to get there from Oxford, in the Bartholomew's *Atlas and Gazetteer* in her father's study. If the worse comes to the worse, she thought, having no inkling of how bad that worse might be, and how much she might need a saviour. . .

The day began much as other days — but later there were variations. Her mother came into her room, and said, 'Come along, girl, we are going shopping. You need some new clothes. You look a fright in your present ones.'

She took a delight in being as unpleasant to Thea as she could, finding a mean pleasure in watching her child wince whenever she reminded her how plain she was. 'How you can imagine that Gis Havilland was genuinely attracted to you. . .' she shrugged when Thea finally came downstairs '. . .is beyond my belief.'

'If so,' said Thea steadily, goaded at last into unwise speech, 'I can't imagine why you should think Hector Dashwood wants me, either. Unless it is my money which attracts him. There can be no other reason.'

'Just thank God that someone is willing to offer honourable marriage to you, without asking why,' replied Lady Edith smartly. She had phoned for a taxi-cab to take them into Oxford, and had arranged for it to pick her up in Carfax at midday prompt. 'And be sure that you are there,' she ordered him brusquely.

Thea hated shopping, particularly for clothes. Since her mother overruled all her choices, she had learned to say nothing. Her mother's idea of a flattering gown for a nineteen-year-old girl, was a knee-length frock in aubergine-coloured velvet, a colour and material whose harsh purple did nothing for Thea, but which, with its saffron lace colour and cuffs, might have been suitable for Lady Edith.

Thea suffered it to be put on, admired — was the shopgirl laughing behind her hand? she wondered — and then added to with stockings of the same hue, aubergine leather shoes, with large gilt buckles and Louis heels, and a kind of lace Alice band to go round her hair, the saffron and purple between them diminishing all its chestnut tones, and even dimming the green of her eyes.

'How charming *mademoiselle* looks!' simpered the manageress, who had come in during the later part of this unpleasant ritual. The shop was called Lucille's and had pretensions to being French, but Thea couldn't help thinking of the beautiful clothes which Diana Troy wore, and what Gis would think if he could see her in this.

'I look a fright,' she said bluntly, to be screamed at in unison by her mother and the manageress. A handbag was added, the only beautiful thing, and later her mother took her to a shop which sold lingerie, and this time her mother chose, not her usual simple cottons, but a decadent-looking camisole in salmon-pink, with knickers and suspender belt to match. And I shouldn't like Gis to see these, was the imp's inner comment which would have shocked her mother into a fit if she could have heard it.

Thea began to feel vaguely worried. Why, she could not help thinking, why is mother dressing me up like this? Like. . .a prize pig being sent to the fair? And why the underwear? In her innocence she could come up with no convincing answer, and as the pile of parcels grew, handkerchieves, and a long rope of artificial pearls — just the kind of thing she most detested — being added to it, her misgivings grew with each unwanted item.

The last shopgirl helped them to carry the parcels to the taxi, and later, laden with her undesirable and undesired loot, Thea staggered into her home.

'You can wear them to dinner tonight,' said her mother when they were safely indoors. 'Here, let

me help you carry them to your room.' Thea was a
little surprised by this unusual concession, but was
less so, when, arrived in her bedroom, and the
boxes piled on her bed, her mother said, in a voice
meant to be cajoling, 'We have a guest for dinner
tonight. Hector Dashwood is coming, and I know
he intends to propose to you again. Now, I hope
you understand what your answer will be. If you
don't, Thea, it will be my duty to remind you. Hard
though it may be, I shall have to persuade you to do
as I ask.'

'Hector,' said Thea faintly. 'You have bought all
this for me to attract Hector!' And she began to
laugh, she couldn't help herself. 'Salmon-pink
underwear and purple velvet. . .curtain material. . .
to help me to lure Hector who usually runs around
with women who look and dress like Diana Troy.
Oh, Mother. . .'

Lady Edith, face on fire at this mockery, walked
across the room her hand, raised to strike her
daughter.

'Oh, don't do that, Mother,' Thea managed to
say, her heart thudding. 'You can't imagine that
even Hector could want to propose to a plain girl
who was also sporting a black eye.'

For a moment, she thought that she had gone too
far, having said aloud what the imp usually kept to
itself. Her mother restrained her desire to teach her
daughter a much needed lesson, said, 'You will
come downstairs to dinner if I have to dress you to
do so. And if you don't accept Hector after it, I
cannot answer for the consequences.'

Thea thought that her mother meant that she
would be beaten again, the true villainy of what

Lady Edith and Hector Dashwood had concocted
between them, was beyond her.

'You hear me, madam.' Her mother was at the
door, the bedroom door-key in her hand — Thea
had not had it in her possession since they returned
to Oxford. 'I'll have your lunch and tea sent up to
you; no chance for you to do anything foolish. I
want you dressed and ready for dinner, by seven-
thirty, sharp,' and she left the room, locking it
behind her, leaving Thea to sink on to the bed
among all the unlovely finery which her mother had
bought in order to sell her to Hector Dashwood,
who needed no such bribe to persuade him to marry
an heiress.

CHAPTER EIGHT

'THEA! Are you dressed?'

Lady Edith had unlocked the door, entered her daughter's bedroom to find it apparently empty. Surely the wretched girl had not managed to find some means of escape?

'Yes, Mother. I am quite ready.' Thea's voice was toneless. She had been standing in the bay, hidden by the curtains, wondering if Gis was somewhere out there, perhaps at the cottage. She had seen Hector's dashing little open tourer arrive; she was not sufficiently acquainted with cars to know what make it was. Lady Edith did not approve of women having anything to do with cars—either knowing about them, or driving them... another of Diana Troy's sins.

What she didn't know was that Thea had persuaded Bates, the Dunstans' chauffeur, to show her how to drive one afternoon when the professor and Lady Edith had been at some grand college garden party.

Like all the servants he was sorry for poor bullied Miss Thea, and admired the quiet unbreakable spirit which the servants could see, if her mother couldn't. It had been a happy couple of hours for both of them, which had been repeated twice. What a thing to be thinking of, when she ought to be worrying about the next few hours with Hector! Perhaps she ought to be worrying about the indifferent dinner

which the temporary cook would be serving to a
man who liked his food!

Now *that* was a comforting thought, mocked the
imp, but doubtless Hector considered that an heiress
was worth a bad dinner or two—and a second
proposal.

He was already sitting in the drawing-room when
Thea and Lady Edith arrived, and blinked a little at
Thea's inappropriate splendour. 'The naughty girl
was late because she was making herself quite ready
to meet you,' simpered Lady Edith, and what a
sardonic contrast that was to what had passed in the
bedroom before Thea was dragged downstairs. The
box on the ear, and the blows and pinches on her
already bruised arms covered by the dress's long
sleeves, all accompanied by the order that she was
to accept Hector or 'take the consequences'—whatever they were. A really brutal beating probably,
was Thea's gloomy thought, with the stick which
Lady Edith had promised her.

Hector was gallantry itself. If she had been Diana
Troy, or the other more famous Diana, Lady Diana
Cooper, he couldn't have been more seductively
charming to her. He took her limp hand and kissed
it, praised her appearance with a straight face,
although the imp told her that he was probably
cataloguing it to entertain his raffish friends with its
horrors once he had won her, and was safely back
in his disreputable London haunts.

Thea replied in monosyllables, agreed that the
weather was remarkable for the time of year, and
prayed for dinner to rescue her. There were apparently, and remarkably, no other guests, and the
knowledge made her uneasy.

'So shy, Thea,' whispered Lady Edith loudly to Hector as she ordered him to take Thea into dinner, 'But, then, these days that must be a rare and valued commodity in any young woman a man might hope to marry.'

As subtle as a sledge-hammer, your mother, commented the imp, who seemed to be working overtime. Hector, having nothing to say to that, said nothing, but later, at dinner, kept up a remorse-less flow of the sort of chat which usually entertained the women he associated with.

The meal was as distressing as Thea thought it might be. She had a sudden flash of Gis and herself laughing together at the Golden Snail over their beautiful food. Hector ate his dinner manfully, even managing to praise the lukewarm soup — brown Windsor — the scorched lamb chops, the over-done peas, the under-done potatoes and the distressing summer pudding, which had not quite 'worked'.

The only good thing about it was an excellent bottle of burgundy, vintage 1910, of which Hector drank far too much, to console himself for the rest of the meal and having to propose — and sub-sequently marry Thea, and acquire Lady Edith for a mother-in-law, after it. Thea wasn't allowed to drink at all, and she had another happy memory of the delicious red she had drunk with her *cassoulet* — and Gis.

It was no wonder that the girl was a poor peaked thing, if this was the stuff they put in her feed-bag! The Dunstans were reputed to keep a good table — but if this was what Oxford thought a good table. . .! Well, his mother-in-law wasn't going to take over his kitchen, that was for sure. The wine cellar, now, that might be different.

Lady Edith alternated between frowning at Thea, and answering for her, saying — a lie — how much she had enjoyed *Chu Chin Chow*, talking about which seemed to be a staple of Hector's conversation.

The clock ticked with agonising slowness. Hector's face grew redder and redder, Thea's monosyllables fewer and fewer, and Lady Edith's strident tones ever more desperate.

'Coffee, afterwards, in the drawing-room,' she announced brightly when the fruit bowl had been removed. 'And I shall leave you two young things together to drink it. You don't want an old woman like me spoiling the party.'

Young things, indeed! sneered the imp, looking at Hector's raddled face, already becoming heavily marked with the signs of his dissolute life, its original beauty fast disappearing — and what party is there to spoil?

Well, her mother couldn't actually make her say yes to him, and if she beats me to death I shan't accept a man I loathe and detest and who, by his manner, detests the idea of marrying me.

Coffee served, the door closed behind Lady Edith. Thea's heart jumped several beats, as she looked at Hector, who desperately needed a cigar, but knew that Lady Edith didn't approve of smoking in her drawing-room. She mustn't let him begin to propose to her, she mustn't. She couldn't face such a farce again, even if her mother killed her when she left the drawing-room still not promised to the man opposite to her.

'Lord Dashwood,' she began, trying to suppress her voice's strong wish to tremble and fail at the enormity of what she was about to do, 'I believe, from what my mother says, that you are about to propose to me again. If so, I should not like to cause you further pain. I have already refused you, and nothing has occurred since then to cause me to change my mind. I wish you to remain a friend, but I cannot marry you. I am sorry that my mother brought you here under false pretences when I had already made my wishes known to her.'

There it was out, and she saw with a sinking heart that he was enraged. He might not want her, but he didn't want her to refuse him — *that* he saw as an insult.

'Miss Dunstan,' he said stiffly, 'I don't think that you understand the honour I am doing you in proposing at all. Most young women would be proud and flattered to be offered the chance to be my Countess. I respect your natural diffidence which your mother assures me is great, but I am not flattered by the notion that your shyness compels me to go on begging for the agreement to my offer which your mother assures me you will give me in the end. Feminine flutterings can be over-prolonged. I will be happy to receive earlier the answer you will give me later.'

'With respect — ' a grand phrase which she had heard her father use ' — I am not most young women,' was her reply to that, 'and I am not engaging in feminine flutterings. My refusal of you was an honest one, and nothing that you, or my mother, can say or do will change it.'

It was his face which changed. 'Oh, I think you

will agree to marry me. . .in the end,' he said, and his manner to her had coarsened subtly. 'I had hoped to persuade you pleasantly to become Lady Dashwood, but there are other means.'

Why, he thinks that mother will bully or beat me into agreement, she thought wildly. Well, he is quite mistaken about that. But, alas, it was Thea who was mistaken — as she was shortly to find out. Lady Edith's plan was not based on beating her into submission, but on something quite different.

Thea hoped that she might forestall him by rising to her feet, saying, in her mildest manner, the manner which deceived people into believing that she was not as strong-minded in her way as Lady Edith was in her's, 'I think, in fairness to us both and to save embarrassment, I ought to retire.'

Hector Dashwood realised that he had little to lose by discarding his suave image. 'No,' he said, also rising, and catching her by the wrist, 'I don't think that would be a good idea, Thea. It wouldn't please your mother — and certainly doesn't please me.'

Thea tried to pull her wrist away, but failed, said, and her voice gave no indication of how fearful she was beginning to feel, 'Seeing that I have ceased to wish to please either of you, that is of little moment to me. Please allow me to leave, Lord Dashwood. Such behaviour does not become you.'

Hector merely tightened his grip still further, jeered at her, 'Oh, bravo, Thea, what play did you get *that* from?'

Thea began to struggle. She knew that it was in vain, he was so much stronger than she was. He responded, by seizing her other wrist, bringing her face to face with him. She let out a little cry as he pulled her towards him — but was saved by the unexpected entry of Lady Edith. Thea later thought that she had been listening at the door.

'Oh, am I interrupting something,' she cried, archly. 'Are congratulations in order?'

'You know perfectly well that they are not,' Thea exclaimed, pulling herself away from Hector who had loosened his grip on her at her mother's entrance. 'I wish to leave, having refused Lord Dashwood again, and he seeks to prevent me, a most ungentlemanly act.'

'How's that,' barked Lady Edith, 'refused?' She looked at them both, anger written all over her, and then, to Thea's astonishment looked sternly at Hector, saying, 'Oh, yes, I quite agree. Most unsuitable. Not at all the thing. I'm sure that Hector will agree that this is not the time or place for further offers. Why,' she added brightly and irrelevantly, or so it seemed to Thea, 'Cook and her assistant have not yet left the premises. There will be other occasions for you, Hector. By all means, go to your room, Thea, and think over most carefully the magnificent offer which you are refusing.'

Thea could not prevent herself, the imp broke loose again. She said in her most colourless voice, so sweetly that for a moment or two her mother and Hector hardly realised what she had said, 'Oh, surely, Mother, you have got that the wrong way round. It is Hector who must think over what he is losing in the way of fortune by my refusal of *him*.'

Even then, strangely, although her face constricted, Lady Edith made no riposte, merely murmured graciously, 'I think it would be better if you retired. Lord Dashwood will understand if I leave him for a moment to accompany you upstairs.'

She didn't wait for an answer, seized Thea cruelly by her already damaged left wrist and almost ran her out of the room and upstairs.

Once alone, she flung the door shut behind her, said, her face like thunder, 'You intend to persist in this, then, despite all my wishes, and all my warnings?'

Thea retreated from her, replied through stiff lips, 'Yes, Mother. You heard what I said to Hector, and I meant it. I shall never agree to marry him. Never! Never!'

Lady Edith advanced on her until Thea found her back against the bedroom wall. For the first time she thought of seizing something, anything, as a weapon to defend herself with, but too late, Lady Edith's hand was already in the air, and she was cornered.

She landed two blows before Thea dodged away and ran to the window. Her mother didn't follow her, shouted, 'You can't escape that way. There is a thirty-foot drop. Resign yourself to the inevitable, and think, when it happens, that you have driven me to it, by your obstinacy.'

Thea, struck by her words, turned to face her mother, said, for it was plain that her mother didn't intend to strike her again, 'Driven you to what, Mother? What have I driven you to?'

Her mother made no answer to her question, simply said, 'Get to bed, my girl. You'll find out soon enough, and one day you'll thank me.'

'Thank you for what?' cried Thea, all nameless apprehension.

But her mother said nothing, simply turned on her heel, left the bedroom, locking the door behind her again, leaving Thea to sink on the bed and listen to the sounds in the house dying down as Cook and her helpers left. She didn't hear Hector's car leave, but by then, she was so emotionally drained that she was hardly capable of registering anything.

Slowly, slowly, she dressed for bed, and after turning off the switch by the door she embraced the blessed dark and tried to sleep — which, at length, she did. Her last thought was of Gis as he had looked when they had sat in the wood together after they had first seemed to come to some sort of understanding, and holding that memory to her she let oblivion claim her.

How long she slept, Thea never knew, neither was she sure what woke her. Only that, one moment she was walking in a garden, knowing that someone was waiting for her at the gate, someone whom she dearly wished to see — and who could that be? — when a noise broke into her light dreaming and she was suddenly awake.

At first, disorientated, she thought that the noise came from the window, and then she knew it was the door. In which case, it could only be her mother, and what would she be doing, coming to her room in the middle of the night? For it was pitch black outside, and she could hear the noise of heavy rain.

What could her mother want? A dismal enlightenment seized her — she had come to thrash her, in the middle of the night, when there would be no witnesses, but she would find resistance. For the first time Thea found herself capable of fighting her mother off. She was not going to be struck again without a struggle.

She rose from her bed, to turn on the light switch by the door, just as the intruder entered to slam the door shut behind him.

'Oh. . .!' Thea almost screamed, for the intruder who had unlocked the door and disturbed her sleep by doing so was not her mother — but was Hector Dashwood.

He had been looking towards the bed where he had thought that he might find her, before the light showed her to him, standing, stiff and straight and wide-awake, not at all what he had intended, the advantage of total surprise quite gone.

'What are you doing here, Hector? I thought that you had left for home hours ago. How did you get the key to my room? I warn you I shall scream, and bring my mother here. I wonder what she will say to finding you here — you can have no good purpose?'

I am talking like a mad law-book, she thought, but anything to keep down the hysteria which was threatening to overwhelm her.

Hector had evidently been drinking hard. He advanced towards her, and Thea retreated to the bay window, putting one hand behind her as she did so.

'Scream away,' he said, a dreadful jollity in his voice. 'Where the devil did I get the key? And who the devil do you think gave it to me? Why, your dear mama, of course, desperate for her ugly frump of a daughter to be a countess.'

Thea tried to hold on to her sanity. 'I don't

believe you,' she managed, despair in her voice and on her face.

'Oh, believe me, my dear little scarecrow. Why else do you think she sent the servants away, and entertained me alone—to our mutual pleasure, I may add—until after you were safely asleep and locked away? Don't be any more green than you need be.'

He was still advancing on her, fell intent on his face, taking his time, enjoying her distress; behind her, her hand groped and groped again. 'But why? Why are you here?' she gasped.

'Can't you guess, Miss Moneybags? Why, by morning, after a pleasant night with me, you'll either be desperate to be my countess for the pleasure we can take together, although I dare swear yours will be more than mine, or desperate to marry me, because otherwise, you'll be ruined. Why else should I trouble to invade your bed, my dear? It isn't for the joy of your company.'

Inside Thea something was screaming, Oh, Gis, no. Not this. It's you I want, and if he does as he says. . . I can never come to you. . . I shall be spoiled and defiled. . .

'Mother wouldn't,' she said, 'not even Mother. . .' but she knew that he spoke the truth.

'Mother would. . .and did,' Hector said gaily. 'Mother does a lot of things to both our advantages, to all three of us, really. What a happy little trio we shall make.'

Thea's groping hand found its target. She had learned one thing from her mother in her bedroom, back at Hampstead Heath, and she intended to put

that learning into practice at Oxford, to try to save
herself.

'No,' she said, 'I won't.'

'Precious little choice, have you? Scream away,
I'll enjoy myself all the more if you do. Can't say I
like spiritless chits, and you're one, if I ever met
one.'

Now, thought Thea, now, and as he advanced on
her, catching her nightgown by its throat, to rip it
down, she finally got a firm grip on the curtain
pole — a much stouter and stronger object than the
one at Hampstead — and brought it round to bring
it down on his head, as he stepped back from her,
grinning his pleasure at her revealed body.

To Thea's horror, her first blow was not enough;
he merely reeled away, blood running from his
temple, eyes wild, to reach for her again, so that
she was compelled to strike him once more, even
harder. This time, he fell to the floor and lay there
unmoving.

If she had killed him, she didn't care. She half
hoped that he was dead, to rape no more girls, for
he had done this before, Thea was sure. But no time
to think of that. She couldn't stay here. She wasn't
safe; if her mother could do this to her, what else
would she not do?

Sobbing with relief, Thea stepped over Hector's
prone figure, a worm of blood running from his
head to stain the carpet, and ran to her wardrobe.
No time to change, to dress. Time only to put on a
heavy winter coat, to thrust her feet into the only
shoes she could quickly find, her light ones, to pick
up her handbag, take from it the key to Gis's cottage
and the paper with the map on it to push them into

her pocket where they would be handy. Thank God, she thought feverishly, since all is quiet, Mother will think Hector at his wicked work, won't interrupt him.

She ran to the door, stood for a moment, turned back, and throwing down her bag, picked up the curtain pole which might be more immediately useful. Hector had begun to stir, was groaning. She hadn't killed him, after all. But his recovery meant that she must get away before her mother discovered what had happened.

She took the door key from where it had fallen by his hand, locked the bedroom door, and ran lightly down the stairs. Not lightly enough. Her mother must have been in the drawing-room, listening, for she opened the door, her face eager — to stare at. . .not Hector, but Thea, the curtain pole in her right hand, the bedroom door-key in her left.

Thea dashed across the hall towards the front door. She had only one idea in her head, to reach Gis, to find safety, and perhaps, who knows, love.

She heard Lady Edith, who had been temporarily immobilised by shock, suddenly run towards her, turned, and raised the curtain pole as she did so.

'Keep back,' she said, 'or I'll do to you what I did to Hector, and damn the consequences,' and then, sorrowfully, the full enormity of what had so nearly been done to her striking her, so that for a moment the pole wavered in her hand, 'How could you, Mother, how could you? To your own daughter!'

'You fool!' said Lady Edith contemptuously. 'Yes, a fool. I was marrying you to an idiot you could control, your money would have been tied up so he couldn't get at it, and you would be a countess.'

'For that?' Thea's voice broke, and then, seeing that her mother was about to advance on her, hoping that filial duty, long exercised would cause Thea not to use her advantage, she raised the pole again. 'I mean what I say, Mother. . .and Mother, remember who taught me to use it! Besides, I think you ought to go and rescue Hector. I think I might have killed him.'

Lady Edith knew when she was beaten. Recognised that the Thea before her was not the one she had always known and dominated. 'Where are you going, in the pouring rain? Like a drab to your lover? To walk the streets? To. . .'

Thea took no notice of this, said, 'If you don't want a dead man on your hands and a major scandal, Mother, you'd better go upstairs to look after Hector.' And then she smiled, held up the key, 'Oh, I forgot. I locked the bedroom door. Now, Mother,' and she ran swiftly, to the front door, which she opened, her mother, for once, paralysed behind her, and threw the bedroom key into the garden with all her strength, shouting, 'But before you rescue Hector, you'd better find the key!'

So saying she galloped through the door, down the drive towards Hector's car which stood there still, awaiting its semi-conscious owner.

Lady Edith lumbered behind her for a moment, thought of the possible dead man upstairs and the scandal which Thea had threatened, and with a stricken wail fell on her knees on the wet lawn in the pouring rain and began to search for the key, her breath hissing and sobbing, all her plans awry.

She looked up once as the car roared into life —
Bates had taught Thea how to start a car as well as
the rudiments of driving one — let out a shriek as the
car wheeled clumsily, its headlights sweeping across
the lawn, across her scrabbling figure, to run down
the drive, through the open gates at the bottom,
erratically steered by a novice in a state of distress,
who was rapidly becoming soaked to the skin as the
rain blew in through the open sides below the canvas
hood, but no matter, Thea was heading for Barton
Dene, Gis Havilland and salvation.

CHAPTER NINE

GIS HAVILLAND had gone to bed very late and couldn't sleep. The problem in aerodynamics which he had spent all day trying to solve refused to leave his brain in peace. He sighed, rose and lit an oil lamp. The bedroom he occupied was at the back of the cottage and the wind was driving the heavy rain, which had started in mid-evening, hard against the window panes.

He had arrived at Barton Dene several days ago, after checking that the Dunstans had left Hampstead. He had driven into north Oxford, past the Dunstans' home, had parked his car beneath a tree and walked up and down, as unobtrusively as he could, and had come to the conclusion that Lady Edith and Thea, at least, had returned home. He saw no sign of the professor, who, as Thea had said, must have left for Paris before his family's return to Oxford. As an undergraduate he had no right to be in Oxford during the long vac, but fortunately no one noticed his presence there.

He didn't know whether to be reassured or not as he drove slowly home to Barton Dene, but the knowledge that Thea was so near kept him at the cottage in case she should need him.

Gis finally picked up a book, *Sanders of the River*, an Edgar Wallace of pre-war vintage left behind by the man who had previously owned the cottage, and tried to interest himself in the lively and exciting

narrative. To no avail, and it was as he was about to
put out the lamp and try again to go to sleep that he
heard a thunderous knocking on the front door.

Surprised, he looked at his watch: it was half-past
three on a wretched night. Surely it couldn't be poor
Thea down there at this hour? He sprang out of
bed, pulled on a brocade dressing-gown, picked up
the lamp, walked downstairs to open his front door,
for Thea to fall forward against him, sobbing with
relief. She had his door-key in her hand and had
been about to use it.

He put the lamp down and drew her into the
living-room — there was no hall — to discover that
she was soaking wet and shivering, whether from
cold or from shock he couldn't tell. He muttered a
curse under his breath, laid her down on the settle
in front of the fireplace and then shut the front
door.

'Thea,' he said, and her eyes which she had
closed, opened to look steadily at him before closing
again. Shocked, as well as cold, he decided, and,
bending down, put a match to the sticks and coal in
the cast-iron grate. What she needed most was
warmth, and dry clothes, and then bed.

'Thea,' he said again, 'did you bring anything with
you, a bag, clothing?'

She shook her head, speech seemed beyond her,
but after a moment she managed to croak, 'Nothing,'
and then, 'just myself. Oh, Gis, you don't know
what a relief it is to find you here. I feel safe again,'
and she clutched at him, so that he drew her into his
arms, never mind that she was wet through. He held
her for a little, because that was what she seemed to
want the most, until he muttered in her ear, 'Thea,

we must get you out of your clothes and into something dry. Let me help you.'

The fire had taken hold and was beginning to flare up. Thea said, 'Yes,' dazedly, and then, when he went to go upstairs to find clothing for her, she said, 'Please, don't leave me,' and clutched at him again.

He was feeling shocked himself because he had suddenly discovered that she was wearing only a badly torn nightgown beneath her coat, and that her footwear was a pair of light slippers, wet and muddy. He suddenly felt a terrible fear for her, and his heart began to hammer, as he suspected the very worst — that she had been sexually assaulted.

After a time, when she had quieted a little, and her breathing had returned to normal, he went over to a cupboard by the side of the fireplace where he kept a few bottles of spirits, fetched out brandy and a glass, and, sitting by her, took her in his arms, and said gently, 'Drink this, Thea. It might warm you a little.'

She lay there as though she were a small child again, obediently drinking the brandy, shuddering a little between each swallow. When she had finished it, he said through the blind rage which was beginning to fill him, 'Do you think, if I gave you another, only a small one, that you would allow me to go and fetch you some towels and dry clothing?'

She didn't speak, merely nodded agreement at him, mute, her eyes huge, purple stains under them, and when she turned her head, he could see a great bruise on her cheek, disappearing into her hair. The rage gripped him again.

Gis rose, ran rapidly upstairs in the dark. There was a candlestick on the small landing, a box of

matches by it. He lit it, went into a small room
which acted as a closet, fetched out towel, and a
clean shirt, then went into his bedroom to take an
old heavy pullover out of a chest of drawers, and
some socks, which might be huge, but would serve
to keep her feet warm.

He dared not leave her too long, ran downstairs
to find her sitting up, the empty glass in her hand, a
flush on her thin cheeks. Gis felt that he wanted to
kill someone, but was unfortunately prevented from
doing so because he didn't know who the someone
was.

'None of this is very. . .' He hesitated, said, trying
to smile at her, 'Very glamorous, I believe the new
word is, but it will keep you warm. The only thing
is, you will have to take off your wet clothes while
I'm here. You're so shocked, I don't want to leave
you. I promise to turn away when you do so.'

Thea looked at him and tried to stand up in order
to remove her coat. Her face suddenly lost what
small colour it had possessed: she was about to
faint. Gis swore to himself again, caught her, said,
roughly, because to speak to her gently was beyond
him, 'Let me help you, Thea. Pretend that I'm a
doctor.'

She gave him a watery but gallant smile. 'Forgive
me,' she muttered, her voice a thread, 'for behaving
like a fool. But I can't seem to stand or to do
anything. I'm sure it's the brandy. I'm not used to
it.'

They both knew it wasn't the brandy, and Gis
began to help her to remove the coat, to reveal her
nightgown, also wet through, and clinging to her
body. Worse, he saw the bruises on her arms where

Lady Edith had pinched and struck her, and the rage rose again, like bile in his throat. But he contained it, and, since she didn't seem to mind, he stripped and dried her as gently as possible, trying to preserve as much of her modesty as he could.

'I must tell you,' she said once, 'what happened to me. I wouldn't have come if it weren't necessary. . .' Her voice wavered and Gis could see the effort that she was making. It was as though, Thea thought later, as though having survived Hector's attack and the knowledge of what her mother had done, and having driven a strange car ten miles on a wild night on roads she hardly knew, her body and spirit had decided to give up the moment she had seen him.

'Tell me tomorrow,' he said, 'not tonight.'

'No,' Thea was firm. 'I must tell you tonight, I must. I. . .couldn't sleep.'

'Very well.' Gis couldn't avoid seeing, as he helped her to dry herself, what a perfect little body she must have when she was not haggard through strain and under-eating. He suspected that she had been suffering for some time from her mother's brutality, and he knew that it was Lady Edith that he wanted to kill, but he suspected that there was more behind Thea's flight than that, wretched though her mother had been making her.

'Later, you must tell me later, when you are warm.'

She let him dress her as though she were a child as he helped her into his shirt, lifting her arms for her. 'It's yours, isn't it?' she asked gravely, smoothing the shirt down, as though to say so were the most important thing in the world. Next she was tucked into the pullover, which was huge on her, and finally she put on his socks. That done, he produced a blanket, and wrapped that round her, for although the small room was growing hot she seemed unable to stop shivering.

'Now let me make you some tea,' said Gis gravely. 'It's in all the best novels, you know. The heroine, and sometimes the hero, is under the weather, and tea is always the solution, something which cures everything from a broken leg to a broken heart. Let's see whether it will work for you.'

The green eyes looked warily at him over the blanket. He had put a cushion behind Thea's head, which he had wrapped in a towel—she didn't seem to have the strength to dry her hair—and gradually, her shivering seemed to abate. He had put a kettle on the fire, fetched out cups and saucers, a teapot, milk jug and sugar bowl from a cupboard, and made the tea as coolly and professionally as though it were the most normal thing in the world to be doing it for a drowned young woman in the middle of the night.

Thea sat up when he came over with her cup and saucer and a plate of plain, sweet biscuits. He watched to see that she could manage her teacup properly, and when it was obvious that she could he sat down in an old Windsor chair with a pad tied to its seat, and began to drink his own.

'How did you get here?' he asked. His rage had abated somewhat at the sight of her beginning to recover a little.

'By car,' she said, and then fell silent.

Gis was surprised. 'By car? I didn't know that you could drive. Where did you leave it?'

'Outside your gate. On the road. I don't suppose many people come this way,' and then, 'I don't know what we ought to do with it. It's Hector's, you see. I stole it, and I can't drive, or at least not before tonight. Bates showed me. I never thought how useful it might be.'

Gis fastened on one piece of this answer. '*Hector's* car!' He began to understand what had probably happened and felt murderous all over again. He wanted to take her in his arms, kiss her and pet her, tell her that she was his little love, and no one would ever hurt her again. But he was fearful of what that might do to her. It was obvious that she was on the very edge of mental and physical collapse, and, given what he thought might have occurred, loving her was not perhaps a good idea. It might push her over the edge.

Instead he said politely, 'Another biscuit?'

Thea considered. 'Yes, I think so. These are rather nice. Our dinner tonight. . .last night. . .was awful. Mother has sent the servants away,' she added, apparently inconsequentially as she ate her second biscuit.

This combination of curate-like tea-party and disgraceful revelations, for Gis's analytical mind had already and rapidly grasped the point of Lady Edith's sending the servants away, was fortunately calculated to prevent him from jumping up, driving to north Oxford in order to kill Hector Dashwood and Lady Edith, in any order, although both at the same time might be the most satisfactory.

'I want to tell you all about it,' said Thea frown-

ing, and when he nodded she began, hesitantly at
first, her voice gaining strength as she went on,
althought at times the effort was too much for her.

'And then I hit him with a curtan pole,' she said,
and fell silent.

'The curtain pole?' Gis was fascinated by this
revelation.

'Yes, Mother gave me the idea. She hit me with
the one in my bedroom at Hampstead. It was a lot
lighter than the one I hit Hector with. At first I
thought that I had killed him, but I hadn't, and then
I locked him in the bedroom. I hadn't time to dress
properly.'

The halting voice continued with its dreadful tale.
At the end, Gis rose, for she had looked away from
him, her mouth beginning to tremble, and went to
sit by her. At last he took her in his arms, not to pet
or to love her, but simply to hold her, to let her
know that he was there, and would protect her from
Hector, Lady Edith and the whole world.

'And he never touched you, or hurt you?' he
asked, knowing that if Hector had done so he would
hardly be responsible for his actions.

'He tried to. He tore my nightie, that's all. I
stopped him from doing what. . .he wanted to. The
most awful thing was. . .' her voice faltered '. . .that
Mother helped him. Gave him the key to my
bedroom. . .' She choked back her tears, and
clutched at Gis's hand.

After a little time, when he had thought that she
had gone to sleep, she said, into his chest, 'How did
you know?'

Gis could not immediately think what she meant,
murmured back, 'Know what, Thea?'

'That I might need to come to you for refuge. How could you possibly know?

How to tell her that it was a combination of things, his ability to pick up the signals human beings gave off and interpret them correctly, the strange empathy, mixed with intuition, which he had possessed all his life. Oh, he didn't always read possibilities aright, but he had done so with Thea.

'I can't tell you,' he said, almost humbly. 'Just that sometimes, the future seems very plain to me, particularly when it affects people for whom I have begun to care.'

He cares for me, then, was Thea's inward comment, he really does, but she said nothing of that, instead, 'But you saved me, Gis, by guessing correctly. I don't know what I would have done if I hadn't known that somewhere, there was a refuge for me. There was nowhere else for me to go. No one who cares. I might have been Hector's wretched victim by now.'

This last was said in such a low voice that Gis had to strain to hear her. He said nothing further to her, merely tightened his grasp of her a little. He thought that now she had told her tale she might be able to sleep—which meant that he needed to make a bed up in his second bedroom.

'Thea,' he whispered, 'would you mind very much if I left you to prepare a bed for you? You really ought to try to sleep somewhere more comfortable than this.'

'Nothing could be more comfortable than I am now,' she said in a voice so low he could hardly hear it, 'but you may be right. I might be stiff by morning.

I feel awfully strange, Gis. As though I might fly to pieces any minute, and my head is swimmy.'

Gis thought that shock and exhaustion might be taking their toll of her, but he was also a little afraid that there might be more to her distress than that. He left her, having first fetched his trench coat from the back of the door, to give her more warmth. And presently, the bed made, he came downstairs again to carry her up to it.

She was so light, and lay so confidingly against his heart, that it was a wrench to put her to bed. 'I'll bring you a hot-water bottle,' were his final words. 'I shan't be long, the fire is still high.' He was worried that she seemed unable to get warm, and once out of his arms and in the bed she had begun to shiver again.

While the kettle boiled, he went outside; the rain had let up, and the moon had come out. It shone on Hector's car, standing by the gate. He ran down to it, started it up, and then drove it into the field, next to the cottage, part of his property, up a pebbled lane and into a derelict barn, where he threw a tarpaulin over it. If Hector reported its loss to the police, and goodness knew how, in the circumstances, he would account for its disappearance, they would have difficulty in tracing it; it was as lost as it could be.

Back in the cottage, the kettle had boiled. He filled a stone bottle with hot water, and wrapped it in an old sock. He then fetched a lemon from his drinks cupboard, sliced it up, sugared it heavily, and poured the remaining boiling water over it, to make a soothing drink.

By the time he returned to her, Thea had acquired

a flushed face, and a *distraite* manner. She looked at
him, almost as though she didn't know him, and
when he touched her forehead it was burning. Gis
put the bottle in the bed, went into his own bedroom, fetched out a small medicine chest, found
two aspirin tablets, and took them back with him.

'Come on, my darling,' he said, his heart full of
affection and pity combined, 'sit up if you can. Take
the aspirin and then drink some lemonade. They
will help you to sleep.'

She was as obedient as a child. She looked at him
with great burning eyes, and did as she was bid.
Then she gave a long sigh and lay down again, not
before saying, 'Oh, Gis, I don't want to be alone.
Could you stay with me until I sleep, please? I know
it's selfish of me, after all you have done for me.
But I should feel so much safer. Mother can't find
me here, can she?'

'Not tonight,' said Gis gently, for it was all that
he could truthfully promise, and he sank into the
elderly basket chair by the bed, also elderly, a brass
one, which had come with the cottage. He sat there
until she fell asleep, and by then, tired himself, he
decided that going to bed was pointless, and slept
where he sat, to be awoken by the sun coming into
the room.

For a moment he couldn't remember why and
how he came to be where he was, until memory
returned with a rush, and he looked over to the bed,
to see that Thea was half awake, drowsy, and, as he
had feared she might be, firmly in the grip of a high
fever. She was not yet saved.

* * *

Whether it was an illness Thea had acquired before the attempt on her by her mother and Hector, exacerbated by the rain and by what had happened to her, or whether the trauma she had experienced was the cause, Gis was never to know, nor did it much matter. She was ill, she was in his cottage because of his intervention in her affairs, and she was his responsibility.

He didn't think that her fever was life-threatening, which was fortunate, because he was reluctant to fetch a doctor to her, unless she became dangerously ill, for fear that through the doctor she might be traced to Barton Dene, and Lady Edith would arrive to claim her. Lady Edith would be reluctant to admit that Thea had fled from her home in the middle of the night, and he wondered what action she might, or could, take — but he was sure of one thing. If she discovered where Thea was, she could come at the run to snatch her away.

For the next two days, Gis nursed Thea, and in the doing, if he had doubted that he loved her, all doubts fled away. Performing the most intimate of tasks for her, changing her damp clothes, sponging her down, making her drink the liquid which would help to break her temperature, listening to her wandering talk in her delirium, his emotions ranged from pity, to affection, to love and to anger.

That he should feel the first three was easily explained. The anger rose from the revelation of her life with her mother, the suffering which she had experienced, the sense of being unloved and unwanted, the cruelties practised against her, both mental and physical. Once she caught him by the hand to look blindly at him, exclaiming, 'Oh, don't

send me back, please. Next time I might not be able
to escape.'

What touched him the most was his discovery of
the simple hero worship which had been her first
feeling for him, but which, her ramblings revealed,
had rapidly turned into love. It made him feel
unworthy when he remembered how lightly he had
treated her in their early days together at Padworth.

On the second day he fetched scissors and carefully cut off her long chestnut hair, which was damp
and unpleasant about her; she spent much time in
her fever plucking it away. Shortening her hair did
more for Thea than relieve her distress. The weight
of its length had kept its natural curl from revealing
itself, and now, when dry, it sprang around her face,
and even in her illness it no longer looked so thin
and extinguished.

Gis cancelled his charwoman's visits until further
notice, paying her for the days she wasn't attending.
He carried his weekly laundry bag to the washer-
woman, his heart in his mouth during the whole
time he was away from Thea. He bought extra
provisions from the small general store in Barton
Dene — his cottage was half a mile outside the
village — he had chosen it for its privacy, and he had
never valued it more. No one knew that young
master at Rose Cottage had a guest.

He galloped upstairs to find Thea still sleeping,
hardly having moved since he had left her. It was
three days since she had arrived on his doorstep,
and it was the first peaceful sleep she had enjoyed.
He watched her for a moment, his heart bursting
with the strange emotion for her which he had first
experienced at Padworth. It was a fierce protective-

ness, mixed with an enormous affection, an affection which, with every day that passed, was flowering into passionate love. He was beginning to want to climb into the bed with her, to take her in his arms and comfort her—no, if he were honest, he wanted to do more than that. And it was all quite different from what he had felt for Diana Troy and the others.

Gis stood and looked down at what he now knew was his true love. How it had happened that she had wound herself around his heart was a mystery to him. He had always kept himself aloof from others, making no commitments, even before he had discovered the secret of his birth. But Thea had broken through all the barriers he had erected against the world.

He thought of the broken words she had murmured to him as he had supported her in her delirium. 'Does he care for me? I can't believe he can. He can have anyone he wants. Why should he want me? Even if I love him, and the others don't.'

'Oh, but I do want you, my darling,' he murmured. 'No doubt about that. And I want to love and protect you, and punish those who have hurt you—but only if *you* want that.'

He stayed watching over her for some time, before he went downstairs to make soup with some vegetables from the garden, and some beef bones he had brought from the village. He had never been more happy that he had learned to look after himself during the war—for now he could look after Thea.

He remembered one of the privates with whom he had enlisted, who had amused the lofty and unheeding young aristocrat he had been by talking about 'his woman'. Well, he, Gis had a woman now, and she was Thea, and he knew what the private had meant. Yes, she was his woman, no one else's, and he would look after her and care for her, as no one had ever done before.

He had thought that she might be recovering, so when the soup was on the fire, in its black iron cauldron, he ran upstairs again, to find that she was awake, struggling to sit up, her eyes clear, water running from her hair, and his shirt, which she was wearing in lieu of a nightgown, was quite sodden.

She looked at him, and for the first time since she had arrived, the expression on her face was its normal tranquil one. 'Oh, Gis,' she said, voice husky with emotion, 'I thought that I had dreamed you. Have I been an awful nuisance? I seem to remember calling out, and you holding me.'

Gis went on his knees by the bed, took her hand, said fervently, 'No, no nuisance at all,' and when she would have thrown the covers back, added, 'No, my darling, you must keep them on. It's essential, now that the fever has broken, that you don't catch cold.'

Her face broke into an expression of sheer delight, 'Oh, Gis, you called me your darling!' Anxiously, 'Do you really mean that?'

'Always,' he replied gently. 'Always. And now, we sponge you down and change you into something dry.' He had placed towels by the bed, and another of his shirts in anticipation that this might happen. Thea tried to sit up fully to help him to change her, but found that she was dreadfully weak, and sitting up made her head swim.

'I'm sorry,' she sighed, 'sorry that I can't help you. How long have I been ill?'

'Three days,' answered Gis; he was towelling her hair dry, having eased her into yet another shirt, the hair drying made much more rapid since he had cropped her long mane.

Thea suddenly realised that her hair was short. 'Oh,' she exclaimed, 'my hair! You've cut it off! Oh, do I look an awful frump? Mother said I would when I asked if could have it bobbed.'

'You don't mind then?' Gis had finished drying it, was teasing the chestnut curls into shape with a brush. 'And your mother was wrong—look.' And he fetched a hand mirror from the dressing-table and held it up before her.

Thea's lips parted at the sight of her new self. Despite the pallor of her face, and the purple smudges of illness beneath her eyes, she could see the improvement losing her long hair had brought about.

'A pixie,' remarked Gis, grinning happily at her delight, 'you will look like a very pixie when you have recovered your normal colour. No one will know you.'

'And what a good thing that will be,' retorted Thea. 'Mother will never be able to find me.'

Gis laid her back on the pillows. 'Forget her, Thea,' he said earnestly. 'I know it's difficult, and when you're better we are going to have to face the world again, but for the moment concentrate on getting well. If you don't mind me leaving you, I will fetch you some soup—do you think that you could drink some?'

'A little,' Thea smiled. 'It smells delightful.' Ill

and weak she might be, but she felt happier than she had ever felt in her life. No one had looked after her so uncomplainingly as she knew that Gis had done. She lay back on her pillows and tried to remember what had happened since she felt ill, but all that she could recall was that, in her brief lucid moments, Gis had always been there, comforting her and helping her.

Whenever he was absent and she thought of him, as she was doing now, it was more than ever true that she never called up his handsome face, or his graceful body, although they both pleased her, but it was his other qualities which seemed to matter most. She remembered how tender and gentle his hands had been, how his voice had soothed her, when, breaking free from her delirium for a moment, she had clung to him for comfort, asking him to help her to banish her memories of her mother and Hector who stalked her dreams.

And how strange and odd it was that she did not mind that he had done the most personal and intimate tasks for her while she lay ill, tasks that she could not imagine a man doing. . . She had reached this point in her reverie, and her eyes were beginning to close when he returned, carrying a tray with a bowl of soup and a bread roll on it.

'Sleepyhead,' he smiled, sitting on the edge of the bed and manoeuvring the tray expertly in front of her. 'Well, you shall sleep—after you have tried to drink a little of this.'

Sitting up, and trying to drink the soup, were such simple tasks, but made her head swim, so Gis took the spoon from her, propped her high on her pillows, and began to spoon the soup into her mouth. 'Tell me to stop when you have had enough.'

It was like feeding a baby bird, he thought as she obediently accepted the spoon, looking so happily at him as she did so that such a rush of love overcame him that he had to put the spoon down, in order to kiss her, gently, on the cheek. But she didn't remain passive beneath his caress, but turned her head, to kiss him back, on his cheek, her eyes giving him a message which he couldn't mistake, especially when she put out her hand to take his.

'Later,' he promised, 'later, when you are better. For now, the soup, and perhaps some bread, if you can manage to eat a little more.'

She could, but not much, and presently lay back on the pillows again, turning her head to watch him, as he gathered up the tray, to carry it downstairs to the shallow stone sink in the kitchen.

He stopped at the door to say, 'I'll be back, Thea.'

Thea nodded at him. The little nourishment she had taken had reinvigorated her. She felt clean and cared-for, wearing Gis's shirt, with new sheets on the bed. A mindless joy seized her, she gave a great sigh, and fell into her first natural sleep since Hector had surprised her in her room.

Gis returned to find her, a small smile on her face, the chestnut curls springier than ever since he had dried them, no longer plastered about her head by the sweats from her fever.

He was carrying a book, for he had thought that she might sleep, and Thea's first sight, when she awoke again later, was of the still face of concentration he wore as he read, and she watched him for

some time, before she spoke to let him know that
she was back with him.

'Fifteen-two, fifteen-four, fifteen-six and eight make
fourteen,' crowed Thea joyfully, 'and the game and
rubber are mine!' She and Gis were playing their
evening game of crib at the kitchen table. By the
end of their first week together, it had become a
ritual. Gis had taught her to play while she was still
confined to bed. The crib box, which contained two
packs of cards and ivory pegs, was a beautiful thing,
like all Gis's personal possessions.

Thea had rapidly recovered, once the fever had
broken and had been allowed up on the second day.
'No staying in bed too long,' Gis told her. 'The RAF
doctor always said that it was bad for the patient
and slowed recovery. I thought that he said that to
get us back on ops as quickly as possible, but I
noticed that I, and others, did seem to get better
more quickly the sooner we were out of bed.'

Thea was wearing Gis's shirt underneath his brocade dressing-gown. Gis was driving to Banbury the
next day, he had told her, to buy her some clothes.
'You having been inconsiderate enough to arrive
without any.'

'How thoughtless I was,' Thea had retorted gaily
to this teasing. 'I am sure that Diana Troy would
have packed three trunks, all while holding Hector
and Mother off with the curtain pole.'

'True,' said Gis, grinning at her, 'and now you
must help me with the supper. Another step in your
recovery. You may lay the table, while I prepare
the food. Afterwards you may, as a special treat,

dry the pots. You see that I mean you to work in return for your keep.'

He had shortened his over-long dressing-gown for her by turning up a great hem at its bottom, and rolling back the sleeves. He had cleaned and dried the slippers in which she had arrived, and she was fully equipped, he said, to play her part in the running of his mansion.

She had told him, shyly, that morning, that she was happier in his cottage than she had ever been in any mansion, and he had put out a finger to stroke her nose, and said, in a lordly voice, 'My cottage? Whatever do you mean, Miss Dorothea Dunstan? I'll have you know that this is my mansion,' and the stroking finger had been followed by a kiss on the tip of her nose. Ever after the cottage was known to them as Gis's mansion.

So, Thea laid the table, fetching out the cloth, the knives, forks and spoons, the plates, cups, saucers and the wine glasses. Gis had promised her a glass of wine after their supper, which was to be poached eggs on toast, prepared on the kitchen range. 'Another day, when you are properly dressed, you can toast the bread,' Gis had promised. 'Today, when you have set the table, you can brew the tea.'

They sat down to their simple meal. Gis had sliced some tomatoes to go with the egg and toast, and he had bought a fruit cake back from the village shop. His practicality, his self-sufficiency in looking after the cottage, in feeding himself, in nursing her when she was ill, always surprised Thea, it was so at odds with his romantic appearance. Remembering the handsome young aristocrat whom she had met at Padworth, who barely seemed able to do the most simple task for himself, she had difficulty in realising that this Gis was the same man.

Presently, the meal over, the table cleared, pots washed and meticulously put away, Gis sat on one side of the fire he had made — Thea still had difficulty in keeping warm — darning a sock. He had given Thea *Sanders of the River* to read.

She looked across at him; he was darning with the same ruthless concentration he brought to his academic work.

'I could do that,' she offered, 'and then you could go on with your studies.'

Gis smiled across at her. He had the momentary sensation that they were an old married couple, the work of the day done, enjoying themselves in the evening. 'You can darn?'

'Yes,' said Thea, and then, as he handed over the wooden mushroom and the sock, she inspected his work and said gravely, 'But you're much better at it than I am. Is there anything you can't do, Gis?'

He had risen, was on his way to the cupboard where his books and papers were stored, he touched her lightly on the shoulder as he passed — a mistake.

For she looked up at him, and her melting glance almost unmanned him. He wanted to wrap his arms around her; living in close proximity to her since her recovery, and she only minimally dressed, was beginning to have a strong effect on him.

'Many things,' he said hoarsely. Behaving myself, was his secret gloss to that.

For a time they worked in silence, Thea's unforced tranquillitiy making her company a pleasure. The darning finished, Thea began to repair the cuff of one of Gis's shirts, which he had placed, with his little hussif, on the dresser, ready to begin work on it once the darning was done.

Like Gis, Thea felt as though they had been together for years, and when in a pause in his work he looked up at her and said, 'Don't you think that you ought to go to bed, Thea? You've had a long day,' she flushed and said,

'No, don't send me upstairs please, Gis. I promise to be quiet.'

'You are always quiet.' He was suddenly as grave as she was, and walked over to sit on the settle beside her, and say, 'We shall have to talk about the future, Thea. Perhaps tomorrow, when I have bought you some clothes. I find it difficult to talk seriously to someone who looks like my young brother wearing my castoffs.'

Thea's hands stilled. 'Do I really look like a boy?'

'Not at all,' he said, 'a joke, merely.'

'Oh, I'm glad,' she replied artlessly. 'There are times when I thought that I might like to be a boy, but not now.'

Gis could not resist temptation. 'Why not?' he enquired gently.

Thea looked down at her work, a vast blush enveloping her. She couldn't tell him, she couldn't. If I were a boy, then you couldn't love me, and oh, how I want you to.

Gis was remorseless, he leaned forward to take her by the chin and tilt her face up. 'Why not, Thea?'

'You know,' she murmured breathlessly.

'Do I? What do I know, Thea? This?' And he pulled her towards him to kiss her on the lips. Not a passionate kiss, but a kiss.

She had half risen, and suddenly was lax against him, so that it was easy for him to lift her on to his knee.

'Is this why?' he murmured into her ear, and kissed her again.

Thea was in heaven. To be with him was bliss; to be on his knee, in his arms, alone, was beyond anything. This time the kiss was passionate, and, untutored though her response was, the passion in hers was plain.

I shouldn't be doing this, thought Gis, and did it again. Her response this time was so forthright — it involved putting both her arms around his neck, and kissing him back with vigour — that he gave a slight groan and pulled away, to sit her by him on the settle.

'I have work to do,' he announced hoarsely, anything to stop himself from beginning something which had only one logical end. 'And we must behave ourselves, Thea. You're still not fully recovered.'

She looked at him beneath her lashes, her face naughty. 'And when I am?'

'Why, then,' said Gis gaily, 'we'll decide what to do when you are.'

Thea pulled a face, which was childish, she knew, and picked up her mending again. She was discovering new things about herself every day, and one of them was that her body was beginning to welcome the idea of Gis actually loving it. In her own way, which was untutored and inexperienced, she was reacting in the same manner as Gis — she thought, If we begin to make love it can have only one end. The difference was that Gis had experienced that end, and Thea had not, and that as a result Gis knew that sexual fulfilment was also a beginning, and not merely an end, and that the consequences which flowed from it were by no means always those which we would wish.

Gis didn't want to go too quickly with Thea, for fear that he might go further than her brave spirit could cope with. He was also fearful how far his own self-control might stretch before it snapped. The situation they were in was acting as a forcing-house, and he didn't want to make her his true sexual partner, and then find that she bitterly regretted what they had done. No, he must be patient and careful, make her understand that what they might do must not be done lightly, must be done only when she was ready, and at the right time — which was almost certainly not when they were alone here, at the cottage.

So he sat down to work again, and shortly afterwards Thea yawned, her mending done, and said that she would like to go to bed now, please. Which she did, but only after Gis had made her a drink of Ovaltine to take upstairs with her. 'For we must put the roses back in your cheeks,' he said, while avoiding any opportunity to touch and caress her, however much he wished to do so.

I wonder if he thinks I am only a little girl, thought Thea ruefully, as she carried her candle and her Ovaltine up to bed. I don't suppose he's so respectful to Diana Troy. I doubt he gave her Ovaltine and not himself! But common sense told her, as she settled herself for the night, that he was only taking care of and for her, and she was most

manifestly not Diana Troy, so it was useless hoping
that he might treat her as though she were!

'Oh, they're lovely! Just what I always wanted to
wear, and Mother never let me.' Thea was admiring
the clothes which Gis had brought back with him
from Banbury. Besides a lemon silk dress with a
broad cream-coloured sash, there was a bluey-green
crêpe de Chine one, which favoured her eyes, being
more green than blue, fine silk stockings, and cream
kid court-shoes with Louis heels—Gis had taken
her slippers with him as a guide to the right size.
The lingerie he had chosen was perfect, too, fine
cotton with feathery lace, and baby-blue ribbon
threaded through tiny eyelet holes. He had also
bought her a cream cardigan, and a pale green
coatee in fine wool to wear with the bluey-green
dress. A cream straw hat, trimmed with lilies of the
valley, would do to wear with either of the dresses,
he said.

'I am fine enough to go to a royal garden party,'
Thea exclaimed. 'Whenever am I going to wear all
this? I can't do the housework in them, for sure,'
but she lifted the beautiful crêpe de Chine dress
reverently and held the fine stuff against her face.

'No need to worry,' exclaimed Gis gaily, and
handed over parcels with gingham dresses inside
and overalls to wear with a pair of heavy shoes. 'For
when you do the rough stuff,' he explained. 'You
can't get out of doing the scrubbing now!'

Not, he thought, that Thea ever got out of doing
anything. She was the most willing worker.

Thea carried all her parcels up to her room, and
laid them on the patchwork counterpane before she

changed into one of the blue and white gingham
working dresses. She found the aprons tucked away
in pink tissue paper and put one of them on. Gis
was going to give her a cookery lesson, he had said,
once she was properly clothed. He had discovered
that she had only been taught to make elaborate
sweets and 'messes', as he called them. Making a
beef stew — 'boeuf en daube' to the posh, Gis had
told her in what he called his private's voice — and
apple tart, with pastry made with butter, were to be
his first demonstrations for her.

'When did you learn to cook and clean?' she
asked, astonished all over again at his grasp of the
menial practicalities of life.

'I was put to work in the kitchens before I trained
to be a mechanic,' was his answer to that, 'and what
I learned there has been of more use to me than all
the airy philosophy for which they are going to give
me a double first.'

'Will you give me a double first if I manage to
cook a decent beef stew and make a good apple
pie?' was Thea's spirited reply which earned,

'No, but you can have this,' this being a brotherly
kiss — Gis couldn't quite prevent himself from reacting to the provocation of the saucy face turned up
to him.

'And tomorrow,' he told her, when the stew was
safely in its brown pot, cooking in the oven, and the
pastry for the apple tart was cooling in the larder,
having been rolled out and used to line an enamel
plate, 'we must discuss what we are going to do.
We're living in fairyland at the moment, hidden
from the world, but this cannot last for ever.'

Thea involuntarily showed the whites of her eyes and shrank away from him.

'I. . . I'm not g. . .going back to M. . .m. . . mother,' she stammered, 'You can't make me.'

Gis put an arm around her shaking shoulders, 'No, my darling, never. But there are ways and means to talk about and now you are so much better, talk we must.'

Thea had to be satisfied with that, but she managed to contain herself and went to fetch her book to read while Gis got down to work, there being three hours before the slow-cooking stew would be ready to eat.

She leaned over his shoulder to look at his work. His papers were laid out on the table, and she saw that today they were technical drawings. 'Is this what you're doing at William and Mary?' she exclaimed in some surprise, for, untutored though she was, she could see that the drawings were of an aeroplane, or rather, bits of an aeroplane, and that Gis was examining them in a most dissatisfied way.

He looked up at her and said, 'No secrets from you, Thea. These are nothing to do with Oxford. Before I came here I finally made up my mind what I wanted to do with my life. I've decided that when I get my degree I shall go to work at Handley-Page — I have already been in touch with them — to learn how to design aeroplanes. Flying them made me want to design something I might feel happy with. The mathematics I did at Oxford will be useful, but I don't know what I shall do with my enormous knowledge of German metaphysics.'

'I heard Papa say once, when Mother was complaining about you, that the talk was that you had the best mind of any student who had been at Oxford for years.'

'No credit to me,' said Gis briefly, 'I find that kind of thing easy. Now this——' and he put a finger on the drawing before him '—is hard. If I make a mistake, someone, some time, might die because of it. No one is going to die because I might interpret Herr Hegel and his world spirit incorrectly.'

'No,' Thea was thoughtful, 'that never occurred to me before. I suppose I thought that aeroplanes and motor cars just grew, like Topsy in the novel.' She looked respectfully at him. 'It's an enormous responsibility, isn't it?'

'Well, I can lessen it by test-flying any plane I design myself,' said Gis slowly. 'That should make me careful, if nothing else does.'

'You like flying?'

'Oh, yes.' Gis was suddenly abstracted. Thea thought that something in the design before him was talking to him, but she couldn't prevent herself from saying, 'Would you take me up some time, Gis? Please? I have never been in an aeroplane.'

His attention swung immediately from the problem before him to her. 'Yes, of course. All the more reason why we should have our serious talk tomorrow, but let us enjoy ourselves tonight.'

He looked at his wristwatch, smiled at her and said, 'Would you do something for me, Thea? Let me set the table for dinner tonight while you go upstairs and dress yourself for it—put on the green one, I'm longing to see you in it. Don't be too long. I have a little surprise for you.'

Thea leaped to her feet, 'Oh, yes,' she said gladly, and made for the open staircase in the corner of the

room. Gis watched her running up it, heard her
door open, and, his smile still on his face, he went
back to his work and the problem before him which
had solved itself while he talked with her as such
problems sometimes did, so that he put the papers
away, and began to set the table as he had promised.

Upstairs Thea threw off her new working clothes,
washed herself carefully in the floral washbowl on
the deal washstand, reminding herself to carry up
more water; she had emptied the large matching
pitcher. Then she slowly dressed herself, lamenting
the lack of the long mirror left behind in her north
Oxford bedroom. He hadn't bought her a corset,
but a small suspender belt, which took a little getting
used to. But once she was fully prepared for dinner,
she brushed her hair with the new brush he had
brought for her from Banbury, and admired the
curls which, now that she was feeling better, sprang
around her face so that she was beginning to look
like the pixie which Gis had promised.

She had a little colour in her cheeks, too, and
happiness was making her eyes shine. I'm wicked,
she thought, shameful. I haven't once worried about
Mother, and what she must be thinking, now that I
have disappeared, and oh, since I have been with
him, the imp has deserted me, probably because
now I can say what I think without fear of
punishment.

She put her hands to her face, stared at her new
self in the tiny mirror—I don't want to go back to
her, I can't, it would kill me, surely he won't make
me—and thinking of Gis made her face softer than
ever.

She had to walk carefully down the stairs, what

with them being so steep and her new shoes having higher heels than she had ever worn before.

Gis saw her appear, drew in his breath a little at what good food and happiness were doing to her. The gaunt drawn look which she had worn ever since he had first met her at Padworth had quite gone.

Daringly Thea twirled around for him, as Monica had told her that mannequins did when they showed off their clothes.

'Will I do?'

Gis leaned back in his chair, inspected her, and said, 'You look splendid. That colour suits you. I thought it would. But an honest answer would be almost. I think that we might try to gild the lily a little.'

Now what could he mean by that? He had turned to the dresser and was fetching a collection of little pots and boxes from it, and a large and beautiful bottle which could only be scent.

'Make-up!' exclaimed Thea. Lady Edith had never allowed Thea to wear any. 'No lady ever plasters herself with such stuff', being her usual acid comment.

'Come here,' Gis commanded pulling out a chair. 'I see that you have already made a good fist of dressing your hair.'

Obediently Thea sat down, and, a little awed at such expertise, watched him open the pots, and prepare to make up her face. 'Not too much,' he said, to have her reply earnestly,

'Oh, it's a waste of time, Gis. I'm not like Diana and the others, not pretty.'

Gis laughed and began to rub cream into her

cheeks. 'Diana doesn't look quite so stunning without her war-paint,' he said, 'nor do any of the
beauties. Wait.' And for the next few minutes he
did things to her face, wielding brushes and a
powder puff. Finally he picked up a pale pink
lipstick in an exquisite gold and enamel case, and
applied a little, a very little, to her lips.

And then, saying, 'A last loving touch,' using a
scent spray into which he had poured the liquid
from the large and beautiful bottle, he surrounded
her with a small cloud of the most delicate floral
perfume. That done, he produced from behind his
back a small hand-mirror and held it up before her.
For a moment Thea thought that he had done
nothing, so subtle had he been, and then she
realised that the glow she had already seen in the
small cracked mirror in her bedroom had been
enhanced, that the hint of rouge, the careful appli-
cation of the mascara brush, and finally the lipstick,
had given her the polished look which she had so
often admired on Diana Troy.

Her lips parted, and were it not that Gis was
feeling rather proud of his new role as make-up
artiste and didn't want to spoil what he had done,
he would have kissed her there and then.

'Where ever did you learn to do that?' she
exclaimed. 'Surely not in the RAF?'

'No, indeed. Watching, noticing. I used to love
being in Mother's room when she prepared for some
great do. Putting on her face, she called it. Not that
she ever wore much, but she always said that
discretion was the thing, and Aunt Torry was the
same.'

Telling Thea this brought on a pang of remorse

and regret for the days when he and his mother had been so close. He began to pack the make-up away in a pretty lacquer box which he handed to her. 'That's for you, Thea. Next time you use it, you must try to put it on yourself. I don't like to see it in the day, but a discreet use at night under artificial light does wonders for modom.' And his final flourish was that of a shop-walker in Harrods or Selfridge's.

Another present! But before Thea could fully enjoy it, Gis was serving dinner. He had already opened the bottle of red wine — 'To celebrate your being properly dressed for company' — and had lit some red candles, instead of the oil lamp.

It was even better than lunching at the Golden Snail. They could take their time, and the pleasure of eating good food, prepared by one's self, was something which Thea was beginning to enjoy.

Afterwards they drank coffee, and if the crockery was coarse, and the cutlery not silver, and the glasses were from Woolworth's, no matter. 'A little music for *madame*,' said Gis, coffee drinking finished, and he went over and began to play the small cottage piano in the corner of the room, which didn't sound a bit like the beautiful instrument he had performed on at Padworth, but that mattered no more than the crockery.

First he played a movement from Beethoven's *Moonlight Sonata*, all haunting loveliness, and then swinging around on the stool, said, 'Let's have something jolly,' and launched into 'Ta-ra-ra-boom-de-ay', which he sang with great verve. 'And now for an encore.' He played her 'If you were the only girl in the world', from *The Bing Boys*, which he later told her he had been to see on leave from France.

At the second chorus he threw over his shoulder, 'Come and join me, Thea, I know you have a good voice.'

She did as she was bid, and began to sing the hauntingly sentimental words, taking Violet Loraine's role. When she reached the last line, and sang, 'And you were the only boy,' Gis stopped singing, took her hands, and, as she finished, asked her gently, 'Am I your only boy, Thea?' to have her answer,

'Oh, yes, Gis, yes,' her face on fire with such love for him that all his good resolutions flew away, and he took her in his arms to begin, for the first time, to make real love to her.

Thea's response was eager and immediate. He lifted her up and carried her over to the settle, and began to kiss and stroke her, all his fire and passion now for her. As their embraces grew stronger, she whispered to him, 'Oh, Gis, yes,' on her face an expression which was the strangest mixure of apprehension and expectation.

It soon became clear that whoever cried halt, it wasn't going to be Thea! For the first time, she was giving herself unreservedly to another, and where Gis led she was prepared to follow. Some remaining vestige of sanity stopped Gis at last. Her head thrown back, her dress opened to allow him access to her body, her own hands, learning the arts of love from him, had roused him to the degree that he was ready to consummate what they both so obviously wanted, brought him to the realisation that were they to go on he would be incapable of exercising the kind of restraint which might prevent her from becoming pregnant.

Worse, he would be betraying them both if he took her as his love when she had come here trusting him to save her from another man's willingness to rifle her virginity. Everything they had done that day had served to bind them closer together, and the shared joy of the music had been the final seal on their pleasure. Lady Edith would be vindicated if he violated her child, however willing that child was, for he had partly created that willingness.

Thea, in the grip of physical sensations of such delight that she could hardly believe what was happening to her, felt Gis begin to pull away. Frantic, she put her arms around his neck, and tried to draw him back to her. He resisted her as gently, but as firmly, as he could.

'My love, my love,' he whispered. 'My fault. I should never have begun this. We must stop before we go too far.'

She showed him blind eyes, whispered, 'I don't want you to stop. I want you to go on. I. . .love you, Gis.'

'Oh, and I love you, too, Thea.' It was the first admission of love he had made to her, and he heard the small cry of joy which she gave on hearing it.

But he must not go on. He said hoarsely, 'Oh, Thea, I do so want to make proper love to you, but it's because I love you that we must stop. Think, Thea, when at last we return to the world, as we must, or if they track us down, and Lady Edith and the rest accuse us of eloping to enjoy an illicit love-affair, we must be able to say — even if they don't believe us — "No, you're wrong. We may have been tempted, but we never fell".'

'Oh,' said Thea, almost triumphantly, 'if they're

going to think that, then why not oblige them?
They'll never believe us.'

It was the hardest thing Gis had ever done. His
whole body was protesting. Soft and warm in his
arms lay the one woman. 'No,' he said. 'No. I have
done too many wrong things already to do another.
I know that my father and mother think that I have
only pursued you to ruin you, and Lady Edith thinks
the same. You know that's not true. Don't let us
make it true, for both our sakes.'

Thea, passion forgotten, sat up indignantly. 'Your
mother and your father think that? How can they?
Why, it is always I who have been the naughty one,
not you. And I am being naughty again today,
asking you to go on.'

'But I am the older and the man. Thea, I have
only one thing to say to you. Will you marry me?
Don't say yes out of gratitude — only say yes if you
feel for me as I do for you.'

Thea reared back a little, showed him great green
eyes in a blazing face, said exultantly, 'Yes, oh, yes,
and for love only, Gis. You *are* the only boy,' and
on seeing his face light up as hers did, threw her
arms about him and almost shouted, 'And if we're
going to be married, we needn't stop tonight. Oh,
I'm a little afraid, Gis, if the truth be known, but
not with you, not with you.'

Her shout of laughter was echoed by Gis's. He
lifted her out of his arms to sit her by him, 'Why,
you wanton baggage! I have created a monster! No,
Thea. If we are to marry it is more than ever
imperative that we behave ourselves. I shall go to
London as soon as you're fit to be left and get a
special licence to marry you. No waiting, no need

for worry. And, when we are married, then and only then shall we celebrate. But let's talk of this in the morning. For now, we must button ourselves up,' for Thea's hands had been as active at undressing him as he had been to undress her, 'and clear the pots away, and read the dullest improving book we can find, to douse our fire, and have a cold water bath before we go to bed. There we can dream of a future where Lady Edith and the world cannot touch us.'

CHAPTER TEN

LADY EDITH was in a quandary. On the one hand she dare not let anyone know of the disgraceful events which had caused her daughter to fly from her home — presumably to the protection of a dubious young man. On the other hand she needed to recover her daughter before the professor returned home, and before people began to query her disappearance.

She dare not go to the police — for if they found Thea for her, Thea might tell them why she had left home. For the moment she avoided trouble by informing her Oxford friends that Thea had gone to stay with relatives — in Scotland. There was no one to contradict her.

But Thea — and Hector's car — seemed to have vanished from the face of the earth. Hector was in a similar dilemma. He wanted his car back, but had to be so evasive in informing the police of how it had come to be stolen that it was virtually impossible for them to help him to trace it.

Lady Edith was certain in her own mind that Thea had gone to Gis. She had no proof of this, but the girl must have gone somewhere, and to disappear without trace — there were no reports of abandoned cars or dead girls found in fields or rivers — argued that she had known where she was going and was lying low. She consulted a London telephone directory and then rang Gis's flat. There was no answer, even though she rang again and again; he was manifestly not there — but where was he? The trouble was that she could think of no valid reason to ask his parents where he might be found — particularly since she had no real evidence that Thea had gone to him.

She did ring Payne's Court, Sir Richard Havilland's country house, to ask for Gis, giving a fictitious name, only to be told that Mr Gis Havilland did not live with his parents, was not currently staying with them, and his whereabouts were unknown. Would she care to speak to Lady Havilland?

No, Lady Edith wouldn't — she dared not risk her voice being recognised. Baffled, angry and now frightened, for the days were slipping by, Lady Edith rang off, and when Hector, also desperate for his reputation, rang her to find out if the wretched girl had returned home, she was as murderously short with him as he was with her. Both of them were becoming frightened.

And then she sat down to write another weekly letter on Thea's behalf, keeping up the fiction of Thea's damaged hand — and how long would that answer. . .? She would search the girl's room again and try to discover some clue to where she might have fled. Nemesis loomed nearer and nearer, and even the strong-minded Lady Edith began to feel like shrieking at the heavens as the days flew by and no Thea arrived home, penitent or otherwise.

Gis taught Thea how to blacklead the two grates, the big cooking range in the kitchen and the smaller, basket one in the main living-room. Once fully recovered she had done her share of carrying water in from the pump in the small paved yard at the back of the cottage. Hauling the ashes, as well as carrying in the coals, were other tasks, she found, and which she insisted on performing. 'Oh, no, you're not going to wait on me, Gis.'

After the blackleading they both prepared breakfast. Thea had discovered a hearty appetite, where once she had pecked at her food, and she ate bacon, eggs and fried bread with gusto.

'Love,' commented Gis, watching her eat, 'seems to have improved your appetite, not destroyed it.'

'Mother always did say that I was contrary,' observed Thea cheekily. 'I think all this slave-driving around the cottage is making me hungry. I never knew how hard servants had to work. I shall hesitate to ask anyone to do anything for me again.'

'Now you know how I felt when I joined the RFC,' said Gis, pouring her another cup of tea from the big brown pot. 'But you know, Thea, there is a satisfaction in doing things for one's self. The only problem comes when it takes so much time that there is none left over to do the things you want to do.'

'Like design aeroplanes?'

'Mmm, I must say that you've learned to cook well in quick march time.' For Thea had cooked the breakfast this morning while Gis had done the more menial tasks around their home.

'The only trouble is,' remarked Thea ruefully, 'that it wrecks the hands,' to have Gis nod agreement, but,

'Honourable scars,' he said softly, taking her hand across the table and kissing it.

'And now. . .' he said, once all the early morning chores were finished, the room cleaned and dusted, pots washed, beds made, and they were sitting in front of the open back door — the only annoying thing being that Thea couldn't go outside very much, for fear of being seen, talked about and traced before all Gis's plans for their future came to fruition.

'And now, we must talk seriously. I must leave you today, to go to London, to take out a special licence so that we can marry. And then we shall have to face everybody, Thea. Are you prepared for that — for the anger and the mud-slinging?'

Thea shivered. 'Yes, if you are with me, Gis. I feel that I could face anything, even though I'm not very brave.'

'Not very brave!' Gis gave an angry snorting laugh. 'How can you say that, Thea, when you held off Hector and your mother, and drove a car, never having driven solo in your life before, to a place which you only knew from my crude map ——?'

'Oh, I'd looked it up in the *Gazetteer*. That was easy,' Thea explained seriously.

'Easy! What a girl you are. Facing down the dogs of war and scandal should be child's play after that.'

'Yes, but,' and Thea looked across the table at him, hoping that he would understand what she was about to say, 'there is one thing, Gis. I don't want to tell anyone. . .about the beatings. . .or what Hector, with mother's help, tried to do to me. I couldn't bear it. To think that people should know that my own mother. . .' She choked back a sob, said, 'You do understand, say you do.'

He rose and came over to her, knelt by her chair

and put his arms around her. 'Yes, I do, only, Thea, you do realise that if you don't tell anyone why you left home they will think that you did so simply to run off with me for. . .bad. . .reasons—even if we do marry. I don't mind that people will think me a seducing rake, to persuade a girl of nineteen to leave her home and family so that I could take my pleasure with you, but think what not knowing the real truth would do to your reputation.'

Thea used a bad word for the first time in her life. 'Oh, damn my reputation, Gis. Who's going to know or care? If you go to work for Handley-Page, I don't suppose you'll live there as a young aristocrat going from Payne's Court, I know you too well for that. We shall be Mr and Mrs Havilland, I hope, nobodies living in a little villa, if we can't live here. Reputations are for the society we shall be leaving behind. I never liked society much, anyway. That was Mother. I've spent too much time hiding in cloakrooms at balls to disguise the fact that for all my fortune young men didn't particularly want to dance with me, to want to go back to it.'

Gis had already told her that he had no intention of keeping up a life in society once he had left Oxford, that he wished to join the working world, and had not yet made up his mind what to do with his enormous wealth.

'Well, you'll never be short of a partner if you marry me,' he said practically. 'But I know what you mean. I want to do something with my life, Thea, and one reason that I love you is that I've found out, since you came here, that you're prepared to help me, not try to tease me out of it.'

'So, that's that!' Thea was brisk. 'And you do agree with me, over Mother and Hector?'

'Yes, so long as you understand how much more difficult it will make your position,' he said gravely. 'Remember, you have a father and friends and other relatives, most of whom will be quick to condemn you.'

It was Thea's turn to take his hand and to kiss it. 'But I have you, Gis, and no one has ever looked after me and cared for me as you have done. Why, yesterday, you thought of me before your own pleasure, and I shall never forget that. Never.' Her voice broke on the last word, and they clung together as though both of them were innocents, as though Gis had not already led a hard life in love and war, but was as unspoiled as Thea was.

Society called London empty in early September, but that was the idle talk of the idle. Even many in society still remained in town, pursuing their own interests, most of them having little to do with the country — to which society was supposed to retire.

Gis had left Barton Dene at dawn, to arrive early in London, and, having completed his business over the special licence, was asked to call back later on in the day to collect it. He decided to take lunch at the one club to which he belonged, the Wanderers, situated like many another in Pall Mall. It might not be a bad idea for him to be seen, he thought, if there were any suspicion that he might have run off with Thea.

He had left her after an early breakfast. She hadn't wanted him to leave her, had clung to him a little, before straightening herself up, and saying,

'What a baby I am, Gis. The sooner you go, the sooner you get back, and the sooner we can live here together legitimately, and I needn't hide indoors. I am in danger of turning into one of those blind white fish in Persia that father talks about, all strange and odd because they never see the sun.'

This brought a laugh, as well as a kiss from Gis. Professor Dunstan had had a lively turn of conversation with his daughter, by the sound of it, and he, Gis, was getting the benefit of the professor's desire to pass on his erudition. He could only wish that the professor had been as careful for Thea's welfare as he had been for her education.

Thea had watched him go from the window. She had had strict orders to stay out of sight, and not to answer the door, but all through the lonely day no one came, and she sat in her bedroom, and read, and stitched some old sheets which the housekeeper at Payne's Court had given to Gis—useful if they're turned, she had said, and Thea was busy turning them, sides to middle, practising to be the prudent housewife that she hoped to become—particularly if Gis chose to renounce his fortune and live on his pay.

He had had second thoughts about that. Making corrections to one of his drawings he had said to Thea, 'Suppose I think, no, suppose I know, that my designs are good, and no one else likes them, what then?'

Thea had considered what he had said very carefully, the oil lamp making a golden aureole around her short curls. 'I suppose,' she had said doubtfully, 'that you are rich enough to finance yourself.'

'I'd thought of that,' said Gis, 'one argument

against renouncing my fortune, and a potent one. But you're a clever girl to think of it. You wouldn't mind me spending it all on research, then, and not on parties and new dresses?'

He knew what the answer would be and having got it was the signal for further gentle lovemaking; one result of having decided to marry was that both of them felt that they could wait — so long as they didn't get too near to one another!

Gis was thinking about Thea as he turned into the Wanderers, greeting old Benson at the door, handing over his hat, and making for the dining-room. Whenever he came, which wasn't often, he felt as though he had never been away.

And then, at the bottom of the grand staircase with the portrait of H. M. Stanley at the top, he saw Hector Dashwood coming down, and his heart sank — the very last person he wanted to see. Hector wasn't sure whether he thought the same about seeing Gis. He had had a telephone call from Sophie Moreton that morning, which had finally dashed his few remaining hopes of making money out of her.

Another telephone call to Lady Edith had proved equally abortive. The wretched girl was still missing, and Lady Edith had finally told Hector that she thought that Thea might have gone to Gis Havillnd. Gis Havilland! He was sure that it was Gis who had been advising Sophie Moreton, and he was almost certain that Gis had stolen her letters back for her. He ran down the stairs at the gallop, blood boiling.

The big hall had filled with people. Lunch was a busy time at the Wanderers, but that didn't restrain Hector.

'What the devil are you doing here, you infernal

puppy?' he snarled at Gis, who had been about to
pass him with a distant nod, cutting a man being a
bit final, and Gis had no wish to quarrel with
anyone, not even the swine who had tried to rape
his Thea: his errand was too precious to be
jeopardised.

He made to pass Hector, but Hector caught him
by the arm. 'Did you hear me, Havilland? I'm not
surprised that you have no manners; your sort
seldom do. It goes with cowardice and running after
little girls.'

The whole hall heard the insult. Gis stopped
dead — and the red rage was suddenly on him, and
brooked no dealings with common sense.

'What's that?' he said, voice low. 'Manners? Little
girls? Cowardice? Mind what you're saying,
Dashwood, or I'll teach you a lesson you won't
forget, since, from what I hear, you're much in need
of one.' But he still retained enough control not to
strike Hector or to mention Thea's name.

No such considerations affected Hector. 'I'll have
you black-balled,' he roared, white-hot with anger
at the thought that the young man before him had
twice helped to balk him. 'Coward and thief,' he
howled, and, still infected with last night's drinking,
and that of the night before that, *ad infinitum*, he
struck at Gis.

Gis was in the strange state which the rage
created. Everything seemed to be happening very
slowly. Hector's fist appeared to float towards him:
Gis caught him by the wrist and wrenched him
forward so that for a moment they were face to face.

Into the void in which Hector's face hung, Gis
said in a deadly whisper, which the fascinated watch-

ers couldn't hear, but Hector could, 'By God, Hector, you deserve a thrashing for what you tried to do to poor Thea Dunstan, with the help of her harpy of a mother, but, looking at you, I'm sure that your sins will catch you up without my assistance, but God help you, if you ever go near her or Sophie again, I *will* kill you,' and he relinquished the wrist to strike Hector a light blow in his raddled and bloated face which was enough to send him spinning away, but not enough to stun him. He was fearful that a brawl with Hector might result in detaining him in London, and he had Thea to think of.

Hector fell against a group of other Wanderers — the young ones were entertained by such a scene; their elders were shocked. One of them seized Gis by the arms and said severely, 'Now, then, enough of that. Such behaviour is intolerable in a gentleman's club.'

The rage was passing. Gis said, in as sweet a voice as he could, 'Oh, I do so agree,' and to the men holding the spluttering Hector, 'You hear that, Dashwood? Fenton doesn't like your manners any more than I do.'

'You damned young swine,' cried Fenton. 'It was you I was reprimanding. I'll have you barred from the club.'

That brought him no change, either.

'Do so,' said Gis cheerfully. 'That will prevent me from enduring Dashwood's presence again.'

At this a cheer rose from some of the younger men. Hector was thoroughly disliked. One of them shouted, 'I might have known, Gil Schuyler, that when I found you again, you would be duffing up the ungodly. Time someone gave that cheating swine what he deserved.'

'Schuyler?' said Fenton stiffly, still retaining his grip on Gis's arm, with Gis making no attempt to break free — he was beginning to enjoy himself. 'This man is Havilland, Ghysbrecht Havilland, and he won't be allowed in here again, if I have my way.'

'Never,' shouted the young man; he had an Australian accent and was not to be denied. 'Don't tell me I don't know my old cobber Gil Schuyler, pride of the squadron. I flew with him too many times not to know him when I see him. Like me to help you teach this old fool a lesson, Gil? This place needs livening up a bit. Wanting to throw you out for duffing up a known cheat at cards — what infernal cheek!'

The small group of ex-airmen who were with him were all guests of a Wanderer who had begun to ask himself what he had been doing to bring them along.

Gis began to laugh. What the hell, if his secret was out it was out, and since meeting Thea, and talking to her about it, none of it seemed to matter any more. He retrieved his arm from Fenton, said, 'Don't worry, I'm going, and I shan't come back,' and to his old comrade-in-arms, 'Yes, I'm Gis Havilland and Gil Schuyler, too, and you may, for all I care, tell the world who and what Gil Schuyler was, and what he did,' for excited questions were beginning to be asked, and how they were answered he neither knew nor cared.

He walked to the door, but the Australian ran after him. His companions were beginning to explain that Gil Schuyler had been a bit of a world

war air ace, had been decorated, and the story of
Gis Havilland who had shirked the war away was
beginning to be destroyed.

'Wait, Gil,' he shouted, 'I'm not losing you again
now I've found you. If you came here to have lunch,
forget it. I'll fetch the others and we'll eat somewhere a little less stuffy.'

On any other day Gis would have been pleased to
oblige him, but at least he could answer, 'I'll have a
beer with you, Bill. I've not forgotten you all, you
see. Bill Searle, and that was Alfie Ricketts with
you, wasn't it?'

'Oh, Gil, you never forget anything,' grinned Bill.
'Wait here, and I'll fetch the others.' For now they
were in Pall Mall, and interested spectators were
beginning to surge around them. Hector emerged,
helped away by friends, more shaken than hurt.
Soon the much inflated story of how Gis Havilland
had added to his reputation by thrashing Hector
Dashwood, and then it had turned out that he had
spent his war — four years of it — in the RAF, not in
America, was running around London and the
Home Counties to reach his father and mother as
one more example of his wildness.

'And that was that,' said Gis, tucking into the
meal which Thea had waiting for him when he
returned from London with the licence that night.
'I'm ravenous. I never got any lunch and spent far
too much time drinking beer with Bill and the rest.'
He hadn't drunk anything like as much as the
others, for when they had all been thrown into the
street at two o'clock his last sight of his old friends
had been of them, drunkenly exclaiming over the
fact that good ole Gil Schuyler was a millionaire,

propping each other up, and staggering off to spend
a night of it up west.

'And did you have too much to drink?' asked
Thea, practically.

'Faked it,' said Gis briefly, 'and not for the first
time. I couldn't arrive at an ecclesiastic office, dead
drunk, reeking of spirits. And I had to drive home
to my love. Couldn't have a hang-over tomorrow,
I've a wedding to arrange,' and he kissed her on the
tip of the nose.

The rest of the evening was a happy one. Gis left
Thea for a short time to go to set the date for their
marriage. The rector of Barton Dene parish could
not marry them the next day, but agreed to perform
the ceremony on the day after that.

But that night — perhaps it was the mention of
Hector — Thea had a nightmare, and Gis had to go
to her room when he heard her crying out. That
ended with her spending the rest of the night
chastely in his arms, Gis on top of the bed, Thea in
it. 'Very frustrating,' said Thea severely.

'Not long now,' said Gis, before they fell asleep.

Lady Edith had not been idle. Furious and frightened, she searched Thea's room again, this time
much more thoroughly. And finally she found
Thea's dressing case, hidden away at the back of a
closet, inside an innocent-looking carton, with some
old exercise books on the top of it.

It took her no time at all to break it open — for
why was it hidden away? — and to discover Thea's
journal which told her everything she wished to
know, except the most important thing of all —
where she had gone. Thea had recorded the miseries

of her daily life, but that was no matter. What mattered was that she had written that Gis had offered her sanctuary — should she need it — but that the wretched child had not written down the sanctuary's address.

Lady Edith's blood, like Hector's, boiled with wrath. The two-faced little bitch! Playing the innocent, and all the time plotting to run away to that wretch if things did not entirely go her way — which was Lady Edith's polite version of, 'If she didn't want Hector to rape her in order to coerce her into marriage'.

She now had the proof she wanted — even if she dared not actually show anyone the journal with its faithful and pathetic record of her brutalising of Thea, and her earlier attempts to force her to marry Hector. With it in her hand she could go to the Havillands and demand to know where their son might be found, and threaten them with the law, if they refused to help her. But she did not think that they would. It was well known that Gis Havilland was at odds with is parents.

She looked at her watch. Six o'clock. The matter would have to wait for the next day. She would telephone them in the morning, and then Miss Thea Dunstan might find out what it meant to run away from her loving parents — and one parent might not even find out that she had run away. . .if Lady Edith were lucky.

Kate Havilland was sitting in the garden room at Payne's Court. Earlier that morning her brother Gerard had telephoned her to tell her the latest scandal about Gis which was running round London.

'Yesterday, at the Wanderers!' she exclaimed. 'I can't say that I either like or admire Hector Dashwood, and neither does Richard, but all the same Richard will be furious. What was it about this time?'

'History does not relate,' said Gerard cheerfully. 'I'm bound to say that it seems that Dashwood started it. The usual thing—he's been saying it about London for weeks, but this time he said it to Gis. Red rag to a bull. From what I hear, Gis behaved with some restraint. I think that the whole thing blew up with the telling. One version has him half killing the man, but Hector turned up last night at Diana Troy's unmarked. Try to persuade Richard not to be too hard on Gis.' He hesitated. 'It also came out at the Wanderers about his war service, and about time, too. He did himself no good by hiding it, even if I think I know why.'

'Why Gis does things these days is wrapped in mystery,' said his mother sadly. 'I'm frightened of what I might hear next. But thank you, Gerard, for telling me. I shall be a little armed when Richard finds out, as he will. Some kind friend is bound to ring up to tell him.'

Some kind friend did, and then, half an hour later, the telephone rang again, and it was Lady Edith, asking for Sir Richard Havilland, and the matter was urgent.

And what could Lady Edith want? Richard had not yet had time to inform poor Kate of Gis's latest outrage; well, it would have to wait. She was probably telephoning him about some charity matter, for which his support was required, he supposed. But no. Of all things, it was Gis again, and this time he had really gone too far. Brawling at the Wanderers was one thing, but abducting a nineteen-year-old, taking her from her home, presumably for sexual purposes, was quite another. He debated about telling Kate what the woman had wanted, but really he had no choice.

Lady Edith had told him that for the moment she had no transport of her own, and had begged him to drive over to north Oxford immediately so that she might inform him of all the sordid details of her daughter's disappearance. It was impossible for her to speak of such a thing on the telephone, she had said tragically, and then she had broken down and begun to cry.

Her story was so muddled that when Richard told it to Kate, she stared at him and said blankly, 'I don't believe it. Gis! Kidnap that dab of a girl. What for?'

'For God's sake, Kate, don't say that to the woman when we see her,' said Richard, goaded. 'She has asked that we go to north Oxford at once; she has no transport. She also wants us to tell her where Gis is, and take her there. It's the least we can do, she says. Which means, if we agree, that we must break our promise to Gis that we keep his cottage refuge a secret. I know that we gave him our word — but this. . .'

Kate was numb. If true, this was the end. She had defended Gis, even if she deplored his habits, ever since the day he had come home from Eton, and confronted them with his knowledge of who and what he was in such a bitter fashion that the love and affection of sixteen years had flown out of the door for good.

But kidnapping plain girl-children! It was not believable.

'You're not going to tell her where he is, Richard? You know, I suppose, that he's at Barton Dene at the moment. He's been there for the last month.'

'Highly convenient for anyone wishing to kidnap or abduct an under-age girl in north Oxford,' said Gis's father drily. 'It's a criminal offence, you know, Kate. If proved, it means prison. And, what's worse, the girl's an heiress, as her mother kindly pointed out.'

'And Gis is even richer, as I must point out,' riposted Kate sharply. 'We have only the wretched woman's word about this unlikely tale. Gis with Thea Dunstan! Words fail me at the very idea.'

'Kate,' said Richard, as kindly as he could, 'if there's anything in the woman's story — of which I am not certain — we have a duty to tell her where he lives, and take her there, if only to prove that she's mistaken. In all decency, the woman has lost her child. . .she's been missing for a fortnight.'

'A fortnight! And only telephones us now!'

'She says she only found proof that Gis abducted her late yesterday afternoon. Be fair, Kate, she couldn't contact us on an idle suspicion. But I'm afraid that she does have evidence to support her story. She refused to discuss the matter on the telephone. Says that she doesn't trust them.'

'She doesn't trust anyone.' Kate was acid. 'I can't say I ever liked her, and the child is such a poor bullied thing, with that dominant mother. Lady Edith's handsome in her way, I suppose.'

'Hector Dashwood seems to think so, by all
acounts,' murmured Richard, who normally never
talked scandal.

'What are you saying, Richard?'

'Nothing, anything,' replied her harassed husband. 'I wish to God that Gis could behave himself
for five minutes. Now, go and get ready, Kate. I
shall drive us. I don't want servants gossiping about
all this — particularly if there's nothing in it.'

'Oh, my poor child, so innocent, so unsuspecting.'
Lady Edith held her handkerchief to her eyes. A
wronged mother ought to be crying. She had told
the Havillands of finding Thea's journal which lay
on the table before them. She hadn't allowed the
Havillands to examine it; she didn't want anyone to
examine it, particularly the police.

Sir Richard, his face grey, had said at one point that
if her story was true the police should have been
informed before. He could not, he said, reprovingly,
understand why she had not immediately informed
them of her daughter's disappearance.

'The scandal, Sir Richard, think of the scandal,'
she sobbed. 'My poor Thea would be ruined.
Abduction,' she said again; she had said it before,
looking at Sir Richard over her handkerchief. Kate's
eyes she avoided. There was something steady and
dispassionate in Kate's gaze. Kate would not, could
not, believe that Gis had run off with the wretched
girl, but Lady Edith roared on, 'She has engaged in
secret meetings with young Mr Havilland in
London, behind my back. I had expressly forbidden
any such thing!'

Kate interrupted Lady Edith ruthlessly. 'Secret

meetings in London?' she asked. 'You are sure of this?'

'The poor child was seen, Margery Veryan told me, and she confessed it. He took her to the zoo,' she lamented, 'and Soho.'

'Soho?' frowned Sir Richard.

'To a restaurant,' moaned Lady Edith, all tragedy.

'Oh, a restaurant.' Sir Richard was relieved.

'But who knows what they did?' cried Lady Edith. This was going better than she had expected, but Kate's eye was still on her.

'And her father?' enquired Sir Richard, still unwilling to believe that Gis could have carried off, or wanted to carry off the unassuming little dab of a thing which Miss Dunstan was.

Fresh outbreaks of sobbings from Lady Edith, more handkerchief wielding.

'Alas, he doesn't know. The professor is travelling through France, his research, you know, and so far I have not been able to get in touch with him. It has all fallen back on to me!'

'And she disappeared one night, you say, without a word?' This was Kate.

'Yes. I kissed the poor child goodnight,' Lady Edith lied, paused to give vent to yet another sob — it seemed required, and she was certainly disarming Sir Richard, if not his lady, 'and then in the morning — she was gone. It's a criminal offence, abduction,' she ended pathetically, and boldly, for the last thing she wanted was a proper investigation of what had caused Dorothea Dunstan to fly her home. There were holes in her story, she knew, but sobbings and exclamations glided over them. She had to get Thea back; the professor was due home any day, and it would be harder to convince him of her story than Gis's parents, one of whom appeared quite ready to believe the worst of his son.

'This is beyond anything,' Sir Richard announced suddenly, and then to Kate, whose scepticism was now overt, 'It relieves us of any duty to Gis to keep his whereabouts to ourselves. He has a small cottage at Barton Dene, and I am prepared to take you there. At least if we visit him we may have the opportunity to discover whether he has abducted your unfortunate daughter, whether she went with him willingly or not. We must also face the possibility that neither of them may be there.'

Lady Edith gave a muffled shriek at this, almost commanded, 'Oh, if you would only take me to Barton Dene, Sir Richard—the hope of having my mind set at rest. . .'

'I shall most certainly go with you,' replied Sir Richard, through his teeth. 'It is time that Master Gis was taught a lesson. The one thing which I don't quite understand is that if he is still at Barton Dene why was he in London yesterday. . .brawling with Hector Dashwood at the Wanderers?'

'Brawling with poor Hector.' Lady Edith was suddenly frantic. 'Oh, let us go at once, I beg of you.' And her cries and, now, her genuine tears were almost enough to convince Kate.

But I don't think Lady Edith is telling the whole truth, Kate thought; there is something wrong about all this, and as for Gis running off with Thea Dunstan, now *that* I do not believe.

* * *

So soon to be married! Only one more day to go.
Thea was in heaven that morning. Gis had made
her stay in bed, had prepared the cottage for the
day, made the breakfast, brought it up to bed, and
then had asked her to wear her bluey-green dress
again for him, 'Seeing that you are going to be a
lady for the day,' he said. 'Ready for tomorrow. I
would like you to be married in the lemon silk —
you don't mind not wearing white do you?'

'I wouldn't mind being married in a coal sack, so
long as you were the groom,' replied Thea inele-
gantly, but truthfully.

She couldn't believe it. That she, poor plain Thea,
was going to marry dazzling Gis Havilland, that he
loved her — no, more than that, that he loved her so
passionately that they feared to as much as touch
hands lest they. . . Thinking about it made her go
all hot and weak.

'I wish I could take you into Banbury,' Gis said,
he was making salad, slicing tomatoes, cucumbers
and hard-boiled eggs, washing lettuce and arranging
them all in a large wooden bowl before mixing a
vinaigrette dressing in a small glass jug. He had
refused to allow Thea to help him. She must put her
feet up, he had commanded, and be ready for the
great day.

Lunch, taken early, was a light meal consisting of
cheese, the salad, and a cottage loaf from the one
shop in Barton Dene. 'I am longing to go there to
see this treasure house of food,' Thea had said, for
the meal had ended with Victoria plums from
Evesham, also supplied by the general store, and
small sweet Marie biscuits served with their coffee.
Gis had brought the coffee from London, he said,

from Harrods to be exact, the general store not being up to such luxuries.

After lunch Gis worked for an hour on his designs while Thea began to turn another sheet. Presently, he yawned, threw his pencil down and said, 'Let's have a sing-song. All work and no play. . .'

'It's all play at Rose Cottage,' Thea informed him gravely, fastening off the hem she was working on.

'So it is.' Gis was laughing as he sat on the piano stool. 'A regular doll's house, with Gis and Thea playing at being father and mother. Do you want to be a mother?' he asked, dropping his hands on the keys after playing scales to loosen his fingers. The question was not a light one, he was in earnest.

'Oh, yes, please,' said Thea eagerly. 'Soon, I hope; you don't mind, do you? I always wanted a baby brother, or a baby sister, but Mother said that I was the last because I was quite enough.'

'*Quite enough* would better describe Lady Edith,' remarked Gis naughtily. 'You shall have half a dozen babies if that is what you want, and I promise to love them all. Not at once, and not all at once, I hope, but I look forward to being a paterfamilias.'

He began to play a wild noisy melody, stopped a moment to say, 'This is to further your education, Thea. It's an irreverent thing we used to sing in the mess at night — I was always being called on to play; its title is "The Bells of Hell",' and he went straight into it from the jazzed-up improvisation with which he had begun,

'Oh, the bells of hell go ting-aling-ling,
For you but not for me,

Oh, death where is thy sting-aling-ling,
Oh, grave thy victory. . .'

And, as he sang, Thea could almost see him back in the War, no older then than she was now, the wild boy he had been. Carousing with his mates — and now it was all for her. He sang it again, and this time she joined in, to his shout of, 'Bravo, Thea!'

'And do you know this tune?' he asked her, and began to play another which she had never heard before. 'I remember that this was always a great favourite in the mess, too. It's a parody of a sentimental ballad called "Little Redwing", about an Indian girl, and some versions are rather naughty, but I'll be a good boy and sing you a clean one.' And he broke into song.

'Oh, the moon shines bright on Charlie Chaplin,
His boots are cracking,
For the want of blacking,
And his little baggy breeches want a-mending,
Before we send him,
To the Dardanelles. . .'

'Altogether now,' he called, looking wicked and thinking that his poor love had never had a proper childhood, and with his help she might make up for that now. Thea sat by him, her arm around his shoulders, as happy as she had ever been in her life, and Gis taught her the words, so that by the third time he played it they were singing together, light soprano and mellow baritone mingling, the noise of the piano rebounding off the cottage walls.

At first neither of them heard the knocking at the door, indeed, Thea was so excited that she never

heard it at all, but Gis did, cocking his head on one
side, and suddenly fearful. So near, he thought; to
fall at the last fence would break both our hearts,
and then as he passed the window and looked out
to see who was calling, his worst forebodings were
fulfilled.

He opened the door, and spoke loudly, to warn
poor Thea, who had risen from the piano stool she
had been sharing with him, her back to the piano,
her face paling as she heard him say in his most
sardonic voice, 'Why, Father, Mother, and Lady
Edith, what a surprise. A little late for lunch, and
too early for afternoon tea, but never mind, I
suppose I must ask you all in. Too much to hope
that you are merely passing!'

CHAPTER ELEVEN

LADY EDITH'S rescue party, for so she melodramat-
ically named it to herself to try to put the unpleasant
truth about Thea's flight out of her mind, heard the
triumphant sound of the piano and the two happy
voices, male and female, floating through the open
windows of Gis's cottage.

Kate turned white at the sound. On the short
journey to Barton Dene she had sat beside Lady
Edith on the back seat, silently refusing to believe
that Gis could possibly have made off with Thea,
that they were on a fool's errand, and that if they
arrived and found Gis alone they would have the
unpleasant task of explaining why they had revealed
his hideaway to Lady Edith.

She saw Richard's face grow even sterner than it
usually was, and knew that there was nothing which
anyone could say or do to lessen or mitigate in any
way his profound anger at his son's behaviour. This
must be the end of any hope that father and son
could ever be reconciled.

She closed her eyes at the sight of Gis's face — as
forbidding as that of the father whom he so greatly
resembled — closed her ears to the sound of his
mocking voice, walked numbly in behind her husband's implacable back and a Lady Edith whose
every foreboding had been justified.

Gis preceded them into the cottage, manners
abandoned, in order to go to Thea, whose colour

began slowly to return, who closed her own eyes for a moment as Lady Edith brayed triumphantly, 'So! There you are, you wicked girl, side by side with your seducer. I knew it,' and out came the pocket handkerchief again, to be wielded as a weapon now.

Kate, her own face white, stared at her son, who had never looked more handsome, whose strength of will was written on his face, on his whole manner, stared at a transformed Thea Dunstan who was hardly recognisable as the little dab of a girl which she had named her to Richard. The short chestnut hair curled round a face which a fortnight's love and good food had begun to round and soften. Thea's pretty body and her shapely legs were revealed by the beautifully cut dress, whose delicate colour enhanced Thea's best feature, her large and blazing green eyes, which were blazing now at her mother.

'I'm not going home with you, Mother,' she cried, in a voice whose firmness belied her inward quakings. Beside her, Gis stared implacably at the enemy, for so he thought of them; Father, Mother, Lady Edith, they were all one.

Perhaps not his mother. He registered his mother's extreme pallor, guessed a little of what she was suffering, decided to take a hand in a game which he could not win, so far as his own integrity was concerned, because he was made defenceless by Thea's wish that the true story of her life with her mother and her flight could not be revealed.

'I have asked you in,' he said, 'because the etiquette which rules our lives compels me to do so, but I must assure you that I shall not agree to Lady Edith, or anyone else, taking Thea away from me. You must also understand, Father and Mother, that

I have good and sufficient reasons for behaving in such a fashion, and I would like to think that you would respect them.'

He saw his father's face change, become even more dour if that were possible, heard Lady Edith's gasp, saw his mother's stunned reaction.

'You damned scoundrel,' said Sir Richard coldly, rejecting his son's plea for understanding. 'You take an under-age girl from her home at night, bring her here for your own wicked purposes, persuade her to reject her mother, live with her for over a fortnight, telling no one of where she is, and then say you will not release her to her own parent! Are you aware that the law provides for such behaviour as yours? That the abduction of a girl minor, compounded by the fact that she is an heiress, is a criminal offence for which you could be sent to prison? I came here not fully crediting Lady Edith's story, but now that I have seen that she is telling the truth, and that you are persisting in your wicked folly, I have no alternative but to send for the police to deal with you. You are no son of mine, sir, if you do not release this poor child to her mother at once.'

The last thing Lady Edith wants is the police, was Gis's inward and grim response to this, and, Oh, Father, you have handed me an advantage.

He tightened his grip on Thea's shoulders as he felt her begin to shake, said in a voice scarcely distinguishable from Sir Richard's, so alike were father and son, 'By all means, Father, send for the police. At once, if not sooner. I shall be happy to answer to them,' which was taking a risk, he knew, for even if Lady Edith did not demur, there was Thea, who began to say,

'No, Gis, no. . .'

But she needn't have troubled herself. Lady Edith, her own colour coming and going, said rapidly, 'By no means, I want no scandal to ruin my girl's good name. No wish for the world to know that she lived here for a fortnight, unmarried. . . It is good of you, Sir Richard, to wish to protect my daughter and myself, but can we not settle this matter between us, without the world knowing?'

Gis spoke before his father could, 'Oh, by all means, Lady Edith, I do so agree; none of us would come well out of a police investigation. If you and my dear father and mother will leave us immediately, Thea and I can continue with our piano practice, and prepare ourselves for tomorrow's wedding. So good of you to wish for no scandal; a marriage should settle that. I'm sure that Sir Richard agrees.'

He thought for one moment that he had overdone it, that his father was going to strike him. Such a possibility would once have appalled him, but the only consideration which he now allowed himself was for Thea—and his determination that she should never go back to suffer Lady Edith's abuse.

'Wedding! Marriage!' Lady Edith cried. 'What do you mean, sir? Is it not enough that you have ravished my child away from her home, turned her against me, lived with her illicitly for over a fortnight, and now you prate of marrying her, without her parents' permission.'

'No prating, Lady Edith.' Gis would have enjoyed himself baiting his future mother-in-law—it was all that she deserved—but doing it with his father and mother present, registering the distress on their

faces at his apparent villainy, was hurting him, for
all his defiant manner. His father's face had changed
a little on the mention of the word marriage, which
proved that his errant son was not lost to all
decency.

'I went to London yesterday for a special licence,'
he said, moderating his tone, 'and I have arranged
for Thea and me to be married tomorrow.'

'You were,' almost shrieked Lady Edith, 'were to
be married. Thea will come home with me, where
she belongs. There will be no hugger-mugger marriage. The child is under age. I will not allow it, her
father will not allow it!'

Sir Richard said coldly, eyebrows raised, 'You
were in town yesterday, obtaining a special licence?
It is my understanding that you were at your club,
the Wanderers, brawling with Hector Dashwood.'

Gis eyebrows's rose, too; father and son, both
proud, were both refusing to give way to the other.
'Oh, really, sir? I gained the distinct impression that
Dashwood was brawling with me. And if you wish
to see the licence, why, I shall be happy to show it
to you — and to Lady Edith.'

Thea spoke at last, and Gis didn't seek to stop
her, even though he knew that once Lady Edith
realised that Thea would keep silent over her reasons for her leaving home the advantage would pass
to her, but Thea was entitled to have her say. Above
all else he must not be to her another, if kinder,
Lady Edith, stifling her development and her bud-
ding individuality. He dropped his arm from around
her shoulders to allow her to stand free.

'No,' she said. 'I won't go home with you,

Mother. I wish to stay here with Gis, where I have been happy, and be married to him tomorrow.'

'You cannot be married tomorrow, girl,' bellowed Lady Edith, forgetting all decorum, wishing that the curtain pole were handy, and no strangers present, so that she might beat sense into her defiant daughter. 'You are under age. Tell her, Sir Richard, it is your duty, seeing that it is your son who has run off and corrupted my daughter, turning her away from her own mother.'

'I'm sorry, my dear,' his father's voice was gentle; Gis noted that in his favour, 'but your mother is right. You *are* under age. It was very wrong of Gis to abduct you and live here with you alone, without marriage, and were Lady Edith not so kind as to refuse to take action against him he could be facing criminal charges. You must go home, for both your sakes, before any decisions about marriage can be made. These things must be done in proper form.'

Oh, there speaks the diplomat, Father, was Gis's sardonic reaction to that. Oh, yes, let Lady Edith beat Thea senseless — so long as it is done 'in proper form'.

'My mother! Kind!' Thea permitted herself to say at least that. 'My mother knows perfectly well why I don't wish to go home. And I love Gis dearly and he loves me, and I want to marry him and live here permanently, and he has not so much as laid a finger on me in a wrong sense, even though I asked him to. You are not so shout at and reproach him, any of you. I am the wanton one, not Gis.'

None of which did him any good at all, Gis was sure. But Thea's defence warmed his heart, even if it served only to persuade his father, and perhaps his mother, that he was hypnotising her, engaging in an almost Svengali-like domination of her, so that he might use her for his own purposes. What Lady Edith thought was another matter. She was patently beginning to understand that Thea was not going to reveal the beatings or the attempted rape by Hector, encouraged by her mother, which had caused her flight.

She became bolder in her denunciations. Kate was sorry for her for the first time, although at the back of her mind she still felt that there was something awry in Lady Edith's story, that some things were not being said, that there were false notes being played.

'Gis. . .' she said at last, hardly able to speak, her throat almost closed with unshed tears. 'Play the man, tell Thea that it is her duty to go home with her mother. She will listen to you.'

'Precisely.' Gis couldn't prevent himself from being harsh with the mother he loved, but saving his truest love of all, the girl whom he hoped to make his wife, who stood staunch beside him, refusing to be daunted, took precedence over everything. 'And that is why I shall not allow her to go home with her mother. I cannot say more than that, Lady Edith knows why.'

He was prepared for the torrent of abuse from Lady Edith which followed, for his father to turn away from him after his refusal to give way, for his mother to sink into a chair, her legs failing her — they had all been standing, glaring at one another like characters in a Greek tragedy, Gis thought, all that was wanted being masks and buskins.

Perhaps he might feel better if he were allowed to

weep and scream — offstage, of course, seeing that
neither his mother nor his father were prepared to
believe anything but the worst of him.

'May I remind you all,' he said, and again his
voice was his father's, 'that you are in my home,
and that I might choose to call the police, and have
you removed? Would that please you, Lady Edith —
or not?'

Of course, it didn't please her, and then she
played what she saw was her trump card, and Gis
had been expecting it, but his heart sank when it
came.

'Come, Thea,' she said, speaking directly and
almost pleasantly to her daughter for the first time,
'come home with me. If you don't, I swear I'll see
that Gis will go to prison. Only my consideration
for his mother and father prevents me from sending
for the police at once. You say that you love him,
so you can't want that, can you?'

Oh, she was no fool, Lady Edith, Gis had to grant
her that, she had seen at once the advantage to her
if Thea refused to tell the whole truth about the
reasons for her flight, and he could see where Thea
got her common sense from and her strength of will.

Thea's lips began to tremble, and Gis felt her
leaving him — to save him.

'No, Thea,' he cried, 'hold firm and she can't
touch you, nor can my father and mother. We know
that we have done nothing wrong. Hold on to that.'
He had fallen on his knees before her, regardless of
the watching trio, and he took her hands in his to
kiss them. He heard Lady Edith's indrawn hissing
breath at the sight, and knew, as never before, that
sexual jealousy informed her whole opposition to

his courtship of her daughter, and that to overcome
that would need a major *coup*.

'Trust me,' whispered Thea as she bent to kiss
him on the lips, and then she straightened up,
bowed her head, so that her mother couldn't see
her face, said, 'Yes, I will come home with you,
Mother, only let me fetch my things from my room,'
and, although her mother began to demur, she was
prevented by Kate, who said,

'Yes, Lady Edith, let the child do as she wishes,'
her voice thick with unshed tears, for she could
recognise, as well as Lady Edith, the true passion
which lay between her son and the girl whom she
had once dismissed as a nonentity — but no one Gis
loved could be a nonentity.

Head bowed, the picture of submission, Thea
walked towards the open staircase which led upstairs
to her room. Gis's face had become as expression-
less as one of the Greek masks he had so recently
visualised — he couldn't let any of the watchers know
what the sight of his departing love would do to
him.

Thea reached the last step before the stairs turned
on to the tiny landing, but before they turned she
did. 'No,' she called down, 'I'll never go home with
you, Mother, whatever you and the Havillands,
whom you have deceived, think, or can do. I am
going to lock myself into my room, and you must
fetch the police, to break the door down, and they
will have to knock me unconscious to carry me out
because I shall never leave my darling Gis willingly — and think what a scandal that will cause — so
you had better let me marry him tomorrow.'

'Oh, you wicked, deceitful child,' screamed Lady

Edith, making for the stairs, but too late. Thea was gone and the bedroom door was locked against them, and Gis's laughter followed her inside, something she could hug to herself as she sat on the bed.

Lady Edith, thwarted, was letting the world know about it. Finally, after about ten minutes' ranting, she fell silent. Sir Richard, condemned to remain at Rose Cottage until Lady Edith announced her intention to leave, like his wife, sank into one of the easy chairs. Lady Edith refused to seat herself, stood against the window, a tragedy queen, her handkerchief a club, a weapon, and a means of drying her — tearless — eyes, something which a critical but unhappy Kate had already registered.

In the immediate aftermath of Thea's departure, Kate had said, her eyes filled with tears, 'Please, Gis. Do the honourable thing and go up and encourage the poor child to go home, and then we might be able to talk about marriage,' but her plea was lost in Lady Edith's storming rage.

Gis lounged against the other wall enjoying the way in which his little love had stalemated everybody, Couldn't have thought of anything better myself, being his inward comment. She's learning, my Thea, yes, she's learning. She going to be as formidable in her quiet way as Lady Edith is in her noisy one. What a pair we shall make! But he said nothing until Lady Edith had quieted, and then, in as bland a manner as he could summon up, came out with, 'Tea, anyone?' like a juvenile lead in a play at the Garrick.

His father glared at him, Lady Edith glared at him, his mother looked at her hands.

'No?' he drawled. 'Then excuse me if I indulge. I have work to do.' And he strolled into the kitchen to put the kettle on the fire, set out a tea tray, and then returned, bringing with him an egg timer — he knew exactly how long it took to boil a kettle on the range fire.

Ignoring the others, he sat down at the table, picked up his pencil and resumed where he had left off when he had begun to play the piano for Thea, pausing only to make the tea. His look of acute concentration was not assumed; he had always had the power and capacity to shut off the outside world at will.

Lady Edith said suddenly into the silence, 'I shall not leave until I take my child home.'

Gis looked up — his other ability was to do two things at once — and said succinctly, 'My poor father and mother have a long wait, then. Unless you are prepared to allow them to leave and stay yourself, although I warn you the cottage has only two bedrooms, and I have no intention of surrendering mine to you.'

What Lady Edith or his irate father would have said to this was never to be known. The front-door knocker sounded vigorously: Gis's parade of visitors was about to be added to.

'Excuse me,' he said politely and went to see who it was. An unusually boisterous Sophie hurled herself at him as he opened the door, threw her arms around his neck and said gaily, 'Gis, I knew you must be in, and Father and Mother, too — I saw their car. I came to thank you.'

She didn't wait for him to invite her in — she and Gis had always been soulmates despite the difference in their ages—but walked into the room, and then stopped, surprised at the gorgon-like apparition Lady Edith presented.

'So sorry, Lady Edith, not to greet you properly,' she said, not sorry at all; she had never liked the woman, had disliked her public treatment of Thea. 'I thought that it was only family Gis had here. What is it, Gis, a party?'

Gis choked back a laugh. 'Not exactly, Soph,' and then, a trifle mischievously, 'What brings you here, so unexpectedly?'

Sophie stared at her grim-faced father, at Lady Edith, at her mother, looking sad about something, Gis presumably, and then wilfully leaned forward and kissed him on the cheek. 'Why, I came to say thank you, Gis. I knew that I could trust you to tell me to do the right thing. Yes, I did what you said— and it came right. Bless you, baby brother. You always did know how to fix things.'

Sophie was no fool. She could feel the anger in the room, and all of it directed at the brother she loved. 'What hanging-judge faces,' she exclaimed, 'What has Gis supposed to have done now?'

When Gis said, a grin on his own face, 'Leave it, Soph,' no one else feeling able to answer her, her own grin was the feminine image of his—they resembled each other greatly.

'Don't they know you yet, Gis?' she answered him. 'Don Quixote in person, fixing everyone else's lives, but not trusted to fix his own. I won't stay, Gis. I know when I'm *de trop*—see me to the car— I came in George's tourer—and I'll tell you all my news.'

She walked over to her father and mother, kissed

them, said reprovingly, 'Be kind to the poor darling for my sake,' held out a chilly hand to Lady Edith, remarked, 'Give my best wishes to little Thea, I'm sorry to have missed her.'

There was an insouciance about Sophie that neither her father nor her mother had seen before. Richard, who had stood up when she came in, said stiffly, 'Must you go, Sophie? Your mother and I see so little of you these days.'

'Of course, I must, Father,' said Sophie. 'I can see that for whatever reason I am, as I said, *de trop* and, as for seeing me, I'll telephone you at the weekend and arrange a visit. George said only yesterday that it was too long since we had had you all over. Give my love to Richie and the girls. Goodbye, Lady Edith. Gis! Come with me.'

They reached the car before Sophie kissed him on the cheek, said, 'If you want me to know, I suppose some day you'll tell me what that was all about. Lady Edith looked like the angel of death about to execute you with her sword. What ever have you done? Run off with the virginal Thea?' and at Gis's expression, 'No! You haven't! Why? No, don't tell me if you don't want to.'

'I've done nothing wrong, Soph,' he said quietly.

'Fixing things?' she said shrewdly. 'Where is she?'

'In her bedroom; she's locked herself in. She's refused to go home with the gorgon. I've been looking after her, here, for the last fortnight. Don't ask me why. I'm going to marry her, Soph. Tomorrow, I hope, with a special licence.'

'Good for you,' said Sophie simply. She kissed him again. 'I told George, like you said. It worked out beautifully. Turned out he'd had an affair with a WREN, was feeling all guilty about it, and my guilt cancelled out his, so to speak. We fell into each other's arms amid scenes of mutual forgiveness. I can't thank you enough. I'd never have worked up the courage to tell him if you hadn't encouraged me to do so.'

She got into the car, kissed him again, and roared off waving and shouting, 'Good luck, little brother.'

Grinning, Gis walked back to the cottage, Sophie's trouble solved, perhaps his own affairs might turn out as well. He sincerely hoped so.

Professor Theodore Dunstan had an uneasy conscience. It spoiled his Paris visit for him. He could not stop thinking about his daughter, her white face, her thinness, the unhappiness written in every line of her body. He had been wrong to leave her to his wife, but he had thought that a young girl reaching maturity was best cared for by her mother.

But he couldn't ignore his daughter's patent misery, and he had become a little suspicious of Lady Edith; it was even possible that she might be mistreating the child.

And then, Thea's weekly letters, which he always enjoyed reading, had stopped. Instead he had received some written by Edith, ostensibly dictated by Thea, which was nonsense; they were totally unlike anything she normally wrote, the excuse being that she had a damaged wrist.

Finally, no letter arrived at all, not even one from Edith, and his misgivings grew so strong that they began to affect his research: it was time to go home, to see Thea again, to protect her a little from her mother, perhaps — a father had rights in his child,

too. He could ensure that Edith was not too harsh
with her, persuade her that, if the child did not wish
to marry Hector Dashwood, that was no great
matter for which to persecute her.

He arrived home some time after Lady Edith and
the Havillands had left for Rose Cottage. To his
great surprise the house was empty of servants,
except for a rather slatternly woman whom he had
never seen before, who grunted something at him
when he went into the kitchen to look for Lady
Edith, or Thea. It became patent that neither of
them was in.

The professor went to his study and began to
unpack his briefcase. He had had to carry his
luggage in himself, the man who usually did such
things for him also being absent. And all the time
his unease grew. It went against the grain to gossip
with servants, but after a time, when no one
appeared, he went down to the kitchen again, and
began to question the woman.

'Your mistress, Lady Edith,' he asked, 'where is
she? Have she and Miss Thea gone to Beauclair?'
He did not ask about the servants, assuming that if
his wife and daughter were at Beauclair, the servants would have gone with them.

The woman sniffed, said, 'No, sir. Lady Edith
went off, early this afternoon, rather suddenlike,
with a lady and gentleman what came in a Rolls-
Royce — I think she sent for 'em. As for Miss Thea,
the good lord knows where she is. She's *supposed*
to have gone to Scotland, a fortnight ago, to stay
with friends, or so the missis says, but seeing as how
she was here the night Lady Edith entertained the
gentleman, and was gone the next morning when I

came in at nine o'clock. . .' and she let the sentence trail off.

'Miss Thea vanished,' said the professor numbly, and then, 'The servants, where are they?' The whole story seemed most unlikely — Thea vanishing — was it possible? The woman must be mistaken.

'Lady Edith sent the servants away the week before Miss Thea vanished — and a wonder she never went before. Her mother knocked her about something cruel. She hired me and another woman to do the dirty work — I do the cooking and the light cleaning.' She stopped and turned back to her work, mumbling, 'I've a lot to do and she's not the easiest of missises to work for.'

No, indeed not, thought the professor unhappily. Thea had mysteriously disappeared, after having been repeatedly 'knocked about' by her mother, if the woman servant could be believed, supposedly gone to Scotland — on her own, a likely story — the servants sent away, and Lady Edith jaunting off for an afternoon's pleasure — and no word of all this to me.

'I suppose you have no idea of where Lady Edith went this afternoon?'

The woman smiled slyly at him. 'Oh, yes,' she said. 'She rang for 'em, didn't she? Havilland, I think she called them. Had a right set-to when they came — all about Miss Thea — I couldn't quite catch what was said, but they all piled off in a posh motor to Barton Dene. Rose Cottage was mentioned.'

Professor Dunstan had never visualised himself cross-questioning a glorified charwoman, who had obviously been listening at doors, to find out what she had heard, but he had no choice if he wished to discover what his wife and daughter had been doing.

'The gentleman who was entertained, the night before Miss Thea. . .left. Have you any idea who it might have been?'

The woman shrugged. 'No, sir. Sorry, I can't help you there. But the missis made an awful fuss about everything being done right before he came.'

The professor found out little more. He stood irresolute. Thea gone, Lady Edith chasing off to Barton Dene with the Havillands. Oh, the connection was plain enough. A colleague had told him that Gis Havilland had a cottage at Barton Dene where he stayed in the Long Vac. He had not yet taught Gis Havilland, but he knew him, thought of his golden grace, his charm, his intellectual mastery, and then of his poor Thea who had been charmed by him — and who had disappeared.

He made his mind up, went to the telephone and arranged for a hired car to be sent to him immediately, his own apparently having gone to Beauclair with the servants. He would go to Barton Dene and find out what his wife and his daughter had been up to in his absence. He should never have left Lady Edith alone with Thea — but too late to worry about that.

CHAPTER TWELVE

SIR RICHARD HAVILLAND had time on his hands: he
could not, in decency, compel Lady Edith to leave
before all chance of retrieving her daughter from
Gis's clutches had disappeared. For lack of anything
else to do, he did what he afterwards told himself
sternly, he should have done before — he put his
good mind to analysing Lady Edith's story and
comparing it with Thea and Gis's behaviour.

Where Kate had instinctively mistrusted Lady
Edith and her story, Richard began to dismantle it
logically using his intellectual powers. The main
sticking-point was the fortnight which had passed
between Thea's disappearance and Lady Edith's
doing anything about it. Why had she not informed
the police immediately? Why did Gis keep offering
to send for the police? For Lady Edith, the plea of
not wishing to cause scandal would surely have
taken second place before the need to find an under-
age girl who had always been heavily chaperoned
and protected. Had he known of the missing servants Sir Richard would have been even more
uneasy.

And Gis, when all was said and done, had
arranged to marry the girl — hardly the act of a
callous seducer — and why was Lady Edith so ada-
mant against him? He was of a good family, handsome, rich — and, his father was compelled to admit,
enormously clever, with a brilliant career in front of

him, although what he might choose to do was unknown to his father, since the breach between them.

Perhaps the most worrying thing of all was Thea's shuddering rejection of her mother, her refusal to go home with her. And, since she had been with Gis, she had changed in many ways from the timid nonentity he had been used to see about society, and that they loved one another was hardly to be doubted — the little scene between them before Thea had fled upstairs had touched him, as he knew it must have touched Kate. Hard though it might seem to her, it was time that he began to question Lady Edith a little more severely — after all, Gis was still his son.

He had begun to frame a series of polite, but pointed questions, the kind of thing for which he was famous in the Corps Diplomatique, when the need for him to do so was removed — Thea's father, the professor, arrived at Rose Cottage.

Gis lifted his head when the door knocker sounded — rapped by a demanding hand. The Professor had seen the Havilland's Rolls-Royce at the gate of Gis's humble home, and knew at once that his Thea had run off with Gis Havilland, and a less likely story the professor had seldom heard.

'"What!"' Gis drawled, quoting *Macbeth*, the play which should never be quoted, but the temptation was irresistible, '"will the line stretch out to the crack of doom?" How many more visitors am I to expect today? I shall need an extension built on to the cottage,' but his face changed when he opened the door to see Professor Dunstan standing there, a look of enquiry on his mild face.

'I believe, Mr Havilland,' he said, his voice gentle, 'that my wife and daughter may be here. I wonder if you would allow me in to speak with them.'

Gis had had little to do with the professor, although he had sat in his lectures, and knew of his reputation, that his intellect was supposed to be formidable — all the more shame, was his conclusion, that he was apparently unable to protect his daughter from her mother. He bowed his head, said politely, 'Oh, do come in, sir — what is one visitor, more or less? But I had better warn you that although you may speak with your wife, your daughter is quite another matter: she is at present — by her own wish, you understand — incommunicado, and will speak with no one, myself excepted.'

He stood back to usher the professor into his small living-room, which was now intolerably crowded. All the parties stood at his entrance. Sir Richard saw immediately that Lady Edith was unpleasantly disturbed by her husband's unexpected arrival.

'Good gracious, Theodore,' she greeted him frostily, 'I thought that you were not due home for another week.'

'Quite so, my dear, that was my intention. But I was a little troubled by your non-communication with me and was consequently afraid that matters might have gone amiss at home. You told me that Thea had broken her wrist — but there seemed to be more going wrong than that. And when I did arrive home, I was greeted with the most disturbing news.'

Before his wife spoke to him, the professor had already gone through the rituals etiquette demanded with Sir Richard and Lady Havilland. He now turned to them to say, 'Pray forgive me for inflicting this family business on you both, but the matter is urgent, as I believe you are aware.'

Gis had begun to enjoy himself, and when his father said to his mother, 'I think, Kate, that we ought to leave the professor and Lady Edith to sort this matter out between them. Gis is of age, and we can only be in the way,' both Gis and Kate began to speak together to the same effect.

'No.' Gis's voice and expression were suddenly steely. 'No, Father, Mother, I insist that you stay. Lady Edith involved you both in this, had you bring her here, and you have been witnesses to what has passed. In fairness to myself, you must not leave now.'

His mother, who had subsided when he began to speak, pleased him by adding her voice to his, so that Richard was obliged to give way, and the professor indicated his willingness that they should remain.

'For,' he said, 'I think a duty is owed to you that we get to the bottom of this, speedily. Edith, my dear, do I understand that Thea left her home a fortnight ago, shortly after she broke her wrist?'

Gis's enjoyment grew. 'Broke her wrist?' he enquired. 'Well, if so, she's managed to conceal the fracture from the world most successfully. Did you notice that Thea has a broken wrist, Father, Mother?'

Lady Edith broke in petulantly, 'Oh, I am being grossly misrepresented, Theodore. I am sure I did not say that her wrist was broken, only slightly sprained.'

The professor's look grew stern. 'Oh, no, my dear. I have your letter in my luggage at home. You distinctly said broken — which was why she could not correspond with me. But that is a mystery to be cleared up later. . .' He broke off, changed tack, said to Sir Richard, 'Do I understand that what Mr Ghysbrecht Havilland said is true, that my daughter is incommunicado? I see she is not here.'

'She has locked herself in the bedroom which she has been occupying during her stay with my son, and refuses to come out to return home with her mother,' replied Sir Richard.

'I see,' said the professor. 'Thank you, Sir Richard. Now Edith, I think that further explanations are in order. Am I to understand that our daughter left home over a fortnight ago, without you knowing where she had gone, and that you neither informed me nor the police, and did nothing until you asked Sir Richard to bring you here on a suspicion that Mr Havilland had abducted her?'

Gis, who had thought that he might be the one to have to explain matters, was happy to watch Lady Edith wriggling beneath the professor's relentless inquisition.

'Oh, Theodore,' she exclaimed, thinking that only boldness would serve her, 'why are you quizzing me in this fashion? You should be questioning *him*.' And she pointed at Gis, who was leaning against the piano, a half-smile on his face. 'It was he who abducted your daughter, kept her here for his wicked purposes. I'm sure you agree that scandal must be avoided at all costs, *that* was why I didn't contact the police, and as soon as I discovered from Thea's journal that she had not only been meeting this young man in London, behind my back, and against my wishes frequently expressed, but that he had encouraged her to leave home by giving her the key to this cottage and his address, which she slyly did not write in her journal — why, then, I asked Sir Richard and Lady Havilland to tell me where he might be found, and they brought me here, and, lo and behold, here the guilty pair were hiding. He is fortunate that I did not at once demand that the police be fetched, and he be charged and sentenced for seducing away our poor girl.' And she looked triumphantly round at three pairs of eyes which, with a sinking heart, she recognised were already looking dubiously at her.

'My dear Edith,' said the Professor. 'Which is it? First you say that Mr Havilland abducted her, took her away in the night, and then that he gave her the key to come here, which would mean that she fled here herself. And how did she do that? I find that our car has already gone with its chauffeur and all the rest of the servants to Beauclair. Why was that, Edith? Why should you, who like your creature comforts so much, send the servants to Beauclair three weeks before you intend to go there — on my return?'

Lady Edith had never had the professor's remorseless dissecting intellect turned on her before, his powers of analysis trained like great guns ready primed to demolish her position. That damnable woman whom she hired must have been talking to him. Any moment it might all come out, even the. . .disciplining of Thea, so necessary to keep her behaving herself.

Her voice high, face frightened, she began to stammer, to say, 'I don't understand you, Theodore,' to have him reply, relentlessly,

'But I think you do, Edith, and I warn you, I am determined to discover the truth.'

'Not like this,' she cried, 'before him,' pointing again at Gis, who had stood motionless, like a statue, trying to avoid looking at his mother and father, 'before strangers. It is not proper, Theodore, it is not fitting.'

The professor sighed, said, 'You leave me no alternative, Edith. You brought them into this, you have threatened their son with prison, and your daughter has locked herself away and refuses to return home. They deserve to learn the truth, as I do. Why should Thea lock herself away, Edith? tell me. And tell me who was the lone gentleman you entertained on the night of Thea's disappearance?'

It was all going to come out, and, despite his promise to Thea, Gis felt that he had no right to stop this. He could see that his mother and father were beginning to suffer, but knew that his father would say nothing. The matter was between husband and wife now — but both had insisted on the Havillands' presence, and, in fairness to Gis, they could not leave.

Gis thought that it was time for him to speak. 'I should perhaps, inform you, Professor Dunstan, that my intentions towads your daughter are strictly honourable. I have taken out a special licence with the intention of marrying her tomorrow. About your daughter's reasons for leaving home, I cannot speak, but Lady Edith knows as well as I do what the truth is.'

Lady Edith, her face ghastly, looked wildly around, began to sob, this time there was no pretence involved. Any moment, now, the truth would be out, and she would be ruined. The Havillands would not talk, she knew that, but what would the professor do? She had to brazen it out, prevent him from discovering the truth, she had to, but before she could lie again, compel him to drive her into the corner where the truth, the shaming truth, would at last be found, her salvation came from a most unexpected quarter. . .

Thea had sat on her bed, quiet. She spent her time reviewing her happy fortnight with Gis, thinking about her wedding, which she still prayed might take place tomorrow. She didn't mind that no one would be there; she preferred that to the suffocating ceremony her mother would have arranged for her. She knew that Gis didn't want spectators, either. She thought, He's a private person, like me.

She ran to the window when Sophie arrived, heard the commotion downstairs, saw her leave again. Saw Gis kiss her goodbye, and was sorry that she had not been there with him, as she would have been if Lady Edith and the Havillands had not arrived.

She was angry with them. They didn't appreciate him. They didn't know how kind he was, beneath his rather cold manner, but they *should* know — he was their son. It was unbelievable that they could credit her mother's story, but she supposed that, between her own presumed naïveté and their view of Gis's villainy, they had no choice.

Hunger might drive her out — no, it wouldn't, she would die first. They couldn't make her hurt Gis in any way, she loved him too much for that. And he loved her—or he wouldn't have agreed that they shouldn't tell anyone of what her mother had done.

Astonishingly, she fell into a half-doze, leaning against the pillows, and was brought back to full consciousness only by the sound of another car arriving. Curiosity drove her to the window. It was her father! In a hired car, which he paid to wait for him, the driver getting out to light a cigarette and lean, smoking, against the bonnet. She watched her father walk up the path, the oddest expression on his face, one which she had never seen before.

Thea's heart began to thunder. What was he doing here? He wasn't due home for at least another week. And why did he look so stern? Was he cross with her? She thought a moment: perhaps not. What if it were Lady Edith—she no longer thought of her as Mother—he was cross with? Well, there was one way to find out.

The old Thea would have lain nervously on her bed, letting the imp speak her thoughts, but doing nothing about them. But the imp had gone, and the new Thea, the one whom her darling Gis had created, had no intention of being helpless, of not knowing what was happening downstairs. She could hear the murmur of angry voices, her mother's high and annoyed.

She went to the door, unlocked it as silently as she could, took off her shoes, and tiptoed to the top of the stairs, just before they turned, where she could hear, but not be seen.

She was right. It *was* her mother he was cross with, and as the relentless inquisition went on she understood that her father was getting nearer and nearer to the truth. She had never heard Gis speak once, nor his father or mother. They were leaving Lady Edith to her husband.

This must stop! At all costs no one, not even Gis's parents, must know what had been done to her. She no longer loved Lady Edith, but she didn't want her wickedness made plain to the world. She couldn't live with that. She would feel guilty as though it were her fault. She slipped on her shoes, began to walk down the stairs.

At first no one, except Gis, saw her. He put up a hand, shook his head at her; she shook hers back, her whole body suffused with love at the sight of him, and as the professor's relentless questioning was bringing him to the truth, she said in her quiet pretty voice, quite coolly, as though she were Gis himself, 'Hello, Father,' and they all turned to look at her.

'My dear.' The professor walked towards her. 'They said that you were locked away.'

'Oh, I was,' she said. 'But I thought I ought to come down again, I have a duty.'

Gis, still standing, apparently relaxed, was lost in admiration for her. She was about to turn the tables on them again, he was sure of it. She had said that she didn't want the wicked truth known, and now, somehow, she was going to prevent it from being known, at least before the Havillands.

'A duty,' shrieked her mother. 'You don't know the meaning of the word.'

'No, Mother,' Thea was still calm, 'you mustn't say that. I know exactly what my duty is. To you, to father, and to Gis, whom I love and who loves me.'

'Duty?' said the professor sternly. 'What I should like from you is the truth.'

'No,' said Thea simply, 'not the truth. You don't want to hear the truth; don't make me tell it.'

'Your truth,' sneered Lady Edith in the truculent voice that had so often brought Thea to heel, but not now, not now.

'Mother,' said Thea, 'you don't want me to tell the truth.'

'Your word against mine,' shot back her mother. 'And we know what yours is. The word of a fool who allows a rogue to snatch her away.'

'No,' said Thea again. 'Gis didn't snatch me away, Father. He thought that I might be in trouble so he gave me the key to this cottage, and the address, and told me to come here, if I needed help. If he wasn't here, he told me to use it as my own. If he were he would look after me. I came to the cottage in the middle of the night, of my own accord because. . . I had to. There was no abduction. Gis never touched me in a wrong way, even when I asked him to. We are to be married tomorrow, Father, and I hope that you will agree to it. I should like you to be there.' She didn't look at her mother as she said this, heard her mother snort.

'A likely story. Pray how did you get here, miss, if he didn't take you away?'

'Oh, Mother,' said Thea wearily. 'No more, please. I came in Hector Dashwood's car, which I admit I stole, but I had to, and if you don't believe me, Father, Gis hid the car for me in his barn. It's there still, under a tarpaulin. Don't make me say any more, Mother, for Sir Richard and Lady Havilland's sake, if not mine. If Father wants to see the car, it's still in the barn. I don't suppose Hector tried too hard to find it or told anyone who took it and why. After I reached here, I was very ill, and Gis nursed me devotedly until I was better. That's all, but I think that it's enough, don't you, Father? Give me your blessing. I would like to be married with it tomorrow.'

Everyone in the room, except her mother, looked at her with respect. Lady Edith's timid and backward dab of a daughter had disappeared without trace. Love and Gis had created a new Thea, the one she was meant to be, a combination of her mother's steely determination and her father's intellect and sweet nature. The story she had told held the ring of a dreadful truth which no one in the room wished to believe but, looking at Lady Edith's stricken face, was compelled to.

The professor put out his arms. 'Come here, my child. I have sadly neglected you. Yes, you may marry Gis, for if your transformation is partly his work, which I suspect it is, then he deserves you. I must say that I cannot understand what all the commotion has been about. A handsome, rich and clever young man, of good family, who was expected to gain a double first before he was twenty, had not the war intervened, a war in which the gossip columns of the popular Press have today informed me he served with distinction, who undoubtedly has a brilliant future before him, although not, I regret, the scholastic one which his intellect could command, wishes to marry our daughter. I cannot understand what your objections have been, Edith, and why you have behaved in what I suspect is a disgraceful manner to keep them apart. Of course you may have my blessing, my dear.'

Lady Edith, even at this pass, would not surrender.

'You do not understand, Theodore.'

'No, Edith, I fear that it is you who does not understand. I am sure that you do not wish Dorothea to tell the whole unpleasant truth. I also advise you to apologise to Sir Richard and Lady Havilland for the slanders you have uttered against their son, and the threats which I understand that you have made.'

He turned to Gis. 'You seemed to have behaved in an exemplary fashion in all this, saying nothing to defend yourself, nor which might have hurt my daughter, even when threatened with the worst. Sir Richard, Lady Havilland, I must apologise to you, for it has been my inattentiveness to my daughter's needs which has helped to bring this about.'

Sir Richard inclined his head. There was really nothing he could say. He might have defended his own role in bringing Lady Edith to confront his son and her daughter, but he knew, after the fact, that he should not have been taken in by her, that the analysis he had undertaken after he had reached Rose Cottage should have been undertaken before.

As for Kate, the misgivings which had plagued her ever since Lady Edith had begun her story had been proved even more nightmarishly true. Thea might have prevented the truth from being spoken aloud, but no one in the room had any doubt what it was. The only thing which Thea had managed to stifle was her mother's physical, as well as mental abuse of her. Kate put her hand in her husband's and pressed it: she could almost feel his distress as he said, quite simply, 'Your apology is accepted, sir.

Mine has yet to be made — to the proper persons.'
He avoided looking at Lady Edith as he spoke.

'You will agree with me, I think,' said the professor, who was determined to spare the feelings of all the participants by bringing the whole wretched business to as speedy a close as possible, 'that, bearing in mind that Mr Havilland has a special licence, and has arranged to marry my daughter tomorrow, there are now no barriers to that marriage. Furthermore,' and he looked sternly at his wife, 'I wish to spare my daughter as much pain as possible on the day before her wedding: she has already suffered enough. Consequently, I am prepared to agree that she should remain here with her future husband. To cavil at another day added to those she has already spent here is not greatly to the point, seeing that she will shortly be spending all her days with him. I hope, Sir Richard, Lady Havilland, that you will agree with me in this.'

He did not ask his wife's permission, nor did he look at her. He shook Gis by the hand, and kissed Thea gently on her cheek. She had been staring at him with an expression of profound gratitude — as though all her dreams were coming true at once.

'Come, Edith, my dear,' said the professor turning to his wife at last. 'You will surely wish to kiss your daughter goodbye before we leave — and assure her that you will be happy to support her in church tomorrow morning.'

Gis couldn't remember ever having seen or heard Lady Edith bestow an affectionate word on her daughter, let alone a caress, and Thea couldn't recall when her mother had last kissed her.

Lady Edith assumed a 'Must I?' expression, and

put her cold lips to Thea's cheek; it was more an emblem of her surrender to her husband than an expression of affection for her daughter. Impulsively Thea raised her arms to embrace her mother as one last attempt at reconciliation, to gain some acknowledgement that perhaps her mother loved her, despite everything.

Her mother drew back. Nothing had changed, other than that she was now to be dominated by the husband who, until this afternoon, she had always dominated, and who, when she returned home with him, was to extract from her a full confession of her true villainy. To kiss Thea, to show her affection, was to seal her surrender, her loss of power.

But, at the last moment, as she withdrew, she suddenly saw Thea as the loving, generous girl she was, saw why Gis loved her, for the steadfast way in which she had faced the world, and above all, that Thea had merely had to say the words telling of her brutal mistreatment and she would have been publicly destroyed. Thea had not said those words, and instead words were wrenched from Lady Edith which she had never expected to say.

'Oh, Thea, I hope you will be happy with *him*.' She still could not say Gis's name, but she kissed Thea again, a true kiss this time, not the distant peck previously offered. It was the first loving kiss she had given her daughter for many years.

Gis stepped forward, put an arm around Thea's shoulders, said in what Thea thought of as his true voice, the one which held no hint of mockery in it, either of himself or the world, 'Thank you for that, Lady Edith. Thea and I hope to see you tomorrow morning.'

Nothing could mitigate what she had tried to do, nor the reasons for which she had done it, nor the cruel treatment which she had meted out to her daughter for so many years, but, like all wounded animals, she needed to have her face saved, even if her wounds were self-inflicted.

'Come, Edith.' The professor's voice was gentle as he took his wife by the arm. 'Let us leave our children to their other parents for a little. Lady Havilland, Sir Richard. . .' and he bowed to them. '. . .I know that we shall meet again tomorrow to celebrate a happier occasion than this.'

After the Dunstans' departure there was silence for a moment. Sir Richard and Kate had both risen to face Gis and Thea, in order to make their peace with them. Gis knew by his father's expression, rueful, but a little proud, like an envoy signing an unexpected treaty which had given him more than he had hoped for, that the long-awaited reconciliation between them was at hand.

He held out his hand to his son, while Kate went over to embrace Thea. 'What a brave and resourceful child you are,' she exclaimed, close to tears. 'And how kind you have been to. . .all of us.' She didn't need to elaborate.

'Gis taught me to be so,' said Thea, 'to be brave, to be true to myself. The lesson is a hard one and I am still learning.'

Gis, who had begun to make his peace with his father, heard this, said earnestly to Kate, 'Don't listen to her, she doesn't need teaching. She has taught me to behave myself, to understand that I cannot love and respect myself if I do not love and respect others.'

'But I have wronged you over this.' His father was heavy. 'I thought that your intentions towards your future wife were dishonourable ones. Can *you* forgive *me* for that?'

'No forgiveness needed; my fault entirely that you should misjudge me. I have given you no occasion other than to think badly of me, after the selfish and unfeeling manner in which I behaved to you and my mother after I discovered the truth of my birth — behaviour which was compounded when I went off to the War without telling you, leaving you unaware of whether I lived or died for two years. To say that the experience was good for me is not to excuse what I did. Believe me when I tell you how much I love you, and how proud I am of my future wife.' There was no doubt that Gis meant what he said; all the cynicism of the past seven years had disappeared.

'I am not proud of my own actions today,' admitted Sir Richard, 'so perhaps we are quits at the end.' No one said anything of Lady Edith; nothing needed to be said. There were further embraces, and tears, from Kate and Thea.

'And when your honeymoon is over,' said Kate, 'you must come to stay with us at Payne's Court.'

Thea flushed. 'The honeymoon, I had not thought of that!' And she looked appealingly at Gis.

'Here,' he said, 'the honeymoon will be here — where better, where we have been happy together?' and he looked lovingly at her. Some time in the near future he would tell his father and mother what he hoped to do with his life, that the career in the

Corps Diplomatique, the brilliant social life, on
which his father had set his heart, was not for him,
but today was not the day. He hoped his father
would understand.

And finally, they were alone together. Everyone
had gone. The cottage was theirs, the day was theirs,
and the night too, if they so wished. They stood,
face to face, holding hands.

Gis leaned forward, kissed his dear love on the
cheek. 'A master stroke, my darling; no, two master
strokes from you, which saved us.'

The look which she gave him was enchantingly
naughty, the look of someone who had grown up,
who knew her powers.

'No, Gis,' she said gravely, as his hands rose to
clasp her shoulders. 'Mistress strokes, surely; master
strokes are for men!'

He gave a crack of laughter. 'Whatever, my love.
I shan't quibble with you. The best stroke of all was
your father's to ensure that we were left alone
together, everyone's blessing on our heads, before
the bonds of matrimony tied us. No restraints, my
Thea — if that is what you wish. Your wish always,
my heart, since you have unfrozen mine.' And now
his hands rose to clasp her face.

'Are you afraid?'

'No,' she said, 'I was never afraid of you, Gis,
and I am not afraid now.' She looked at him shyly.
'If I said that I wished to wait until tomorrow night,
after we are married, would you think that I was
being selfish? It is not fear that holds me back, only
what you said before they all came down on us —
that if we truly behaved ourselves, it didn't matter

what they or the world thought of us. I want to carry that with me to the wedding. To be your virgin bride, even if I shall not wear white.'

His hands continued to hold her face. He kissed her on the lips. 'Oh, you honour both of us,' he said softly, 'by wishing to wait, especially if you feel as passionately for me, as I do for you.' He felt her tremble beneath his hands and knew that she did. He dropped them and stepped back.

'Tomorrow night, then. We must burn until then, but until then. . .' And he whirled to the piano and began to play Mendelssohn's *Wedding March* as though no time at all had passed since they had sat there singing in harmony, before their unwanted visitors had come to disturb them.

The moon rose to shine brightly on the cottage, on the music which streamed from it, on the lovers, sleeping in their lonely beds, dreaming of the morning, dreaming of the future, of the three tall sons, the pretty daughter, of Gis's career, of the aeroplanes he would design, of Thea's happiness, of the shared joy of a long and happy life together — they had come home at last.

LEGACY *of* LOVE

Coming next month

BEAU'S STRATAGEM
Louisa Gray
Regency 1814

Lady Allegra Ashley was banished to Bath to stay with her
Aunt Lydia, but on arrival there was no aunt; instead a
strange gentleman was attempting burglary. Luc Fleetwood
was looking for clues to the whereabouts of his brother, the
Earl of Hawkhurst, but, on learning Lydia had disappeared
too, Luc lost no time in transporting Allegra, her young
brother, his tutor, the parrot and the dog to stay with his
grandmother! Certain it was somehow a French plot, Allegra
let her vivid imagination take over, and even Luc was not to
be trusted—whatever her growing feelings for him...

ESCAPE TO DESTINY
Sarah Westleigh
Sark 1571/2

Rescuing a naked man from the sea took all Judith Le
Grand's strength and her fortitude when sheltering him from
the Spanish cost her brother Edward's life.

Part privateer, part spy, Oliver Burnett had to get back to
London to report his knowledge of the Ridolfi plot to
assassinate Elizabeth I, though a little dalliance as he
recovered his strength wouldn't go amiss—but marriage, to
save Judith's reputation? Yes, for the right to bed her! He
could always go back to Sark later, when he was ready to
settle down. Judith had other ideas!

LEGACY *of* LOVE

Coming next month

RANSOM OF THE HEART
Kate Kingsley

New Orleans/Morocco 1824

Her late brother's debts had left Danielle Valmont penniless,
homeless and forsaken by the New Orleans élite whose
conventions she had previously flouted. Still, Danielle was
prepared to pick up the pieces—until that scoundrel De Leon
came crashing back into her life, wreaking all manner of havoc...

Erstwhile pirate Arturo De Leon felt obligated to rescue
Danielle from the danger she unwittingly faced—even if that
meant kidnapping her aboard his brigantine. When Danielle
showed her gratitude by stabbing him, the privateer steeled
himself for what promised to be a long—and intriguing—voyage!

SILVER LINK
Patricia Potter

New Mexico 1846

Antonia Ramirez knew that the tall, blond American was not
to be trusted. Yet Tristan Hampton had awakened something
deep inside her that would not be denied.

Since the moment he had first laid eyes on Antonia, Tris
Hampton had been lost. He was haunted by her dark beauty.
She made him feel he had finally found the completeness he
had been searching for. But her father clearly hated him, and
someone wanted to see him dead. Of Antonia's love he was
certain. The question of her loyalty was still to be answered.